OUTSIDE THE CAVE,
THE THUNDER CRASH

Reeve looked down at me. His face w
clung to his lashes. He said, "Do you kn
thinking, Deb, that perhaps our get
wouldn't be so terrible a thing after all."

I stared at him in astonishment.

"Think about it yourself," he urged.
my money, and you"—he gave me
crooked smile—"you would get all the horses you
wanted to ride."

I pulled his wet jacket more closely around me and
said impatiently, "Reeve, there is more to marriage
than that."

"I know there is." The sound of the rain beating on
the rocks of the shore was very loud. Reeve took out
his damp handkerchief, took my chin in his hand, and
carefully dried my upturned face. Then he said coaxingly, "I think you and I would deal together very well
in other ways, too, Deb."

He bent his head, and a crack of thunder split the
heavens . . .

"JOAN WOLF NEVER FAILS TO DELIVER THE
BEST."

—**Nora Roberts**

"AS DELICIOUS AND ADDICTIVE AS DARK,
RICH, BELGIAN CHOCOLATES."

—*Publishers Weekly* on *The Arrangement*

Please turn the page for more endorsements of Joan Wolf . . .

more . . .

THE GUARDIAN

"The reader is drawn intimately into the story. Only a writer with Joan Wolf's mastery of the language can accomplish this. . . . Wolf meets this demand with a large cast of interesting and individual secondary characters, an intricate and believable plot, mastery of period details, a fallible but untarnished hero, and a storyteller heroine who lets the reader into the deepest recesses of her tormented heart."
—**Lee Gilmore, *Romance Reader* (Web site magazine)**

"Joan Wolf may be considered Ms. Regency Romance, but with this novel she changes her format by placing a strong emphasis on the mystery, a circumstance that brings a freshness to the subgenre."
—**Harriet Klausner, *Under the Covers* (Web site magazine)**

"Sizzle and sparks . . . the humorous, exasperating, and endearing goings-on . . . pack this novel chock-full."
—**Dalton's *Heart to Heart***

"Typical Joan Wolf . . . wonderful, 4½ Bells!"
—***Bell, Book and Candle***

"Delve beneath all the layers of marvelous characters in the book and discover love, deceit, hatred, envy, mystery, forgiveness, great danger, and passion. It's one heck of a story that will keep you turning the pages far into the night."
—***The Belles & Beaux of Romance***

By Joan Wolf

The Deception

The Guardian

The Arrangement

The Gamble

The Pretenders

Published by
WARNER BOOKS

JOAN WOLF

The Pretenders

WARNER BOOKS

A Time Warner Company

WARNER BOOKS EDITION

Cover design by Diane Luger
Cover art by Stanislaw Fernandez
Hand lettering by David Gatti

Warner Books, Inc.
1271 Avenue of the Americas
New York, NY 10020

Visit our Web site at
http://warnerbooks.com

 A Time Warner Company

Printed in the United States of America

First Printing: February, 1999

10 9 8 7 6 5 4 3 2 1

CHAPTER

one

It was three o'clock in the afternoon, on a beautiful but blowy day in mid-May, and I was, as usual, in the Earl of Cambridge's stable office talking with his head groom. I was lounging in my chair, in a most unladylike posture, when there came the sound of a carriage being driven rather precipitously into the stable yard.

Clark jumped to his feet like a shot. "Lord Almighty, Miss, could that be his lordship?"

I said a little dryly, "Since I don't know anyone else who comes sweeping in here quite so grandly, I rather imagine that it is."

Clark disappeared out the door. I slid down a little farther on my spine and idly wondered what could be bringing the Earl of Cambridge back to his ancestral home in the midst of the London Season.

A brilliant ray of May sunshine came slanting in through the small office window and rested on the top of my head. It had been a cold April, and the heat felt delightful. I closed my eyes to savor it.

"You here, Deb?" a familiar voice asked and I opened my eyes to regard the man who had just come in. The Most Noble George Adolphus Henry Lambeth, Earl of Cambridge, Baron Reeve of Ormsby, and Baron

Thornton of Ware, stood in the door looking at me out of his famous dark eyes.

"I'm always here," I returned mildly. "Where else am I to be—at home with Mother, gardening?"

He flashed me a swift, charming grin. "Well, since you put it like that . . ."

He came into the room and sat on the edge of the desk, facing my chair and swinging his leg.

"The really interesting question is what are *you* doing here?" I asked. "Isn't the Season still in full swing?"

"I'm going over to Newmarket tomorrow to take a look at Highflyer," he said. "The Derby is in a few weeks, and I want to make certain that he's training well."

I bolted straight up in my chair. "May I come with you?"

He sighed. "You know you can't do that, Deb. It ain't proper for an unmarried young lady to be alone all day with a twenty-four-year-old man."

"Fiddle," I said vigorously. "You and I have been friends forever, Reeve. No one will think anything odd of me going to see your racehorse."

He snorted. "Won't they? My reputation is not exactly spotless, Deb, and I am *not* going to besmirch yours. I'm sorry, but you just can't come with me."

I glared at him. "But it is so boring here, Reeve. The only thing the local girls do is giggle about boys and talk about getting married. It is enough to make one go stark raving mad. If I didn't have Clark to talk to, I think I *should* go mad."

He looked like a dark angel as he sat there, swinging his booted leg and looking at me out of enigmatic eyes. "You ought to think of getting married yourself, Deb. You can't spend the rest of your life as a spinster, after all."

I could feel my face take on what my mother calls its stubborn look. "No one wants to marry me, Reeve."

"Don't be ridiculous," he said.

"It's true," I insisted. "For one thing, I'm too tall."

His straight black brows drew together. "You're not too tall. Stand up, and I'll show you."

"No."

Two strong hands closed around my wrists and dragged me to my feet.

"See?" he said. "The top of your head comes to my mouth. That's a perfect height for a woman."

I was annoyed. "Reeve, you are several inches over six feet. I don't know if you have ever noticed this, but most men are not quite as tall as that. They like girls whom they can look down upon."

His eyes flicked over me. "They also like girls who wear something more feminine than ancient riding skirts and jackets that look as if they were rejected by the local orphanage."

I scowled up at him.

"It's not as if you were a Valkyrie, for God's sake," he said. "If anything, you're too thin. I could probably fit my hands around your waist."

"Well don't try it," I warned. I backed away from him and folded my arms across my breast. "How did we get started on this conversation in the first place?"

"You started it."

"I did not."

"Yes, you did. You were complaining that all the local girls are on the catch for a husband."

I leaned my hip against the desk that he had stepped away from and shrugged. I hated to admit that I was wrong.

"It's perfectly normal for girls to want husbands," Reeve went on. "I don't know why you should find the topic so boring, Deb."

"It's not only boring, it's fruitless," I said. "Not only am I too tall, but I have no money. Don't forget that little fact, Reeve. Gentlemen are not inclined to marry a girl who is virtually destitute, which is what Mama and I are. We are lucky to have a roof over our heads." I shook my head. "No, I fear I am doomed to permanent spinsterhood."

I must admit I was not as unhappy as perhaps I should have been about this situation. My long legs might have made some of the shorter local swains uncomfortable, but they gave me a distinct advantage in the saddle. In point of fact, except for Reeve himself, I had the best seat in the entire countryside. This was the reason that I had the free run of Reeve's stables, of course. He knew his horses were in good hands when I took them out.

Realizing that he was getting nowhere with his discussion of marriage, Reeve changed the subject. "It looks as if Highflyer is going to be the favorite for the Derby," he said smugly. "What do you think about that?"

"I think it is wonderful," I replied slowly. "But what does Lord Bradford think?"

Reeve scowled. "Bernard is a spoilsport," he said. "All he does is spout prosy speeches about the evils of racing. He has no understanding that racing is something that all real gentlemen do. He lives on that boring little estate in Sussex and does nothing but see to his farms and his flocks of sheep! Wait until Highflyer wins. Then he'll see the value of keeping a racehorse!"

I said carefully, "Reeve, where are you getting the money to have Highflyer trained?"

"Oh, Benton loaned it to me," he replied carelessly. "I'm to repay him as soon as Highflyer wins the Derby."

A note of foreboding struck my heart. "And what if he doesn't win?"

That earned me the famous Cambridge glare. "Of course he'll win! He's by far the best horse in the race. That's why he's the favorite!"

He picked up an iron paperweight in the shape of a rearing horse and slammed it down on the copy of the *Stud Book* that Clark and I had been looking through. "Damn Bernard, anyway. Why does he have to make my life so difficult?"

It was a question I couldn't answer.

Reeve raked his hand through his dark, overly long hair. "You don't think I should have borrowed the money from Benton?" he challenged me.

I looked back at him thoughtfully, taking a minute before I answered. Even Reeve's glower could do nothing to disguise the classical purity of his face's bone structure. The only thing that saved him from being outright beautiful was the bump in what had once been a perfectly straight nose. He had broken it when he was twelve. Someone had been riding too close behind him over a fence and crowded his horse, and both Reeve and the horse had come down. He had been laid up for

weeks with broken ribs and a broken collarbone as well
as the nose.

I had known Reeve since I was five, however, and I
was so accustomed to his magnificent looks that they
rarely got in the way of my reading the inner man. So I
knew now that under the bravado he, too, was nervous
about the money he had borrowed. I also knew that he
would never admit it.

"It is just that I would hate to see the relationship
between you and Lord Bradford deteriorate further than
it already has," I said carefully.

Reeve gave a short bark of humorless laughter. "I
should think that is impossible, Deb," he said.

There was no answer to that, so I pushed away from
the desk. "It's time I was going home," I said. "Mother
will be looking for me."

He nodded. "I really wish I could take you to see
Highflyer, Deb, but even if you could find a chaperone,
I'm not coming back here after Newmarket."

"That's all right, Reeve," I said resignedly.

"Give my best to your mother."

"I will."

And so we parted.

I waited until my mother and I were having dinner
together in the small dining room of our tiny cottage before I told her of my encounter with Reeve that afternoon.

"I wish he had not bought that horse," Mama said.

"Reeve picked Highflyer out as a yearling, and he
has turned into one of the best three-year-olds of the season," I said. "*I* think it's a shame that his pleasure in his

horse is dampened because of that damn will of his father's."

"Deborah," my mother protested automatically.

"Sorry, Mama," I corrected myself. "Rotten will."

Mama sighed. "It is certainly unfortunate that Reeve's father should have decided to keep him from coming into control of his fortune until he is twenty-six. I agree with you that it is humiliating for Reeve to have to go to his trustee, Lord Bradford, for money. But you must admit, darling, that Reeve's father had good cause to doubt his son's maturity."

"Hmmm," I said. I ate a piece of asparagus from the pile on my plate. One of the good things about Reeve's coming home was that he would be sure to send us some big hams before he left for Newmarket. It would be nice to have meat again.

Mama took a small sip of water from her glass. "I saw a notice in the paper today that your half brother Richard is getting married. The young lady is the daughter of Viscount Swale." She took another careful sip. "It's a good match. The Woodlys must be pleased."

I went rigid. "Mama," I said dangerously. "I've told you that the less I hear about that family, the happier I will be. And as for my esteemed half brother—he can rot in hell, for all I care."

My mother looked at me, a small frown between her brows. "Darling, I wish you would not continue to bear this grudge against your brother. I agree with you that the family behaved very badly to us, but I scarcely think that Richard, who was a child of eight at the time your father died, can be held at fault."

I slammed my hand on the table. "*Behaved very*

badly to us! My God, Mama, is that what you call throwing us out of my father's house and banishing us to live in poverty in a poky little cottage!"

Mama winced.

I tried to get hold of my temper. I knew I upset her when I started to shout.

"I'm sorry," I gritted out between clenched teeth.

"Your father left the estate and all his money to his son Richard, with his brother John to act as trustee," Mama reminded me. "I'm sure your papa expected that we would be taken care of, Deborah, but we have no legal claim on the estate." Her voice dropped slightly. "We are lucky John saw fit to give us this cottage rent-free and to pay me a quarterly annuity to keep us fed."

For that was how John Woodly had interpreted his duty: he kept a roof over our head. And even that came at the expense of Mama's promising never to use her title. She was by rights Lady Lynly, but all the world must call her by the lesser name of Mrs. Woodly. John had left her nothing of her pride. All he had left her was me.

I stared across the table at my mother. She had been hired to be my older half brother Richard's governess and, much to the dismay of his family, my father had taken her to be his second wife. When my father had died his family had swept her (and the product of this union—me) out the door of Lynly Manor as fast as they possibly could.

Mama said earnestly, "Don't bear a grudge against your brother, Deborah. None of this was his fault."

"He never tried to find us," I said in a hard voice.

"Nor have I ever tried to get in contact with him," Mama returned.

This was true, and I had never quite understood why.

Mama smiled at me now, and said, "Let the old animosities go, darling. You will be a happier person if you do."

The late-afternoon sunshine slanted in through the window, gilding the coronet of silver-blond braids on the top of Mama's head. Her sky-blue eyes smiled trustingly at me across the table.

We had the same coloring, I thought, but nothing else about us was alike. I had my father's height, and I supposed I also had his nasty temperament. Unlike Mama, I didn't forgive.

I forced myself to smile at my gentle mother. "Do you think it would be wrong of me to pray that Highflyer wins the Derby?" I asked lightly.

She laughed. She was so pretty, my mother, so soft and so delicate. She was forty-four and I was twenty-one and I had been taking care of her for years.

I grinned. "What do you bet that we get some hams delivered here tomorrow?"

"Darling Reeve," Mama said. "He is so considerate. I rather believe that I will pray for Highflyer, too."

The next few weeks went by in the usual fashion. I rode Reeve's magnificent hunters every day to keep them in condition. One thing I had to say for Lord Bradford, he didn't stint Reeve on the normal things that a gentleman was expected to own. It was the gambling that made him put his foot down.

Unfortunately, Reeve liked to gamble.

Ambersley, Reeve's house, was also maintained in beautiful condition. There was an army of servants to keep the house, and an army of gardeners to see to the grounds. In every way possible, Reeve looked like the incredibly wealthy young nobleman that he was.

Except that all the bills were paid by Lord Bradford, and that drove Reeve wild.

During the weeks before the running of the Derby, I went on several expeditions with local friends whom I had known forever. They were the same expeditions that we took every spring, and they were growing rather tedious, but I couldn't spend every waking hour in the stable, and so I went. The expeditions also had the virtue of getting Mama away from the house and her garden, which I thought was good for her.

One afternoon a group of us went boating on the River Cam, just above the university from which Reeve had been so spectacularly ejected five years before. I found myself in the same boat as Cedric Liskey, the new vicar at our local parish church.

It was a beautiful day, and I watched the brownish water eddy around the boat as Mr. Liskey pulled the oars through it. There was scarcely the whisper of a breeze. The bulrushes on the shore were as still as their reflections. The willows trailed their branches in the water, and the irises on the shore were budding. The peace, the sunlight, and the warmth were very pleasant, and I smiled at Mr. Liskey as I trailed my fingers in the water.

"Everyone has been so kind to me since I arrived here," Mr. Liskey said. "Why, I don't believe that I have dined at home more than once or twice."

Of course he hadn't dined at home, I thought cynically. He was twenty-seven, single, and in possession of a very decent living. Every unmarried girl in the parish was after him. In fact, I had been rather surprised to find myself sharing his boat. I rather thought that Maria Bates would have made certain of that place for herself.

"Are you connected to the Cambridge family?" I asked him now. I assumed that he was, of course. The Ambersley living was a good one, and Lord Bradford would not have given it outside the family.

He smiled at me. He was a nice-looking young man with good teeth and warm brown eyes. "Yes. I am a second cousin of Reeve's, actually. We haven't seen much of each other, but our lives did cross briefly at university."

"Oh," I said.

He stopped paddling and leaned on his oars. "My career was longer than his, but far less . . . sensational."

I sighed. It often seemed to me that the prank in which the home of the Head of Reeve's college had been painted daffodil yellow overnight was known throughout England. The joke had resulted in Reeve's being sent down, which was exactly what he had hoped for, of course. He had hated Cambridge.

"I don't like rules," he had said to me defiantly when his father had banished him to Ambersley in disgrace after Cambridge had washed its hands of him. "I want to be in charge of my own life."

Ironically, it was that particular prank which had been the last straw which caused his father to change his will to keep Reeve from coming into control of his inheritance until he was twenty-six. Reeve had accomplished exactly the opposite of what he had wanted.

"Reeve never liked Cambridge," I said now quietly.

"No, he didn't," Mr. Liskey agreed. "It was perfectly evident to me from the moment we met that he wasn't going to last. He was like a . . . a comet blazing across the Cambridge skies. The fiery light he cast was mesmerizing, but somehow one knew that he was going to burn himself out."

I thought that Mr. Liskey had probably described the Cambridge situation very well. I sighed.

Poor Reeve, I thought.

"Tell me, Miss Woodly," Mr. Liskey said, "will you be at the dance the Bateses are holding this Saturday evening?"

I brought my attention back to him. "Yes, I will," I said.

He looked pleased. "Then I must beg you to be sure to save a dance for me."

Dances such as the one the Bateses were throwing were completely informal. There were no dance cards and one simply danced with whoever asked one at the moment. I didn't want to seem to belittle the Bateses' entertainment, however, so I simply smiled, and said, "Of course."

"I shall look forward to it," Mr. Liskey said. He picked up the oars and began to row us back toward the picnic.

CHAPTER
two

HIGHFLYER LOST THE DERBY. HE STUMBLED ON his way up the last hill and pulled up with the lower part of his leg dangling. He had snapped his cannon bone. They put him down right on the Epsom course.

"Oh my God," I moaned when I read the account of the race in the *Morning Post* the following day. "This is terrible. Poor Reeve. What incredibly rotten luck."

"Let me see." Mother reached across the breakfast table to take the paper from me.

"Oh dear, that is too bad," she said in distress when she had finished reading the article. "Lord Bradford will be very annoyed when he learns that he has to pay out training money and now Reeve doesn't even have a horse he can sell."

"It isn't just the training money, either," I said gloomily. "Can you see Reeve not betting on his own horse? A horse that is the Derby *favorite*?"

"Oh dear," Mama said again. She knew Reeve well enough to recognize the truth of what I had just said.

I didn't see him for two weeks after the Derby fiasco. Then, one hazy June morning, as I was helping Mama in her garden, which fed us for most of the summer and half of the winter, he drove his phaeton up to the front of our cottage, pulled up with his usual flourish, and jumped down. I wiped my hands on my skirt and walked over to greet him.

"Hello, Reeve," I said. "How are you?"

"I've been better," he replied shortly.

In fact, he looked ill. He had lost weight, which made his high, classical cheekbones more prominent than usual, and there were noticeable shadows under his eyes.

"I was so sorry to hear about Highflyer," I said gently. "What a terrible way to lose a good horse."

He nodded tersely. Reeve had never been very good about dealing with his own feelings.

At that point, my mother came up. She patted him gently on the arm, and said, "It's good to see you, Reeve. Thank you for the hams."

She, too, knew him well enough to realize that an excess of sympathy would not be welcome.

"I've come to ask Deb to go for a drive with me," Reeve said to Mama. "Will that be all right, Mrs. Woodly?"

"Of course," Mama said. "Change your dress first, Deborah. You cannot be seen abroad in that dirty old gown."

"She looks fine," Reeve said impatiently.

"If you don't mind, I would like to wash my hands at least," I said mildly. "I won't be long."

He gave me a very somber look. "All right."

Good heavens, I thought, as I went into the cottage. *Something must be very wrong indeed. Could Bernard have refused to pay his debts?*

A cold chill struck my heart. *Surely Reeve had not gone to the moneylenders? He would not be that stupid!*

I washed my hands and face, brushed off my dress, and was back downstairs in ten minutes. Reeve was standing beside his horses, talking with Mama and looking high-strung and tense.

"I'm ready," I said lightly, and let him take my hand to help me up to the high seat of the phaeton.

As we rolled away down the country lane, Reeve was very silent, ostensibly concentrating on driving his matched pair of bays. I didn't say anything either. He had obviously sought me out for a purpose, and from past experience I knew I was going to have to be patient until he was ready to bring it out.

Reeve steered the phaeton away from the well-kept paths and splendid gardens of Ambersley and aimed instead toward the river, following one of the local country roads that at this season were lined with leafy trees and small grassy meadows filled with wildflowers. At last he pulled off the road and stopped the horses. We were in a small glade that was hidden from the road by a stand of graceful beech trees.

He loosened his reins so the horses could stretch their necks and turned to look at me.

I could hold my tongue no longer. "Whatever is the matter, Reeve?" I asked. "Did Lord Bradford refuse to cover what you owed on the Derby?"

Dark color flushed into his cheeks. "If I live to be a hundred, Deb, I do not ever want to spend another hour such as the one I spent with Bernard after that race. He is such a clod. Do you know what he said to me? He said that raceowners were a congregation of the worst blackguards in the country mixed with the greatest fools. That is what he thinks me. A fool!"

Reeve's eyes were glittering dangerously, and there was a white line around his mouth.

"Lord Bradford is a very conservative man," I said cautiously.

"You won't credit this, Deb, but he seems to have no understanding that what I owe on the Derby are debts of honor." Reeve thrust his fingers through his dark hair. "I shall be drummed out of the Jockey Club if I do not pay up on my bets, do you realize that?"

"Of course you must pay your bets," I said. I added carefully, "Er . . . exactly how much do you owe, Reeve?"

He scowled. "I bet sixty thousand pounds on High-flyer to win. Then, of course, there is the money I borrowed from Benton for training fees. That is another ten."

My heart sank. Seventy thousand pounds!

"And has Lord Bradford refused to meet your obligations?" I asked.

"He has said that he will meet them, but he has made a stipulation."

For the first time he looked away from me, averting his face and staring out over the shining dappled brown backs of his standing horses.

I looked in puzzlement at his profile, which was shaded by the overhanging canopy of leaves from the beeches. There was a single stripe of sunlight on the left shoulder of his rust-colored coat.

"And what is this stipulation?" I prompted when it didn't seem as if he were going to continue.

I could see a muscle jump in his jaw as he clenched his teeth. "I have to get married."

I was dumbfounded.

"Married?" I echoed. "But what does getting married have to do with your debts?"

He didn't answer immediately, and the truth slowly dawned on me. "Oh, I see. He has found you an heiress."

Reeve's reply was bitter. "I don't need an heiress, Deb. Even Bernard knows that." He turned around to look at me directly once again. "It seems that my esteemed cousin and trustee is a great believer in the settling effect of matrimony on a man. He has hopes that if I take a wife, and begin to set up my nursery, then my wildness will disappear. In fact, he has promised to give me access to half of my money when I marry and the other half if I can maintain what he calls a 'decent life' for a year."

"Good heavens," I said faintly. "Can he do that? I thought your father's will stipulated that you could not come into your inheritance until you were twenty-six."

"Apparently he left it to Bernard's judgment to put forward the time if he felt I showed sufficient 'maturity.'" Reeve's gloved fingers opened and closed on the loosened reins he was holding. He added grimly, "A stipulation that Bernard has not seen fit to inform me of until the present."

I stared at his clenched fingers and tried to make sense of what he was saying. "Lord Bradford told you he will not pay your debts unless you marry?"

"That is what he said."

Here was just another example of the way Lord Bradford constantly mishandled his young cousin, I thought angrily. One of the worst mistakes one could make with Reeve was to put him in a position where his back was to the wall. And Lord Bradford was very good at putting him in that position.

I said, "What are you going to do?"

He growled.

I looked at him with compassion. "If you want your debts paid, it looks as if you are going to have to get married."

He growled more ferociously than before. "I don't want to get married."

"Surely it won't be so bad," I said encouragingly. "I read the papers. According to the gossip columns, there are dozens of young ladies who would welcome a proposal from the handsome Earl of Cambridge. You will have to marry someday, Reeve. Why not sooner rather than later?"

He moved a little closer to me on the seat of the phaeton. Feeling his movement, one of his horses tossed his head. The bit jingled in the warm June air.

Reeve said, "Those young ladies you talk about are the silliest collection of twittering idiots I have ever met in my entire life. It would drive me mad to have to spend my entire life leg-shackled to one of them."

I watched as he moved another inch on the seat, intruding into my space. I felt like a mare about to be herded. He bestowed upon me his most charming smile, all white teeth and glinting dark eyes.

I regarded him warily. I never trusted that smile. I had seen too many times how unscrupulously he could use it to get his own way.

His voice deepened. "I have been thinking about this situation I find myself in, Deb, and I have come up with a splendid idea. Why don't you and I become engaged?"

I stared up at him in utter shock. "Are you mad?" I finally managed to sputter.

"You wouldn't really have to marry me," he said reassuringly. "Once Bernard hears that I am engaged, he will pay off my Derby debts. Why, if I play my cards right, I might even get him to sign over half of my money to me before the marriage takes place. After all, he can't expect us to tie the knot immediately. Weddings take time to plan, don't they?"

"I have no idea," I said firmly. "And, much as I would like to help you out, Reeve, this scheme of yours is impossible."

He moved another inch closer to me. "Why?"

I moved an inch in the opposite direction. "For one thing, Lord Bradford will not consider me a suitable wife for you. You are a Peer of the Realm, Reeve, and I live in a cottage!"

"There's nothing at all wrong with your birth, Deb," he returned. "You're the daughter of a baron, aren't you? You don't need to have money. God knows, I have money enough to support the entire county—if Bernard would only give me control of it!"

I shook my head and repeated, "Lord Bradford would not consider me a suitable wife for a man of your station."

"The hell with what Bernard will consider suitable," Reeve said. His dark eyes flashed dangerously. "He didn't say that I had to marry a duke's daughter. All he said was that I had to marry."

He was bearing down on me with the full force of his personality, which was considerable.

"Stop trying to push me off the side of this phaeton," I said crossly. "I am not going to marry you."

"You won't have to marry me. I promise you that faithfully, Deb. All you will have to do is pretend to become engaged to me. We will inform Bernard, send out an announcement to the *Morning Post*, and then, according to his promise, Bernard will pay my Derby debts."

"And how are we to sever this engagement, pray tell?"

As soon as I said the words, I knew I had made a mistake. I had opened a wedge, and Reeve was sure to move right in.

He did.

"Well, I think it would be a good idea to keep the masquerade going for a few months, Deb. If Bernard thinks that I am really serious about getting married, he might sign over to me the control of half of my money before the deed is actually done."

I folded my arms across my chest. "You didn't answer my question. How are we to sever this engagement?"

He returned promptly, "We will discover that we don't suit."

I frowned. "I don't know, Reeve. It sounds . . . dishonest."

"I'm only trying to get control of my own money," he pointed out. "How can that be dishonest?"

My hair was in its usual style, a single braid down my back, and I chewed on the end of it worriedly while I looked at him, trying to make up my mind.

He picked up my bare hand in his gloved fingers. "Help me out, Deb," he said coaxingly. "There isn't anyone else I could ask to do this for me."

"Mother will not like it."

He snorted. "The last time you listened to your mother you were eight years old."

Still I hesitated.

"Deb," he said, "if you don't help me out, I'm going to have to sell off my stable."

I stared at him, appalled.

"I have to find the money to pay my debts somewhere. The hunters will have to go."

His eyes glittered. He had me, and he knew it.

I let perhaps ten seconds of silence elapse. Then I said tightly, "All right, Reeve, I'll pretend to become engaged to you."

He put his arm around my shoulder and gave me a brief, hard hug. "You're a great girl, Deb. I knew I could count on you."

"You blackmailed me," I accused, as he shortened his reins and backed the horses in preparation for leaving the glade.

He chuckled.

Oh well, I thought, what we were doing couldn't be so very terrible. I had always thought that Reeve's father had done him a terrible injustice in making that will.

And it was certainly nice to see Reeve looking cheerful again.

I made Reeve come with me to break the news to Mama of what we were planning to do. As I had predicted, she was utterly opposed to the scheme.

"It is deceitful," she said. "I cannot like it."

"It isn't really, Mrs. Woodly," Reeve assured her. "All I have to do is assure my cousin that I am engaged, and he will pay my Derby debts."

"But you are not engaged," Mama said distressfully.

"Yes we are," Reeve returned. "We just don't plan to *remain* engaged, that's all."

He looked at me for confirmation, and I rolled my eyes.

We were sitting in the parlor of our cottage, Mama and I on the settee perpendicular to the fireplace, and Reeve on one of the two straight-backed chairs that faced the settee. He always looked absurdly large in this small room.

Mama said next, "It is not as simple as you are making it out to be, Reeve. For one thing, Lord Bradford will most certainly expect to be introduced to Deborah."

Reeve waved his hand like a magician. "No reason for him not to be."

I looked at my dress and thought of the rest of my wardrobe. "Reeve," I said, "I look like a pauper. Mama is right. This idea of yours is simply not going to work."

"Yes it will," he said, "and I am going to tell you why it will work. I had a run of luck at Watier's two nights ago."

I stifled a groan at this news. Watier's was one of the most expensive of the gambling clubs in London, and I hated to hear that Reeve was patronizing it. He surprised me, however, by concluding, "I actually got out of the game with ten thousand pounds in my pocket."

Ten thousand pounds was a huge sum of money to

me, but for a man like Reeve, who owed seventy thousand, it was pin money. I was surprised that he had not tried to increase the money he had won by continuing in the game. He was not known for getting out early.

"Do you know what I am going to do with that money?" he asked me now.

I shook my head, mystified.

"Take you to London and buy you a decent wardrobe," he said smugly.

"*What!*"

"You heard what I said."

"I cannot allow you to do that for Deborah, Reeve," Mama said firmly. "It wouldn't be proper."

"Nonsense," Reeve said. "I look at it as a ten-thousand-pound investment that will net me a great deal more money in return."

"Just a moment, here," I said. "When I agreed to pose as your promised wife, I did not bargain on a trip to London and a new wardrobe."

Reeve stretched his legs out in front of him so that one polished boot rested on the ankle of the other. "Deb, I've said there's nothing wrong with your birth, and there isn't, but there sure is a hell of a lot wrong with your wardrobe."

I scowled at him. "This masquerade is getting a lot more complicated than you originally said it would be."

He gave me a patronizing smile. "Just remember those hunters, Deb."

"Deborah," Mama said, "I forbid you to do this."

I remembered the hunters.

"I have to, Mama," I said piously. "I can't leave poor Reeve in the lurch. It would be terribly unfair."

He gave me a wicked grin. "Now that's the attitude a man likes to hear from his promised wife."

With difficulty, I restrained myself from throwing something at his supremely self-satisfied face.

Reeve had a town house in Berkeley Square, which is where he escorted Mama and me two days after our discussion in the glade. The Season was almost over in London, and Reeve said he would be able to introduce me to the *ton* relatively quietly, as most of the large balls had already been held.

I did not want to be introduced to society at all, but Reeve insisted that it was necessary. We would purchase an appropriate wardrobe—both for me and for Mama, who would act as my chaperone—and I would make my appearance at a few of the end-of-Season balls.

He made it all seem very simple.

It did not turn out to be quite so simple as he had indicated.

The wardrobe part was not difficult. The dressmaker Reeve escorted us to in Bond Street appeared to enjoy herself very much in making me the basic wardrobe that I would need in order to appear in society, and she did the same for Mama.

I had to confess that it was a pleasure to have pretty, fashionable dresses for a change, and the dressmaker was full of enthusiasm for my slim waist and long legs, which she said were perfect to set off the high-waisted dresses that were the current fashion. My flaws were that my bosom could have been larger, and she was horrified to see a slight swell of muscle under the smooth skin of my upper arms and my back.

"I ride a lot of horses," I explained.

"This is no problem with day dresses, but your evening gowns. *Mon Dieu!* I will design dresses with small sleeves to hide this malformation," Mme. Dufand decided. She bit her lip. "Unfortunately, there is nothing I can do about your back."

"Lord Cambridge will not mind my muscles," I assured her. "After all, it is his horses that I ride."

She was doubtful, but after a little coaxing she made me up three gorgeous evening dresses.

Mama, too, was outfitted with a new wardrobe. She fretted and worried and her conscience bothered her, and I tried to get her to relax and enjoy herself.

"Believe me, Mama, the ten thousand pounds that Reeve is spending would just have been handed back to the bank at Watier's if he had not had the incentive to pull off this masquerade for Bernard," I told her with perfect truth.

It took Madame Dufand only two days to have the rudiments of a wardrobe ready for Mama and me, and that was when Reeve sent notice to Lord Bradford of his engagement. He also put a notice in the *Morning Post*. It announced our engagement, and that Mama and I were visiting in Berkeley Square for a few weeks before we retired to the country for the summer months.

I had to admit I got the strangest feeling in the pit of my stomach when I saw my name written down in black and white: *Deborah Mary Elizabeth Woodly, daughter of the late Lord Lynly of Lynly Hall;* then came Reeve's name; then came: *a marriage has been arranged.*

Last week at this time I had been floating down the River Cam with Mr. Liskey. Now here I was in London

with Reeve, preparing to meet London society as his intended bride.

I prided myself on my nerves of steel. I could throw
my heart over any fence, boldly take a nervous horse
across any ground, but the thought of appearing in a
London ballroom made me as tense as a three-year-old
when he first encounters a pack of hounds.

"I have an invite to the Merytons' ball tonight,
Deb," Reeve had said cheerfully at breakfast. "That
should be a good enough place for you to make your
debut as my intended."

His white teeth snapped a piece of bacon in half. He
chewed it with relish.

I narrowed my eyes as I looked at him. "How many
people are likely to be at this good-enough ball?"

"Not above two hundred, I should think," he
replied. "London is starting to thin out as people go to
Brighton or to their country estates."

"I realize that two hundred people might not seem
like much to you, Reeve dear, but it is a great many people to us," Mama said softly.

He reached across the table to pat her hand. "I will
take care of you and Deb, Mrs. Woodly. Never fear. All
will be well."

Hah, I thought. If I was reduced to relying on
Reeve to take care of me, I was in trouble indeed.

CHAPTER
three

I DRESSED FOR THE MERYTON BALL IN A STATE OF nervous apprehension, which I valiantly tried to keep hidden under a calm exterior. The maid whom Reeve had hired to attend to my personal needs did my hair in a deceptively simple knot at the base of my neck. White roses were tucked around the knot, and she used the curling iron to coax two soft ringlets to dangle alongside my ears.

The hairdresser had originally wanted to cut my hair short, which was the current style. However, once I learned that this meant I would be forced to spend hours each day under a curling iron, I had put my foot down and insisted that she leave it long.

The maid was doing up the small covered buttons at the back of my pale blue–silk dress when the door opened and my mother came in.

She looked utterly beautiful. Unlike me, she had agreed to have her hair cut and the short, feathery, silver-blond curls that framed her face made her look so young she quite took my breath away.

"You look beautiful, Mama," I said sincerely.

She smiled. "You look nice too, dearest."

Bless Mama. She knew the last thing I wanted at the moment was effusive comment on my appearance.

"Is Miss Woodly ready yet?" she asked my maid, whose name was Susan.

"I will be five more minutes, Mrs. Woodly," Susan replied.

Mama patted me gently on the arm, and said, "Then I will wait for you downstairs, Deborah."

I nodded.

Exactly seven minutes later, I was walking slowly down the stairs of Lambeth House, still striving to keep my nervousness from showing on my face. As I came around the curve of the staircase I glanced to the bottom of the steps and saw Reeve standing there, looking up at me. His face was wearing an expression I had never seen before.

"Good God, Deb," he said. "You're beautiful."

I reached the bottom of the stairs and gave him a doubtful look. "Do you really think I look all right?"

"All right?" He continued to stare at me. "I think you're rather more than all right."

I smoothed the silk of my blue gown. It was cut lower than anything I had ever worn in my life, and I filled out the décolletage admirably. Madame Dufand had certainly known how to disguise any deficiency I might have in that department. Reeve certainly thought so. He was standing at me with unabashed interest.

Reeve himself looked splendid. His black evening coat fit perfectly over his wide shoulders and was only slightly darker than his eyes and his hair.

"Stop looking at my bosom," I said irritably.

He grinned.

Mama came in from the drawing room, where she had been waiting. "Deborah, darling, are you ready?"

I looked at her again in admiration. She wore a sky-blue gown that brought out the color in her eyes, and she looked as fragile and beautiful as a piece of delicate china.

If I lived to be a hundred, I would never look like a piece of delicate china.

"I shall be escorting the two most beautiful ladies in all of London," Reeve said gallantly.

I gave him a dark look. "If you desert me at this party, I shall kill you," I informed him.

"The men will be swarming all over you," he said. "I'll never be able to hold on to you."

"I won't know anyone, Reeve," I pointed out. "I get asked to dance at home because everyone knows me."

"You don't look like this when you go to dances in Cambridge," he said positively. "Madame Dufand has done you proud."

"She should," I said. "She cost enough."

"Stop complaining." Reeve settled a light cloak around my shoulders, then did the same thing for Mother. "The carriage is waiting, ladies. Let's go."

Mother and I allowed him to hustle us out the door.

The Meryton ball was a revelation. I had never seen so many elegantly dressed people in one place at the same time. Nor had I ever been the subject of such breathless attention.

It began with our hostess, who stared at me with unabashed curiosity. "So you are the lucky woman who has captured our Corsair," she said.

I looked at her in utter bewilderment, not knowing what to reply.

Corsair?

"Lady Meryton, allow me to make known to you Miss Deborah Woodly," Reeve said sternly. "She has promised to be my wife."

"But where did you find her, Cambridge?" Lady Meryton said. "You must know that the *ton* is in a state of shock about this sudden announcement."

Reeve's face was wearing its blackest look.

"Reeve and I have known each other forever, ma'am," I said quietly. "My home is near Ambersley, you see."

"Well, you are a very lucky young woman, my dear," Lady Meryton informed me. "Half the young ladies in London have gone into mourning."

With difficulty, I refrained from rolling my eyes.

We left Lady Meryton in the hall and progressed to the entrance to the drawing room, where the dance was being held. The minute we appeared on the threshold, everyone turned to look at us.

"Good heavens, whatever is the matter?" I muttered to Reeve out of the side of my mouth.

"Pay no attention to them," he said, but I could see that he was annoyed. He took my arm and almost pulled me into the drawing room. Mama walked quietly at my other side.

A little whisper of excitement rippled around the room.

I had never in my life caused such stir. It had to be Reeve.

Whatever was going on?

There was a dance forming up as we came in, and Reeve immediately took my hand and led me to the floor. He didn't say anything, but the set of his jaw was rather grim.

The dance was a quadrille, which required me to pay close attention to my steps and didn't give me much opportunity to question Reeve about what was happening. As soon as the dance was over we returned to Mama, who had found a place among the chaperones, and I was preparing to quiz Reeve about the oddity of our reception when two gentlemen came up to us and demanded to be introduced to me.

Reeve looked resigned. "Deb, these are two good friends of mine. May I present Colonel Angus MacIntosh of the Scots Guards, and Mr. Devereaux Miles, who has been a friend since Eton."

The Colonel was a bluff-looking older man with sandy hair and an unfashionable sandy mustache. Mr. Miles was Reeve's age, with smoothly brushed blond hair and attractive hazel eyes.

Mr. Miles said, "I am so pleased to meet you, Miss Woodly. It was quite a shock to learn that Reeve has decided to get riveted, you know, but now that I've seen you I can perfectly understand his decision."

"Thank you," I said.

I knew as soon as Mr. Miles said Reeve's name that he was in fact an old friend. Reeve had been called by his father's second title, Baron Reeve, ever since he was born. At his father's death five years ago, he had become Lord Cambridge, but to those of us who had known him since childhood, he would never be anything but Reeve.

"Wonder if you would give me the pleasure of the next dance?" Mr. Miles continued charmingly. He looked at Reeve. "That is, if Reeve don't mind my poaching on his territory."

I glanced at Reeve, but all he did was give me a bland smile and tell me to go ahead.

I danced with Mr. Miles.

I danced with Colonel MacIntosh.

I danced with a large number of other gentlemen whom Reeve presented to me.

Except for the two times that he danced with me and the one time he danced with Mama, Reeve didn't dance at all. Instead he spent the evening leaning against the wall next to Mama's chair, with his arms folded across his chest. He talked occasionally to Mama, and the rest of the time he watched the room with hooded eyes and a faintly mocking smile on his lips.

Most of the women in the room appeared to be surreptitiously watching him.

It was not until I paid a visit to the ladies withdrawing room that I learned something about Reeve's London reputation.

It began when a very young lady with a heart-shaped face and huge violet eyes came up to me and said breathlessly. "I am Amanda Pucket, Miss Woodly, and I'm sorry if you find me rude but I will just *burst* if I don't find out how you and Lord Cambridge met."

I repeated what I had said earlier, about Reeve and I knowing each other forever.

"Oh you are so lucky!" This came from another

starry-eyed seventeen-year-old. "To be marrying the Corsair!"

This was the second time someone had called Reeve the Corsair.

"Er, is *Corsair* Lord Cambridge's nickname?" I asked in bewilderment.

The circle of girls stared at me as if I were mad.

"But . . . surely you know *The Corsair*?" Amanda Pucket said.

My face told her that I did not.

"It is Lord Byron's newest poem," she informed me. "Ever since it was published in February people have done nothing but compare the hero, Conrad, to Lord Cambridge."

"Good heavens," I said faintly. Poor Reeve.

"Conrad is supposed to be modeled on Byron himself, of course, but Lord Cambridge is so much handsomer," Amanda told me reverently. "He has sable-colored hair that tumbles down across his forehead, just like Conrad's, and flashing dark eyes, just like Conrad's, and . . ."

Another young lady closed her eyes and quoted soulfully:

> *There was a laughing Devil in his sneer,*
> *That raised emotions both of rage and fear . . .*

"A *laughing devil?*" I had to struggle to keep from laughing out loud myself.

Another young lady quoted even more soulfully than the first:

He knew himself a villain—but he deemed
The rest no better than the thing he seemed.

All of a sudden I didn't feel like laughing anymore.

"You see, Miss Woodly," Amanda explained, "Conrad has this deep dark secret that has wounded his very
soul, and that is why he acts as he does." She gave me
a sunny smile. "You must read *The Corsair*, you really
must."

"Yes," I said. I felt slightly sick, but I did my best
for Reeve. "Lord Cambridge is really nothing like the
Corsair, you know, even if he does have sable-colored
hair and flashing eyes."

The smitten Amanda sighed. "You know what
Caro Lamb said about Byron, Miss Woodly: 'Mad, bad,
and dangerous to know.' Well, my Mama said that
those words are twice as applicable to Cambridge and
that I was to stay out of his way."

All the girls gazed at me with longing.

"*Lucky you!*"

When we reached home, Mama was tired and
went up to bed, but I knew I wouldn't sleep unless I
had a chance to unwind first, and so I asked Reeve if
we might have a cup of tea in the drawing room.

"Come into the library," he said. "You can have
tea, and I'll have a glass of brandy."

I followed him down the black-and-white marbled
floor of Lambeth House's hallway to the library door.
Together we went inside the high-ceilinged, oak-
paneled, book-lined room. Reeve went to a cupboard in

the corner of the room to get a bottle and gestured me to one of the striped silk–covered chairs that was pulled up in front of the carved-oak fireplace.

A minute later he took the chair opposite mine. He put the brandy bottle on a small pedestal table next to his chair, poured himself a full glass, stretched out his legs, crossed his ankles, and took a swallow of his drink.

"I thought you'd be popular, but I didn't quite realize you'd be the belle of the ball, Deb," he said. He took another deep swallow of brandy. "Half of those fellows who asked you to dance I scarcely even knew."

The butler came into the room with my tea in a pretty Wedgwood service, which he set up on a low table in front of me. I poured myself a cup and stirred in some sugar. I sipped it gratefully, looked up, and found Reeve watching me, a tense frown between his straight dark brows.

I said, "This *Corsair* business must be driving you mad."

I could hear him release his breath. "You heard about it, then?"

"A group of very impressionable young ladies got ahold of me in the ladies' withdrawing room."

His brows snapped together again. "You cannot credit what a hell my life has become since that damned poem was published, Deb. I should like to take that bounder Byron and wring his neck. Some people are even saying that he based that bloody stupid Conrad on me!"

I said practically, "From what the girls were saying, I gather you look like him. Surely that is not so very dreadful, Reeve. You know how impressionable young ladies are." I lifted my eyebrows. "In addition to which, you cannot expect to go around London behaving like some arrogant Renaissance prince without stirring up comment."

What I did not mention, would never mention, were the other aspects of Reeve's character that would inevitably lend themselves to comparison with a doomed, self-destructive, guilt-driven hero.

"I am not arrogant," he said, outraged.

"Well you certainly looked arrogant tonight," I shot back. "You didn't dance with anyone but me and Mama. You just leaned against the wall, with your arms crossed, and looked . . . looked . . . well—arrogant. You behave much better in the country."

He finished his brandy and poured himself another glass. "Yes," he said scornfully. "A fine gudgeon I should look if I made out that I was too good to dance with the likes of the squire's daughters."

I understood. It was precisely because the squire's daughters, and the rest of our small village society, were so far beneath his social class that Reeve would not dream of insulting us. Here in London, among his peers, it was different.

He said, "Surely you can see now why it is impossible for me to marry one of those imbecile girls, Deb."

I frowned. "But Reeve, there have to be other women you could court. Certainly the girls who accosted me in the ladies withdrawing room tonight can't be the only eligible females in London!"

"They're the only eligible females that I know," Reeve said gloomily. "This is the way it works, Deb.

Members of the *ton* trundle their seventeen- and eighteen-year-olds into London for a Season or two, and then, if the girls don't get an offer, they're brought back home so that the next daughter can have her chance." He drank some more brandy. "I really don't want to marry a seventeen-year-old, Deb."

I didn't blame him. Such a marriage would be a disaster. Reeve was too complicated a man for a seventeen-year-old to handle.

I sipped my tea. "What about your friends? Don't they have any sisters who would be suitable?"

He shook his head and put his glass down on the table with an audible click. He looked at me, his eyes glittering like black obsidian. "Do you have any notion of how beautiful you've turned out to be, Deb? I had no idea you were hiding so much potential under those dreadful clothes."

I gave him a dangerous glare. "If I find your eyes on my bosom one more time, Reeve, I shall throw something at you."

He grinned, the rare, carefree, joyous smile that made him look as young as his twenty-four years. "Do I make you nervous?"

"You make me uncomfortable," I said.

"Good."

I picked up a small pillow that was tucked in the side of my chair and threw it at him.

He ducked, and then he began to laugh.

"I wonder what Bernard will think of you?" he said. He took another swallow of brandy.

"He will probably think I'm a hoyden," I replied.

"Well, it doesn't matter what he thinks," Reeve

replied stubbornly. "His stipulation was that I get married. He's not in a position to complain about my choice."

I said reluctantly, "I have to confess that I am not looking forward to meeting Lord Bradford."

"I don't blame you," Reeve said bluntly. "He's a stick. But you can't back out on me now, Deb. The notice is in the paper, and Bernard will probably be here tomorrow or the day after. Be brave, keep your chin up, and we'll weather the storm together."

"I hope so," I said gloomily. "Really, Reeve, I don't know how I let you talk me into this."

"You did it because you're my best friend, and you didn't want to let me down," he said. He cocked one eyebrow. "Also, you didn't want to lose your rides on my hunters." He handed me his glass, which was half-full of brandy. "Here, have a shot. It will do you much more good than that mushy tea."

I took the brandy and bolted it down. It made me cough, but the warmth burned its way all the way down to my belly.

"That *is* better," I said.

"Come along," he said. "Time for bed. I'll get you your candle and escort you upstairs."

I stood up and my head spun a little. I staggered, and Reeve reached out to take my arm. "Whoa there, old girl," he said. "All right?"

I took a deep breath. "Yes."

Reeve escorted me to the door of my room. When we were standing there, just before I opened it to go in, he bent to give me a quick kiss on the cheek.

"Thank you, Deb," he said gravely. "I appreciate your help."

I patted him on the shoulder. "What are friends for?" I said lightly, then turned and went into the pretty, chintz-covered safety of my room.

CHAPTER
four

REEVE TOOK ME DRIVING IN THE PARK THE following afternoon at the fashionable hour of five o'clock, and when we returned to the house it was to discover that Lord Bradford had arrived. The butler, Jermyn, informed us that Mama was giving him tea in the front drawing room.

"Courage, Deb," Reeve muttered in my ear, as we turned toward the room in question to make our appearance before Reeve's formidable trustee.

I had never seen Lord Bradford before, but I had certainly heard about him. He was Reeve's father's first cousin, a widower with a daughter and two sons, the eldest of whom was Reeve's age. He owned a decent, unencumbered estate in Sussex, where he happily spent most of his time in country pursuits. His position in the peerage was not high, but his barony was of an old date. In short, I had always judged him to be exactly the sort of stolid, unremarkable, unimaginative man who would have no comprehension of the kind of devils that drove someone like Reeve.

I smoothed the already straight collar of my sky-blue driving dress. Three-quarters of the clothes Madame Dufand had made for me were blue. She had been quite insistent on matching the color of my eyes.

Reeve put his hand under my elbow, gave an encouraging squeeze, and together we went into the front drawing room of Lambeth House.

Mama was sitting on a green-silk-covered sofa dispensing tea to a powerful-looking, broad-shouldered man with a strong, square, blunt-featured face. He rose to his feet as soon as I came into the room.

"Hallo, Bernard," Reeve said. "I trust your journey was a pleasant one."

"I made very good time," Lord Bradford replied. He was not looking at Reeve, however, he was looking at me.

Reeve looked down at me also, a hint of mischief in his eyes. "Deb, allow me to present my cousin, Lord Bradford." His eyes flicked to his trustee. "Bernard, this is Miss Deborah Woodly, who has done me the honor of consenting to be my bride."

Lord Bradford approached me and took my gloved hand into his. His eyes were gray and steady and not quite two inches higher than my own. "I am very pleased to meet you, Miss Woodly," he said gravely.

You could have searched the earth over and not have found a man more opposite to Reeve, I thought, as I smiled and murmured a polite response.

"Will you have some tea, Deborah?" Mama asked. "And you, Reeve?"

"Of course," I replied, going to sit beside Mama on the sofa. I wondered how long she had been stuck trying to entertain Lord Bradford on her own, poor thing.

Reeve took a cup from Mama and went to lean his shoulders against the green-silk-covered wall, next to the white-marble fireplace.

Lord Bradford went back to his chair and took a sip of his tea. "I was delighted to discover that you took my suggestion seriously, Reeve," he said. "Surprised, but delighted."

Reeve scowled. "You didn't leave me much choice, did you, Bernard? I hope that I can count on your paying my Derby debts now."

Lord Bradford looked like thunder. "This is hardly a tactful matter to be discussing in front of your future wife," he said angrily.

"Oh, don't worry about me, Lord Bradford," I said with a sunny smile. "Reeve and I understand each other perfectly."

I found myself the object of a suspicious stare. "Just what do you mean by that, Miss Woodly?"

My mother's gentle voice intruded. "Deborah only means that she understands that Reeve has an obligation to pay his gambling debts, Lord Bradford." She gave him an extraordinarily sweet smile. "May I pour you some more tea?"

He was instantly distracted, holding out his cup to Mama and looking with undisguised pleasure at her lovely face.

"You are going to pay poor Reeve's debts, aren't you, Lord Bradford?" Mama said worriedly. "He is quite anxious about them."

Lord Bradford sipped his tea and ran his eyes from Reeve, who was standing against the wall, to me, sitting beside Mama. I thought I detected the faintest trace of suspicion in his gaze. "I said that I would pay his bills if he would get married, but he is not married yet."

Reeve catapulted away from the wall, spilling his

tea on the Turkish carpet. "You said that you would pay my Derby debts if I became engaged! I cannot keep my creditors waiting any longer. Dammit, honor demands that those debts be paid immediately! You know that, Bernard!"

Lord Bradford scowled. "There are ladies present, Reeve. Do not swear."

If Lord Bradford knew how often I had heard Reeve swear, he would probably have an apoplexy, I thought. I also thought that it was better not to mention that fact right now.

"Bernard," Reeve said tightly, "if you don't pay those bills immediately, you will drive me to the money-lenders."

"Don't try to blackmail me, Reeve." Coldly.

"It seems to me as if you are the one who is black-mailing me!" Hotly.

"Oh dear," Mama said. Pitifully.

I said, "Well, if you are not going to pay Reeve's debts, Lord Bradford, then it seems to me as if the whole point of our marriage has been nullified. We had better send a notice to the newspapers that we have made a mistake."

Everyone's attention swung to me.

"I don't understand you, Miss Woodly," Lord Bradford said. His voice was calm, but his gray eyes looked angry.

"It is very simple," I said. "Reeve is marrying me because he—very understandably!—wants to get control of his own money. For my part, Mama and I are not in the best of financial health, and such a marriage will benefit us also. However,"—and I fixed Lord Bradford with my most steely look—"our marriage is based on the assumption that it will benefit us both. I refuse to take advantage of poor Reeve if you refuse to hold to your end of the bargain."

Silence fell on the drawing room. I took a sip of tea and shot a quick glance at Reeve. He winked.

I swallowed my tea, and said to Lord Bradford, "Reeve told me that you said you would pay his gaming debts if he became engaged. Did he misrepresent your words to me?"

To my infinite surprise, a touch of humor appeared at the corners of Lord Bradford's mouth. "No, Miss Woodly, he did not."

I allowed my eyes to widen questioningly. "Well then?"

"You cannot cry off from this engagement now," Lord Bradford said. "It would cause a scandal."

I saw Reeve's lips beginning to open, and I frowned at him.

"Then will you pay Reeve's gambling debts?" I asked Lord Bradford.

"Yes," that gentleman replied resignedly. "I will pay Reeve's gambling debts, Miss Woodly." He turned to Reeve. "Give me a list of the men to whom you owe money, and the amount of the sums, and I will see to it."

Lord Bradford left shortly after tea. Mama invited him to take dinner with us and then accompany us to the Larchmont ball that evening, and he accepted. He was staying with his sister, not with us, which was a great relief to me. The thought of constantly playing mediator between Reeve and his trustee if Lord Bradford were actually living in the house was an exhausting thought.

"Good job, Deb," Reeve said as soon as Lord Bradford was out the front door.

"What a thoroughly unpleasant man," I said. "For a dreadful moment there I thought he was going to go back on his word to you."

"Oh, Bernard never actually goes back on his word," Reeve said bitterly. "The problem is that he is a master at shaping his words to mean something other than what you thought they meant."

"I did not find Lord Bradford so unpleasant, Deborah," Mama said. "Indeed, until you and Reeve came in, his company was quite agreeable."

I smiled at her. "No one could be disagreeable to you, Mama."

Unbidden, the thought slipped into my mind of my father's brother, John, and my half brother, Richard, both of whom had been far more than merely disagreeable to her. From the moment I had known that I would be coming to London I had wondered if I might run into one or the other of them.

Richard was a few years older than Reeve, and engaged to be marreid to the daughter of a viscount. What if he and his fiancée were in London?

I despised my half brother for his neglect of Mother and me for all these years, but once in a while I admitted to the truth that, deep down inside, part of me desired to meet my father's other child. I wanted to tell him just what I thought of him, of course.

However bad he was, though, Richard's perfidy paled when compared to that of my half uncle, my father's younger brother, John. He was the one who had been named trustee of my father's estate. He was the one who had forced Mother and me out of Lynly Manor. He was the one who was the deserving recipient of my unrelenting hatred.

One day I would like to meet *him*, I thought. And he had better not be standing near the edge of a cliff when I did.

Lord Bradford arrived for dinner with his sister and her husband, and we actually had a pleasant, civilized meal together. Reeve sat at the head of the polished-mahogany table from which all the leaves had been removed, and Mama sat opposite him. Lord Bradford and I faced each other across the middle, with Mr. and Mrs. Stucky beside us.

The dining room of Lambeth House was elegant without being overwhelming. It was less than a quarter the size of the dining room at Ambersley, and the yellow-silk wall and drapes set off the richly polished mahogany furniture most effectively. There was but one crystal chandelier hanging from the ceiling, not three like the ones that hung over the twenty-foot-long table at Ambersley, and I found it an altogether more comfortable room than the one I had seen the single time Reeve had given me a tour of his country estate.

The dinner could have been better. The vegetables were fresh, but the lamb was overcooked and so was the fish. I was hungry, though, and even overcooked meat tasted good to someone who was not accustomed to having too much of it.

Lord Bradford pushed his food around on his plate and looked disgusted. "Your chef leaves something to be desired, Reeve," he said.

Reeve, who had a stomach of iron, shrugged. "That

will be something that Deb can attend to," he said, giving me a wicked look.

"Hmmm," I said.

"Do you have your own sheep and cattle, Lord Bradford?" Mama asked.

Lord Bradford smiled at her. "That I do, Mrs. Woodly. In fact, I may say that I quite probably have the best herd of sheep in all of Sussex."

"How splendid," Mama replied. "I know very little of sheep myself, but I do love to garden."

The elder members of the dinner party conversed genteelly while Reeve and I listened. When finally dinner was over, it was time to leave for the Larchmont dance.

"This is a larger ball than the one we attended last night," Reeve informed me. "In fact, it will probably be the last big crush of the Season. Everyone who is still in town will be there."

I nodded, not quite so nervous as I had been the night before. This evening I was wearing a cream-colored gown with blue-satin trim around the high waist and the puffed sleeves. My hair was gathered high on the crown of my head and allowed to fall in ringlets down my back. The bloody ringlets had taken almost an hour to create, and they tickled the nape of my neck. Reeve told me that they looked just the thing, however, so I supposed the effort was worth it.

This time in London wasn't going to last forever, after all. I figured that I would be home in my own familiar village before another week had passed.

Lord Bradford and Reeve were waiting for Mama

and me in the drawing room when we came downstairs. They looked at us.

"Reeve, I do believe we will be escorting the two most beautiful ladies at the dance this evening," Lord Bradford said gallantly. He was dressed in conventional evening dress of black coat, white neckcloth, and knee breeches, and he looked like a stocky farmer in disguise. Reeve, on the other hand, looked utterly magnificent in his well-cut clothes.

I braced myself to cope with that silly Corsair business again tonight.

Mama and Lord Bradford rode in the carriage belonging to Mr. and Mrs. Stucky, leaving Reeve and me to follow in the Cambridge town chaise. As we traveled toward Grosvenor Square where the party was to be held, I said to my erstwhile fiancé, "I think it would be a good idea for you to dance with a few other ladies beside Mama and me tonight, Reeve. You are only adding to this foolish Corsair image by standing around looking haughty, you know."

He was sitting in one of the corners of the chaise, gazing out into the street, and at my words he turned to look at me. The sky was still light with the softness of twilight, and I could see his face clearly. "There isn't anyone else I want to dance with," he said grumpily.

"Well, you can dance with Mrs. Stucky for one. And it would be polite to dance with your hostess as well."

He scowled at me.

"Lord Bradford will think you rude if you don't dance," I said.

His scowl deepened.

"Stop being such a martyr," I recommended. "Look at me. Last night I spent more time talking about the weather than I have ever done in my entire life, and you haven't heard me complaining, have you?"

He lifted his eyebrows at me in surprise. "Were you bored, Deb? You looked as if you were having the time of your life."

"Let us say that the conversation of most of my partners was scarcely scintillating." I gave him a minatory look. "It seems to me that if I can make sacrifices for this pretend engagement of ours, Reeve, so can you."

He slid down on his spine a little and folded his arms across his chest. I saw his eyes glitter wickedly. "I fail to follow your logic, Deb. If I dance with other women, then people will think that I don't care about you, whereas if I lean against the wall all night and stare at you hungrily, everyone will be convinced that I am madly in love."

I said in my most practical voice, "Reeve, I don't think it is precisely wise to have people think that you are madly in love with me. We are eventually going to call this marriage off, remember? Let's not overdo the love business."

There was silence in the coach for a few minutes while Reeve once more stared out the window. I regarded his splendid profile, and gave him a chance to work things out on his own.

At last he turned back to me. "Oh, all right, I suppose you are right," he mumbled irritably. "But nothing will induce me to dance with those silly chits who always look as if they will faint whenever I come within speaking distance of them."

I thought of Amanda and her friends. "I don't think it's a good idea for you to dance with them, either." I pushed one of the damn ringlets away from my neck. "There has to be a matron or two whom you can safely squire to the dance floor, just to demonstrate your courtesy to Lord Bradford."

He scowled at me. "Why do I let you talk me into these things?"

"Because you know in your heart that I am right," I said.

"No, it's because I owe you a debt for agreeing to this pretense, and you are exploiting that fact shamelessly," he retorted.

I grinned. "How can you think such a thing?"

He grunted, leaned back against the rich brown-velvet squabs, and closed his eyes. We neither of us spoke again until our carriage pulled up in front of Larchmont House in Grosvenor Square.

There was not quite such a commotion when Reeve and I were introduced at this dance as there had been the evening before. For one thing, Larchmont House had a ballroom, so there was room for a very large number of people, and the new guests coming in were not as noticeable as they had been in the Meryton drawing room. We were also a party of six this evening, and much as I disliked Lord Bradford, it was comfortable to be part of a group of ordinary people and not merely an appendage of the famous—or infamous—Corsair.

We stood along the side wall of the ballroom, in front of a large gilt mirror and next to a massive arrangement of roses. Reeve sighed and bent his head to mine.

"Another bloody boring evening," he murmured in my ear.

If Mama or Lord Bradford had heard that *bloody*, they would have had a fit.

I smiled up at him sympathetically. "I'm looking forward to supper," I said. "Your cook is so ghastly that I saved my appetite. I hope they have lobster patties, like the Merytons did last night."

He grinned. "You ate an obscene amount of those lobster patties last night, Deb."

"And I plan to eat an obscene amount of them tonight as well," I replied.

"Is my cook really that bad?"

"Yes."

"That's peculiar. I never noticed."

"It's because your stomach is always in such a wretched state from all the wine and gin and brandy that you drink," I said austerely.

He gave a longing look at my hairdo. "I wish you were wearing your braid so I could pull it."

"Touch my hair, and you die," I informed him.

He chuckled. "All right, all right." His face sobered. "According to the incredibly tedious rules of Lady Jersey and her cohorts on the Ladies Committee of Almack's, I am only allowed two dances with you. We will make one the supper dance—and what about this next quadrille?"

"Certainly, my lord," I said sedately. "That will leave you an ample amount of time to dance with Mama, and Mrs. Stucky and Lady Larchmont."

He sighed. "Oh, all right."

The music ended, and he took my hand and led me out to the floor.

The Larchmont ball proceeded much along the lines of the Meryton ball the evening before. Reeve did dance more, as he had promised me he would, but he also spent an inordinate amount of time holding up the wall with his shoulders. He did not look as bored, however, as a number of his friends were in attendance this evening and so he had some men to talk to. He and his friends also spent a good deal of time frequenting the punch bowl, and by the time he came to claim me for the supper dance his eyes were looking distinctly glazed.

"You need air, not a dance," I proclaimed as soon as I saw him, and taking his arm, I steered him through the French doors at the back of the ballroom, which opened onto a terrace. It was a warm night, and the shrubbery hiding the back garden from the stables gave off a scent that almost made one feel one was in the country.

"I am not foxed," Reeve said in an injured voice.

"I didn't say you were foxed," I replied.

"Well, you implied it."

"Your eyes look glassy."

"That is because I am bored," he said, his voice even more injured than before.

He *was* foxed, I knew, and I also knew that he was foxed precisely because he was bored. Clearly he didn't like these large society balls. Nor had he been happy during the few drives in the park we had taken since our arrival in London. Not for Reeve the slow, stately procession of vehicles that made up the afternoon ritual of the *ton*.

"It seems to me that you are not overly fond of

London, Reeve," I said in a voice that I strove to keep light. "Everything bores you."

He shrugged. "There are a few things that are all right. It's good fun having a go at Gentleman Jackson's boxing saloon, and I like practicing my shooting at Manton's and my swordplay at Angelo's. As for the rest of it . . . the clubs, the dances, Almack's . . ." He shuddered, then raised his voice. "Damn it, Deb, why do you think I bought a racehorse? I needed some excitement in my life!"

You don't need excitement, Reeve, I thought. *You need to have the sole control of Ambersley. You need to be in charge of your own land, your own people, your own heritage. A racehorse is not the answer to your restlessness.*

It had long been perfectly clear to me that one of the reasons why Reeve got into so much trouble was that he had nothing meaningful to do with himself. I had never been able to comprehend why Lord Bradford did not understand this. It was precisely because Reeve had no say in the running of his own property that he avoided Ambersley. And the more time he spent in London, the more dangerous his activities became. The drinking, the gambling, the outrageous stunts, the opera dancers, all of the things that Lord Bradford so deplored, would probably cease if Reeve could only have control of his own destiny.

I believed this most profoundly. In truth, it was the main reason why I had agreed to this shocking masquerade. I had made his threat that he was going to sell his hunters an excuse for me to go along with him. Reeve and I had been friends for a long time, and I felt an obligation to help him if I could.

We stood together on the terrace of Larchmont House, and I looked up at him in the dim glow cast by the light coming from inside the ballroom. I said urgently, "Reeve, don't do anything to cause Lord Bradford to think he has made a mistake in promising to turn over half of your inheritance to you."

His brows drew together. "I have no intention of doing anything to outrage Bernard."

"Then don't let him see you drinking!" I snapped. "You have spent half the night dipping into the punch bowl. Don't you think that Lord Bradford noticed?"

He ran his hand through his hair, causing it to tumble down over his forehead. Amanda and her friends would swoon when they saw it. "I was only having a few cups with my friends," he said, but I could tell he was now on the defensive.

"Listen to me, Reeve," I said fiercely. I stepped closer to him and straightened his neckcloth and smoothed back his hair with fingers that were none too gentle. "You are going to behave yourself while we are engaged, or I am going to back out of this bloody masquerade and leave you hanging in the wind."

"You wouldn't!"

"Watch me."

"Do you know that you are the prettiest girl in the room tonight?" he said unexpectedly.

"You can't turn me up sweet, Reeve, I know you too well. Now come along. We are going to walk around this little garden for a few minutes and you are going to breathe deeply and try to get your head in order. Then we are going in to supper."

"How did I ever get myself engaged to such a shrew?" he grumbled, but he let me take his arm and move him onto the graveled path that went around the little garden.

"You begged me," I reminded him.

"I must have been mad."

"You were desperate," I said. "And you still are. Remember that, Reeve, and remember what I have just said."

I felt a sudden sharp pull on one of my ringlets. I jumped and made a noise indicative of both surprise and pain.

"I couldn't resist," came Reeve's laughing voice from somewhere close to my ear.

"All right," I said. "Touché. Shall we call it even?"

"Even it is." He linked his arm in mine. "How many turns will we need before you can go and attack the lobster patties?"

He actually seemed to be walking fairly steadily on his own. "Ten," I said, and, meekly, he agreed.

CHAPTER
five

WHEN WE WENT INTO THE SUPPER ROOM WE saw Mama sitting with Lord Bradford, and at my urging, we joined them. The fresh air had removed the glaze from Reeve's eyes, and altogether he conversed with perfect articulation and good sense. I was convinced that he had made a favorable impression on his trustee.

It was not until the following day that I discovered that perhaps Reeve had made too favorable an impression. Lord Bradford arrived at Lambeth House during morning calling hours to invite Reeve and Mama and me to a house party at his home in Sussex.

Reeve was at Tattersalls during our interview, so he did not learn about the invitation until he came home late in the afternoon.

"Bernard what?" he shouted when I told him the news.

"He invited us to visit him in Sussex," I repeated gloomily. "He wants to get to know me better, he said. He plans to put together a small house party for our entertainment."

"Entertainment? Bernard? By God, that's a joke." Reeve began to stride around the room like a caged tiger. "The two words don't fit together in the same sentence."

Mama said, "Lord Bradford seems a very pleasant

man, Reeve." She was distressed. "Deborah and I did
not know how to turn away such a generous offer."

"That's easy," Reeve said. "We'll say we're busy."

"Doing what?" I demanded.

"We'll think of something."

"What?"

He glared at me out of outraged dark eyes. "Surely
you can think of something, Deb. You've always been
the one with the imagination."

I thought, *I was not the one who had the brilliant
idea to paint the historic house of the Head of my college yellow.*

I held my tongue, however, and said instead, "Do
stop prowling and sit down, Reeve. I can't think of a single thing." I waited until he was at least leaning against
the window wall before I continued patiently, "Now, let
us look at this situation from Lord Bradford's point of
view. He thinks we are really engaged. He is your closest relative, and he wants to introduce me to the rest of
your family. It makes sense, after all, doesn't it?"

A very strange look came over Reeve's face. "The
rest of the family?" he said. "By any chance did he mention if my cousin Robert was going to be there?"

"Is Robert one of his sons?"

"His eldest son."

"Then yes, he did say that his sons would be there."
Reeve groaned.

"What's the matter with Robert?"

"We don't get along," Reeve said briefly.

Mama was wringing her hands. "I am sorry if you
are displeased, Reeve."

"Don't apologize to Reeve, Mama," I told her. "He

has brought all of this on himself." I turned back to my fiancé. "We have to go," I said flatly. "We have to go, and you have to behave yourself, and if we can convince Lord Bradford that you are indeed a reformed character, then I think perhaps you can get him to sign over half your fortune to you before the wedding."

"Deb, do you know how incredibly boring a visit to Bernard is going to be?"

"We'll have horses, I presume," I said. "The Sussex Downs are supposed to be wonderful to ride along."

He still hadn't sat down. "Wakefield Manor is rather a pretty property," he admitted. "It sits right on the crest of the South Downs in West Sussex, not far from the sea." His scowl deepened. "It's not the locale that is the problem, it's the company."

"Reeve, it will only be for a few weeks. You yourself said that we should probably have to extend this mock engagement for at least that length of time."

He settled his shoulders more firmly against the wall and looked extremely discontented. "I don't want to go to Bernard's."

My patience snapped, and I slammed my hand down on the arm of the sofa where I was sitting. "Stop being so petulant. Do you or don't you want control of your own heritage?"

He glared at me. "Of course I do."

"Then stop complaining and go to Sussex."

At that he flung himself into a chair, stretched his booted legs in front of him, and closed his eyes. "You don't understand," he said wearily. "Going to Sussex means listening to Bernard going on about my lack of responsibility from morning till night. I don't think I can stand it."

"He won't call you irresponsible if you don't act irresponsibly," I said. "And you won't act irresponsibly, because I will be there to keep you in line."

He opened his eyes and looked at me. An emotion I couldn't identify glittered in their dark depths. "You will?"

"Yes."

He gave an elaborate sigh. "All right, all right, I'll go. I only hope you know what you are getting us into."

"I can endure anything for a few weeks if it's in a good cause," I said piously. I narrowed my eyes at him. "And you can, too."

He gave me a mock military salute. "Yes, ma'am."

"That's what I like to hear," I said. "Now would you care for some tea?"

"How about some Madeira?"

"Tea," I said.

"Oh, all right, I'll have some tea."

"Mama, will you ring for the tea tray?" I asked sweetly.

Poor Mama, who had been quiet as a mouse during my skirmish with Reeve, gratefully pulled the bell and summoned the butler to ask for tea.

Lord Bradford left town the following day in order to prepare for our visit to Sussex. During the remainder of the week we spent in London before we followed him, Reeve and I kept busy by making a number of expeditions together. He took me to the Tower of London and to Astley's Amphitheatre, where we saw a wonderful equestrian exhibition. He also put together a party of his friends for outings to Richmond Park and Hampton Court.

Reeve's friends were a high-spirited lot, and I could see why he found them amusing, but except for Dev Miles, his old friend from Eton, I wasn't overly impressed by any of them. I judged them to be friends for good times, not the sort that one could count on when the chips were down.

Richmond Park, on the outskirts of London, was known for its wonderful horse paths, where one could gallop full out to one's heart's content—unlike Hyde Park in central London, where one was constrained to a modified canter at best.

It was faintly overcast when we left London for our expedition to Richmond, but the air seemed to clear as we drew closer and closer to the country. As we rode along, each of Reeve's friends made a point of pushing their horses up alongside of mine so that they could speak to me. I would have thought that this was mere politeness, had I not found myself somewhat disconcerted by the outrageous compliments with which they bombarded me. After all, I was supposed to be engaged to Reeve. Wasn't it inappropriate for them to make me the subject of such continuous and outrageous flattery?

I could see that Reeve didn't like it, either. The young women whom these men were ostensibly escorting didn't seem to mind, however. They were too busy flirting with Reeve.

Once we reached our destination, however, and Reeve gave our admission tickets in at the gate, the tenor of the afternoon changed. Reeve and I were able to give our horses free rein and gallop flat out along the wide, well-trimmed rides, easily outdistancing the rest of our party. It had been a long time since we had ridden together like this, and the sheer pleasure of it more than made up for the annoyances we had been forced to suffer along the way.

Reeve had arranged for a picnic to be brought from London for us, and when we returned to the grassy, tree-enclosed area where such informal meals took place, it was already laid out by several of the Lambeth House footmen. There was champagne for the gentlemen, tea for the ladies, and an assortment of cold meats and breads and cakes to eat.

I took a glass of champagne and a plate of cold chicken and went to sit at one of the simple wooden trestle tables provided by the park.

Reeve left his groom, who had been driving the curricle with the food, and came up to stand across the table from me. "Don't drink too much of that stuff, Deb," he warned. "You've got to stay in the saddle on the way home, remember."

"I believe I can manage one glass of champagne, Reeve, without putting myself in danger of falling off my horse," I returned haughtily.

"I'm sure you can, Miss Woodly," said one of Reeve's friends, a silly, blond-haired fellow named Hampton, who took the seat next to me and looked at me with unabashed admiration. "Dashed if you don't have the best seat on a horse I've ever seen on a woman."

Now *this* was a compliment I could appreciate. "Thank you, Mr. Hampton," I said, giving him a smile that was not a mere social twitch of the lips.

He blinked and beamed back at me.

"Aren't you going to get yourself some food, Hampton?" Reeve growled. "Or do you think making a cake of yourself over my fiancée is sufficient nourishment?"

Mr. Hampton glanced at the expression on Reeve's face, and his silly smile disappeared. He stood up hastily. "Just going, old fellow. No need to fly up into the boughs, you know."

I glanced up at Reeve and was surprised to see him looking so thunderous.

"Why don't you take your own advice and get some food?" I said mildly.

He grunted. He was looking at me with his brows drawn together as if he were not pleased.

"Are you really that upset that I am drinking champagne?" I inquired.

"What? No, of course not."

One of the women in the party, a young widow who was accompanying one of Reeve's friends, came over to us with a plate of food in her hands.

"You are not eating, Lord Cambridge?" she asked archly. She gazed up at him out of sultry green eyes. "Allow me to get you something."

Good God, I thought irritably, *she sounds as if she were propositioning him. And right in front of me!* I scowled.

Reeve caught my eye and suddenly grinned, his temper miraculously restored. "Thank you, Mrs. Wethersby, but I will get something for myself," he said, and went off to fill up his plate with chicken and ham and beef and cold pigeon pie, which he washed down with five glasses of champagne.

He sat solid as a rock in his saddle the whole way home. I suppose one of the results of too much drinking is that after a while one begins to get used to it.

Our visit to Hampton Court the following day was more pleasant than the trip to Richmond Park had been. We went by boat up the Thames, and as we shared our boat with Mr. Miles and his sister, who was a very pleasant, well-mannered girl, I enjoyed the trip upriver very much. Then, once we reached our destination and joined up with the rest of our party, Reeve and I were able to get rid of them by the simple expedient of losing ourselves in the famous Hampton Court maze. We found a bench where we sat for several hours in the pleasantly warm sun and chatted about a dozen or so things that interested us, among them the crying need for parliamentary reform; the injustice of the Corn Laws; and the unfortunate performance of Lord Liverpool as Prime Minister.

One of Reeve's secrets was that he was far more interested in politics than anyone would ever suspect. However, he refused to grace the House of Lords with his presence for the same reason that he rarely came home to Ambersley for more than a few days at a time.

He would never feel himself to be truly Lord Cambridge until he had control of his heritage.

We left London for our visit to Sussex on the last day of June. Mama and I rode in Reeve's town chaise with another chaise following us filled with our baggage and Susan, whom Reeve had brought to attend Mama and me.

"Two maids might be excessive in an establishment

like Bernard's," he had said, "but you will look positively shabby if you do not have someone to take care of your clothes."

"But how much money do you have left from your winnings, Reeve?" Mama had said worriedly. "Are you certain that you can afford this?"

"Yes," Reeve had said uncompromisingly. He gave Mama a look of mock severity. "You will make *me* look shabby if you are unattended, and surely you do not want that."

As Mama never knew how to deal with anyone when they stood up to her, she had immediately ceased to argue. I had enough sense to realize that Reeve would know more about what was expected in such a situation than I did, and so I didn't argue with him at all. Consequently, Susan rode in the following coach along with Reeve's valet, Hummond, both of them keeping watch over the baggage.

Reeve, lucky man, was riding. I looked longingly out the window of the chaise at his tall, long-legged figure and thought for about the thousandth time in my life that he really did have the most wonderful seat on a horse. He was always right over his mount's center of balance, which made all his horses' gaits so much better than they would be if they were impeded by someone leaning forward on their shoulders or backward on their loins (as was the case with ninety-nine percent of the English riders that I saw).

Reeve had always been the model I strove to emulate. His kind of balance was more difficult to attain in a sidesaddle, where one had the use of only one leg, but most of the time I thought I at least came close to it.

"I do hope this party goes off quietly," Mama said.

I heard the nervousness she was trying to hide. Poor Mama. She did not like conflict, and I was certain she was not looking forward to the next few weeks.

"The very fact that there will be other people in the house besides Lord Bradford and Reeve will help to keep things civilized, Mama," I said.

She perked up a little. "That is true."

"I wonder who else will be there?" I said. "Reeve told me that we could expect to see Lord Bradford's three children, but I hope to God it is not just a family party. From what Reeve tells me, he does not get on with his cousin Robert very well."

The chaise hit a rock on the road and bounced. Mama grabbed the strap next to her, and I braced my foot against the seat that faced me.

"Lord Bradford told me that he would invite some friends of his from Hampshire," Mama said a little breathlessly. "A Mr. and Mrs. Norton, I believe. They have a son and a daughter about your age, dear."

I looked at her with surprise. "Is there anything else that Lord Bradford saw fit to impart to you and not to us?"

Mama smiled. "No, dearest, that is all."

I sighed and once more looked out the window at Reeve. "I wish I could ride," I said wistfully.

"You will be able to ride while we are staying with Lord Bradford," Mama said. Her voice became more sober. "I must confess, this whole scheme of Reeve's is making me more and more uneasy. How are you going to call off this engagement after you have been introduced to all of his family, Deborah?"

"We'll just say that we do not suit," I said.

Mama gave me an extremely doubtful look.

I turned my back on Reeve and gave my mother my full attention. "The important thing is for Reeve to get control of his money, Mama. I'm afraid that if he has to wait another two years, he might not be alive to inherit at all."

Mama's sky-blue eyes looked shocked. "Surely you cannot be serious, Deborah?"

"I might be," I said gravely. "There has been a feeling of . . . desperation . . . about him lately that I do not like at all."

Mama was silent, and I turned to look back out the window. We were driving through a forest of beech trees at the moment, and the sun shone in dappled patches through the branches of the trees that overhung the road. Reeve rode in and out of the sunshine, too, now in shadow, now in light. I felt a tightness in my chest.

Please God, I found myself praying, *make Lord Bradford give Reeve his money.*

"Do you think the accident still haunts him, dear?" I heard Mama's voice ask.

For a moment I pressed my forehead against the glass of the window. I felt as if I had a headache coming on, which was ridiculous. I never had headaches.

"Of course it does," I answered. "In some ways, it probably always will. But if he has some kind of purpose in his life, something to think about besides himself and his own guilt, I'm convinced that it will help enormously."

Mama said in a voice that sounded oddly worried, "You care for him a great deal, don't you, Deborah?"

I turned to give her a warm smile. "Of course I do. Reeve has always been my best friend in the world." The ache in my head was growing more pronounced. "Will you mind if I lower this window a little so we can get some air, Mama? I feel as if I might be getting a headache from being cooped up for so long."

"No, of course not, dear," Mama said. "Open it as much as you like."

Fifteen minutes later Reeve shouted something to me and pointed ahead. I rolled the window all the way down and stuck my head out to see what it was he was gesturing at.

We were still driving through the beech woods of the South Downs, but now the chaise was climbing up a long, steep hill. In a few minutes time, we came out of the woods and there, at the end of a tree-enclosed drive, was a welcoming old two-storied house built of a silvery pink brick that was a particularly lovely color. Dormer windows peered out of the hipped roof, and there was a pediment crown over the front. Two single-story outbuilding blocks jutted on either side.

"Don't hang out the window like that, Deborah," Mama said. "It is not good manners."

She was smoothing her skirts and putting her bonnet and gloves back on, and I did the same. By the time the chaise pulled up in front of Wakefield Manor, we were ready to be handed down gallantly by Reeve.

Lord Bradford was waiting to greet us. "Welcome, Mrs. Woodly," he said to Mama. "Welcome, Miss Woodly. I am so pleased to have you as my guests."

He took Mama's arm to escort her up the steps, and Reeve and I followed behind.

"What a pretty house," I said to Reeve.

"You haven't seen the best part yet," he returned. "It looks just like any other house from this side, but when you look out any of the windows on the other three sides you will see that Wakefield is actually situated right on the very top of the Downs. The views are magnificent."

"How lovely."

We were in the hall by now, and Lord Bradford said, "I'll have my housekeeper show you and Miss Woodly to your rooms, Mrs. Woodly. Then perhaps you will join me for tea in the front drawing room and I will make you known to our other guests."

"Thank you," Mama said.

"I believe you have been given your usual room, Reeve," Lord Bradford said next. "You do not require a guide?"

"Not at all, Bernard," Reeve said blandly.

Lord Bradford's steady gray eyes regarded his young cousin. "It has been a long time since you visited Wakefield," he said. "I don't believe you have been here since your father died."

Reeve's face darkened. "You know the reason for that, Bernard."

"Yes, I fear that I do."

Reeve turned toward the stairs.

"Reeve," Lord Bradford said. Impatiently, Reeve swung back. "I am happy to welcome you also."

Reeve nodded his head. "Thank you," he said. He made an infinitesimal shooing motion in my direction, and I turned and walked firmly up the stairs.

*   *   *

Mama and I had adjoining bedrooms, and I had never inhabited such a large chamber in my life. That is, I couldn't ever remember inhabiting such a large chamber. I supposed that in my earlier years, before John Woodly had ejected Mama and me from my father's house, I might have lived in such a room.

It was bright. That was what I liked about it most of all. The walls were painted a pale gold, the old tapestry bedspread was a faded gold, the carpet over the polished-wood floor was also old and faded and lovely and the old four-poster was solid oak.

The room had a large window, and the warm summer breeze ruffled the drapes and filled the room with the scent of grass.

I thought of the low ceilings, small windows, and cramped rooms of our cottage at home. This room alone was larger than our living room and dining room put together.

I remembered what Reeve had said about the views, walked to the open window, looked out, and felt my breath catch in my throat.

From where I stood, Wakefield Manor seemed to be perched on the very top of the world. With no trees to block the view, as there were in the front of the house, one could see how the stretching Downs fell away on the house's every side. I leaned out the window, looked down, and saw in amazement that below me the green turf had actually been allowed to grow right up to the walls of the house itself. I inhaled deeply, and, mixed with the scent of the grass, I caught the whiff of salt air. Sure enough, in the far distance I could see just the faintest glimmer of the sea.

What a beautiful house, I thought. *What a pity that it belongs to a man with as little sensitivity as Lord Bradford.*

I changed out of my wrinkled travel clothes into a sprigged-muslin afternoon dress and knocked on Mama's door to see if she was ready. She was. Reeve was waiting for us at the top of the stairs, and all three of us went down to meet the rest of the party together.

The drawing room was bathed in the light let in by two large windows, and sitting majestically between the windows, on a striped silk sofa, was a white-haired old lady dispensing tea. The remainder of the party were grouped around her in old gilded chairs with needlepoint covers.

"Oh my God," Reeve groaned in my ear, "it's my Aunt Sophia."

Lord Bradford came to the door to greet us and lead us to meet Reeve's aunt, who fixed me with gimlet eyes that I could swear saw through to my very soul. I stared back and tried to look polite yet inscrutable.

"Lady Sophia Lambeth, may I present Miss Deborah Woodly," Lord Bradford said.

"Hah," the old lady with the gimlet eyes snorted.

"How do you, Lady Sophia," I said, and curtsied.

Lord Bradford introduced Mama, who got the same greeting as I had. Then Lord Bradford took both our elbows in a firm grip and steered us away from the tyrant who was sitting on the sofa and took us around the room to introduce us to the others who were present.

First I met Mr. and Mrs. Norton, the neighbors from Hampshire, who appeared to be a pleasant couple in their forties. After them came Lord Bradford's children,

Harry and Sally. Harry looked like his father, while Sally was a pretty girl with hazel eyes and brown hair. I knew from Reeve that Harry had just finished at Cambridge and that Sally was seventeen.

Miss Norton, who was seated next to Sally, looked to be about her age. I hoped that the girls had not read *The Corsair*, but from the looks on their faces as they stared at Reeve, I was very much afraid that they had.

Mama and I took seats, and Reeve went to get us some tea. I found myself seated next to Mr. Edmund Norton, a youthful gentleman who looked to be a few years younger than I. He had big brown eyes, floppy brown hair, and pink cheeks. He gazed at me with wide-eyed attention, and said a little shyly, "Did you have a tiring journey, Miss Woodly?"

"Not really. I don't care to be confined in a coach for such a long period, but otherwise, I can't complain," I answered cheerfully.

He looked as if he wished to say something more but didn't know what.

I helped him out by asking, "Are you at university, Mr. Norton?"

His pink cheeks grew a little pinker. "Yes," he said. "I am at Cambridge."

"Ah," I said, and took a sip of my tea.

He looked at Reeve with a mixture of envy and awe. "They still talk about him there," he said.

"I am sure they do," I replied resignedly.

In fact, the painting of the Head's house had only been the last in a long series of Reeve's transgressions at college. The authorities had been very forbearing with him, really. After all, it had been more than usually upsetting to be forced to eject the heir of Lord Cambridge, who in the Middle Ages had been one of the school's original patrons. But Reeve had been determined to get himself sent down, and eventually, of course, he had succeeded.

Miss Norton, who had her brother's big brown eyes and shiny hair, was conversing shyly with Reeve. He appeared to be treating her kindly.

Then Lady Sophia's voice cut through the polite chatter in the room. "Well, Reeve, what have you got to say for yourself?" she demanded.

We all looked at her. I judged her to be one of those ladies who had grown up in the previous century who had no notion of the modern idea of politeness. She would consider it mealymouthed not to say exactly what she thought, even if in so doing she trampled all over the feelings of the person whom she was addressing.

She had Reeve's dark eyes and his nose, without the bump. In her youth she must have been a great beauty.

Reeve said, "I hope I find you in good health, Aunt Sophia."

"Hah. You can't fool me, young man. I could be dead for all you know or care. I haven't heard a word from you in years."

The corner of Reeve's mouth twitched. "I would have heard about your death, Aunt Sophia. There would have been an eclipse of the sun or something equally dramatic to announce the news to the world."

The old lady laughed heartily. Then, when she had got her breath back, she demanded, "So who is this gel you've asked to marry you? Bernard tells me she ain't got a groat."

Reeve's eyes met mine across the room.

"Nary a shilling to my name," I said cheerfully to the dreadful old woman seated behind the teapot.

Her dark eyes, so disconcertingly like Reeve's, peered shrewdly into mine. "It's a love match then?"

It is very seldom that I find myself at a loss for words, but I was at a loss now. Did she know about Bernard's ultimatum? Should I say anything about Reeve's debts?

Desperately, I looked across the room for help.

"It is a love match, Aunt," Reeve said firmly.

Mama put down her cup of tea as if the saucer had suddenly scalded her hand.

Everyone looked at me. I could feel my cheeks grow pink.

Damn Reeve for getting me into this, I thought.

Then I remembered that I was the one who had insisted that we come to Sussex. I sighed and tried to look sweet, like a maiden in love.

I heard Reeve cough and knew he was covering up a chuckle.

Lady Sophia said to him, "Well, I'm sure that Bernard is hoping that this marriage will put an end to your roguery, but I've always had a soft spot for a rascal." She turned to Lord Bradford. "Unfortunately, you have always been a dead bore, Bernard."

He looked as if he had heard this castigation a thousand times and had ignored it for a thousand times as well.

"Yes, ma'am," he said, his square face never changing its expression.

Mama gave him a sympathetic look. She had such a soft heart.

Lady Sophia turned back to me and began a relentless interrogation that lasted for the remainder of teatime. The rest of the party sat in wooden silence while they learned that I was twenty-one ("almost at your last prayers, aren't you, Missy?"); that I lived in a cottage in the village next to Ambersley; that I played the pianoforte indifferently; that I was a poor needlewoman; that I knew nothing about running a house the size of Ambersley; that, in the eyes of Lady Sophia, I was totally unsuited to be the wife of the Earl of Cambridge.

"Young men," she said maliciously, "they make their choice of a wife with their eyes and live to rue it."

Reeve said, "Deb has the best seat on a horse of any girl I've ever seen. There aren't many men I know who can ride as well as she can, as a matter of fact. Who cares if she can't play the pianoforte? I don't like the pianoforte. I like to ride."

Bernard said to me, "Housewifely virtues cannot be ignored, Miss Woodly. As the mistress of an establishment such as Ambersley much will be expected of you."

Since I would never be the mistress of Ambersley, I was not overly worried about this, but I bowed, smiled, and nodded my agreement, assuring him that I was sure I would be able to learn what I did not already know.

Lady Sophia sniffed loudly, clearly in doubt of my abilities.

Dreadful old woman, I thought.

Reeve's eyes caught mine across the room, and he read my thought unerringly. He winked.

A few minutes later the tea party broke up. We would all reassemble again for dinner in a short while, and at that realization I suppressed a groan.

Oh well, Reeve had warned me, I thought, as I followed Mama upstairs to our rooms, where we were supposed to rest until dinner. It was only for a few weeks, after all. I could endure it. I had to.

Unfortunately.

CHAPTER

six

SINCE RULES OF POLITENESS RESTRICTED LADY
Sophia to conversation with the persons who sat on either side of her, dinner was not quite as nerve-shattering
as tea had been. Reeve was seated to the right of his
aunt, but instead of being the target of her barbs he appeared to be charming the old lady with his most seduc-
tive smiles.

I remembered her comment that she liked a rogue.
Well, she had certainly found one, I thought sourly.

Mama and I sat on either side of Lord Bradford,
who told us all about the activities he had planned to
amuse us during our visit. There would be a dance for
the local gentry, some excursions to local sites of interest, and a large summer fair organized by the local vil-
lagers. Reeve would probably complain that Lord
Bradford's offerings were a complete bore, but in truth,
it sounded to me as if our visit might be rather enjoyable.

We were having dessert when I said to Lord Bradford, "I thought you had two sons, my lord."

A flicker of uneasiness came across his face, then
was quickly gone. "Yes," he said. "Robert is presently
visiting friends in East Anglia, but he will be returning

home shortly, Miss Woodly. As you can imagine, he is anxious to meet his cousin's fiancée."

I smiled and did not reply.

That flicker of uneasiness was not at all reassuring.

After dinner, the ladies were forced to follow Lady Sophia to the drawing room so the gentlemen could be left to the dissipation of their port. Reeve rolled his eyes at me as I went by, and I had to stifle a giggle.

It would never do for Lady Sophia to hear such an undignified sound coming from the lips of the future Countess of Cambridge.

We took our places in the drawing room. Lady Sophia was once again on the sofa, and the rest of us sat as far away from her as we could politely get.

Then she started on Mama.

"I understand that you were employed by the late Lord Lynly to be governess to his son, Mrs. Woodly," she said.

Mama went very pale. "That is correct, Lady Sophia," she said.

"Hmm. You must have been quite young. Odd that such an unprotected young gel would go to work for a widower."

Her implication was that not only was it odd, it was not respectable.

"There was nothing odd about it, Lady Sophia," Mama said. "Lord Lynly needed a governess, and I was qualified and needed a job. His son and I liked each other. Surely there can be nothing odd in that."

"It's demned odd that he married you, you can't deny that," the old lady said with relish. "He did it over the objections of his family, too, I hear."

Mama said with dignity, "I really do not think that my marital affairs are any of your business, Lady Sophia."

Good for you, Mama, I thought.

"Since your daughter is marrying my nevvy, they certainly are my business," Lady Sophia returned. She had a silver-tipped cane which she carried and now she tapped it commandingly on the floor. "For instance, if you are Lynly's widow, why are you living in a cottage? Why doesn't your daughter have a dowry? Why are you calling yourself Mrs. Woodly and not Lady Lynly?" Once more the old lady rapped her cane authoritatively. "I demand to know the answer to these questions, Mrs. Woodly. It is my right as Cambridge's aunt."

By now Mama was white as snow, and I was furious. I said, "If you want to know the answer to those questions, you can ask Reeve, Lady Sophia. He knows everything there is to know about us. And if it doesn't bother him, then it shouldn't bother you."

The old lady's head snapped around. "Hah, do you dare to dictate to me, Missy?"

I said, my voice clear and cold and deadly, "Leave my mother alone."

Our eyes met, and for a moment something that almost looked like respect flitted across her splendid old face.

She sat back on her sofa. "Very well," she said, elevating her perfectly carved nose. "I shall ask my nephew."

There was a moment of tense silence in the room which was mercifully broken by the entrance of the gentlemen. It did not take Lord Bradford long to realize that something had happened, and he moved quickly to defuse the situation.

"Will you play something for us, Miss Norton?" he said genially. "You delighted me yesterday with those charming songs."

Mary Ann Norton shot a glance at Harry from under her long, dark lashes. "I should be happy to, Lord Bradford," she said.

Lord Bradford gave his son a meaningful look, and Harry went obediently to turn Mary Ann's music for her. The rest of us settled down to listen.

The girl did play charmingly. And sang charmingly, too. She looked charming as well, with her pastel pink dress picking up the pretty pink color in her cheeks. She was followed by Sally, who was dressed in pastel green and also played and sang and looked charming.

I crossed my fingers and prayed that no one would ask me to follow.

"And you, Miss Woodly?" said that miserable crone, Lady Sophia. "Surely you can perform something upon the instrument?"

I stood up and went glumly to the pianoforte. I had taken lessons once a week for several years from one of the matrons in the village, but I had not been an apt pupil. I limped through two Scottish songs that I had once memorized for a recital, and when I resumed my seat no one urged me to continue.

"Dreadful," I heard Lady Sophia mutter.

"I thought you played very well, Miss Woodly," Edmund Norton said stoutly.

The boy must be tone-deaf, I thought, as I smiled and thanked him.

Shortly after that, Lady Sophia yawned and announced that she was fatigued after all her great exertions and would go to bed. With difficulty, we all refrained from cheering.

Once she was gone, the rest of us went out onto the terrace, which opened off the morning room in the back of the house. The turf of the Downs had been displaced here by gardens, which surrounded the terrace. Paths wound through plantings of flowers, which I smelled but saw only dimly in the moonlight.

Reeve and I found ourselves walking with Mama and Lord Bradford.

"I do apologize for Lady Sophia," Lord Bradford said. "In retrospect, it was probably not a wise idea to invite her. But I had to have a hostess, and she is your father's only sister, Reeve. At the time it seemed like a good idea."

"What a harridan," I said frankly. "She began to upset Mama by asking her all sorts of painful and embarrassing questions. I told her to ask you instead, Reeve, so if she pounces on you, you will know why."

He grunted.

"Has she ever come to Ambersley?" I asked. "I don't remember seeing her before."

"She came to visit a few times while my father was still alive, but she hasn't been since. I haven't invited her."

Well, that wasn't odd. He never invited anyone to Ambersley.

"Where does she live?" I asked.

"Where do all dreadful old spinsters live? Bath, of course," Reeve said.

Lord Bradford actually chuckled. "She is not as bad as she seems."

"Well, she hasn't been very pleasant so far," Mama surprised me by saying faintly. Normally she would never criticize someone's relation to their face.

"I will speak to her, Mrs. Woodly," Lord Bradford said firmly. "Believe me, she will not bother you again."

I looked up at the sky, which was filled with stars. "What a beautiful night," I said. I inhaled deeply and once more caught the salty smell of the ocean. "Do you think that we might ride to the sea tomorrow, Lord Bradford? I have never seen it."

"Haven't you? Then we must remedy that immediately, Miss Woodly. We will most assuredly go to the sea tomorrow, and take a picnic with us. The rest of the young people will enjoy that as well."

I was immediately sorry that I had said anything about going to the sea. I should have snagged Reeve for an early-morning ride so I could have my first glimpse of the sea with him and not with a group of strangers.

I smiled, and said, "That will be very nice indeed."

The first of July dawned clear and bright. Breakfast was laid out in the bow window of a very pretty morning room, and by eleven o'clock the whole house party was on horseback and heading in the direction of the sea. Reeve had brought horses from home for himself and for me, and the Norton children had brought their own horses as well. Lord Bradford supplied the rest, and I had to admit that the quiet, gentle little mare he gave to Mama was perfect.

Mercifully, Lady Sophia remained at home.

Wakefield Manor was directly north of the small village of Fair Haven on the English Channel and to the west of the village, on the other side of a small bay, was an expanse of beach known as Charles Island. To get to the island it was necessary to cross a causeway made of sand and pebbles and eroded shells, which Reeve told me was covered during storms when the tides became excessively high.

"So Charles Island is only an island part of the time, then," I said.

"That is right," he replied.

He and I were leading the house party parade, as Reeve's horse was one of those who always liked to be in front, and now he looked up into the air at a group of noisy seagulls that were swooping over the shining water to our right, and said, "I used to love to come here when I was a boy. Charles Island was once a great haunt of smugglers, you know, and I used to pretend I was a free trader smuggling all kinds of contraband goods into the country."

I looked up at the crying gulls as well. They looked so graceful and white against the clear blue sky. "Is there still smuggling going on here, do you think?" I asked curiously.

There was a breeze blowing from the west, where the Isle of Wight was visible, and it ruffled the dark hair on Reeve's brow. "Oh, I'm sure some brandy still gets floated in on the tide," he answered. "But free trading is not what it was in the last century."

There were a number of small boats out on the bay between Charles Island and Fair Haven, and I looked at them speculatively, wondering if any of them might sometimes engage in illegal activities. "Did your cousins pretend to be smugglers with you when you were children?" I asked Reeve curiously.

His voice sounded oddly flat as he answered, "Harry used to, but Sally was too young."

"What about Robert?"

Reeve gave me a strangely somber look. "Robert and I don't get on, Deb. The animosity was on his side originally, but to be honest, at this point I think I dislike him fully as much as he dislikes me. I was absolutely delighted when I learned that he was not here at Wakefield when we arrived."

I said, "Lord Bradford told me that he was visiting friends in East Anglia, but that he would be returning home shortly."

"He can't stay away long enough, as far as I'm concerned," Reeve said.

My horse stepped into a puddle that had been left by the tide, and his hooves made a soft splashing sound as he lifted them free.

"Why doesn't Robert like you, Reeve?" I asked.

He shrugged. "Who knows? It could be simply that I'm standing in the place in the sun that he thinks should belong to him."

We reached the end of the causeway, our horses set foot on the island, and I shook off the uncomfortable feeling our discussion of the absent Robert had given me and looked around with delight.

On its north side, where we had come ashore, the

island's causeway connected it to the mainland; on its east side it made up part of a series of small, jagged bays, which indeed must have been hell for the government to patrol for smugglers. On its west side it looked out across a stretch of water to the Isle of Wight. All of these three sides of Charles Island were rimmed by a sandy beach. Behind the beach was a forest of evergreens.

And everywhere one looked the sun glittered down on blue-gray water which smelled like salt.

I gave Reeve a rapturous smile. "This is wonderful."

He grinned. "It is pretty grand, isn't it? It's even better when the tide is all the way out. Then the beach is even wider than it is now. It makes for a great place to gallop."

Lord Bradford said from behind us, "We'll tether the horses on the edge of the trees, Reeve."

Reeve nodded and swung down from his saddle. I got down myself and took Reeve's reins so he could go to assist Mama, but Lord Bradford was there before him. I frowned as I saw the sweet smile Mama bestowed upon our host as he handed her to the ground.

She would have to be careful, or that fellow would think she was making up to him, I thought.

The rest of the party was out of the saddle by now as well, and the grooms who had come in the trap with the picnic assisted with tying the horses to the tether rope they had stretched at the edge of the trees.

"I thought we might show Mrs. Woodly and Miss Woodly about for an hour or so and then return here to have our luncheon," Lord Bradford said.

Of course, I thought, everyone else in the party had probably been on the island many times. It was just Mama and I who were the newcomers.

We started off in a large group, walking eastward along the wet sand, where the going was easier. The tide was receding quickly. The day was warm, and even though I was not wearing a riding habit but was attired in a lighter-weight riding dress and jacket, still I was too warm. I wished I had been able to ride bareback in a cotton muslin dress and no shoes. I looked at Reeve out of the side of my eyes. He wore a riding coat, and he also looked hot.

If we had been alone, we could have taken off our jackets and been more comfortable.

"Reeve, we must show Miss Woodly Skull Rock."

Harry Lambeth had come up on my other side.

I turned to look at Reeve's cousin. "Skull Rock?"

Reeve chuckled. "That is what we named it when we were boys. We used to make up horrible tales of what smugglers did to the revenue men they caught, and one of the things was bashing their brains out against Skull Rock."

"How charming," I said.

Harry's gray eyes smiled at me. "We also used it as a lookout post to keep watch for smuggled goods coming in on the tide."

"I would love to see Skull Rock," I said.

As the two young men talked and reminisced I watched them, making appropriate replies when necessary.

It seemed that nothing but harmony reigned between Reeve and this cousin of his. If Harry had indeed

just come down from university, then he had to be two
or three years younger than Reeve, although he looked
older than twenty-one or twenty-two. There was a gravity about his square face that I found particularly pleas-
ing.

"Is your father looking about for a living for you
now that you've finished school?" Reeve asked. "In
truth, I was very surprised when he gave away the living at Ambersley to Cedric Liskey. I was sure he'd keep
it for you, Harry."

"He wanted to hold it for me, but I wouldn't let
him," Harry returned.

"Oh?" Reeve said. "Why not? Not that there's anything wrong with Cedric, but you would be a good man
to have in the neighborhood."

Harry said intensely, "I don't want to go into the
Church, Reeve. I have told that to Papa a hundred times,
but he doesn't listen. You know how he is, he always
thinks he knows what's better for you than you do yourself."

Reeve kicked at a shell with his boot. "I know that
very well," he said tightly.

Harry sighed.

Reeve turned to look at his cousin over my head.
"What *do* you want to do then, Harry, if you don't want
the Church? You don't strike me as the sort who is army
mad."

"I'm not," Harry said emphatically. His gray eyes
burned. "I want to be a doctor, Reeve. I want Papa to let
me go to the Royal College of Physicians in London.
But no Lambeth has ever been a doctor before, and

Papa doesn't think it is respectable, and so he is trying to push me into the Church."

My opinion of Lord Bradford's insensitivity was increasing by leaps and bounds. While it was true that the Church or the army were the two traditional careers for younger sons of the upper classes, surely that didn't mean one couldn't take into consideration the needs and talents of individuals.

The wet sand squished beneath our shoes as we walked along the water's edge, avoiding tidal puddles that had not yet dried in the sun. Reeve's long legs had easily outdistanced the rest of the party, and since I was used to keeping up with him, we were far in the vanguard of the group.

Reeve raised his eyebrows at Harry. "So you want to be a physician, eh?"

"Yes. It is all I have ever wanted to be, and if Papa were not so stuffy, he would realize that I am far more suited to that than I am to the Church. It is people's bodies I want to serve, not their souls."

"That sounds to me a very admirable goal, Mr. Lambeth," I said gravely.

He gave me a quick, attractive, gray-eyed smile. "Thank you, Miss Woodly."

"You don't have the money to go to school in London on your own?" Reeve asked.

"No," Harry said. "I am completely dependent upon Papa for money."

"That is how he controls us all," Reeve said with deep bitterness.

"Papa is not a bad man, Reeve," Harry said awkwardly. "He just thinks he . . ."

"I know," Reeve cut in. "He just thinks he knows what's better for us than we do ourselves."

Harry sighed. "Yes."

Straight ahead of us, jutting up out of the wet sand like an ancient monolith, was a very large gray rock. Crying seagulls circled around it, as if keeping guard.

"Is that Skull Rock by any chance?" I asked.

"Yes," Reeve said, "it is."

As we drew closer I could see that the lower part of the rock was wet. "At high tide the water is over one's head at the rock," Reeve informed me.

"My goodness." I looked at the two young men. "Did you ever get caught out there by the tide when you were young?"

They grinned at me.

"Once in a while," Harry said. "But there isn't much of an undertow, so it is an easy swim back to the shore."

By now we had reached the bottom of the rock, which I could see had barnacles growing on it. I looked all the way up to the top of it.

"Can we climb it?"

Harry gave me a nervous look. "I don't think you want to do that, Miss Woodly. It is slippery."

"Oh, don't worry about Deb," Reeve said cheerfully. "She can climb like a boy. Come on, and we'll show you the view from the top, Deb. It's grand."

Lord Bradford would probably have a heart attack at the sight of me on top of Skull Rock, but I didn't care. I followed Reeve to the first foothold.

*   *   *

By the time the house party returned to the picnic area, the food had been laid out. The salt air and exercise had made me hungry, and I bit ravenously into a meat pastry, which I washed down with some lemonade.

Lord Bradford had not provided champagne.

Mama had color in her cheeks, and her curls were feathering around her face in a way that made her look extraordinarily young and pretty. I was not at all sure I liked the way Lord Bradford was looking at her.

Sally shared a blanket with Edmund Norton and chatted away comfortably about some people they both knew. Harry and Mary Ann had their heads together over some shells that Mary Ann had collected during her walk. Mr. Norton talked amiably to Reeve about horses, and Mrs. Norton, who had her children's lovely large brown eyes, talked to me about the summer fair that would be held in a few weeks' time. I listened to her and tried to keep an eye on Mama and Lord Bradford at the same time.

Mrs. Norton said, "The fair is a hangover from the midsummer festival that was held from the Middle Ages right through the first part of the last century. The Church was deeply suspicious of the pagan origins of that festival, so about fifty years ago the local parish succeeded in canceling the midsummer festival and substituting this summer fair instead."

"What does the fair involve?" I asked.

"Oh there are games for the children, and dancing and food for the young people and adults. There are horse races and boat races as well. Last year Lord Bradford brought in a dancing bear, which was a great hit.

This year I believe he is sponsoring an equestrian exhibition."

Mama laughed at something Lord Bradford said to her.

"The fair sounds like fun," I said to Mrs. Norton.

She frowned. "Mind, it still has its rowdy side. Too often the young men and women from the local villages sneak out at night and meet in the woods. The old midsummer festival has not quite let go its grip on this part of the world."

I gathered that the young men and women who met in the woods were not there in order to discuss the latest happenings in Parliament.

"Disgraceful," I said gravely.

She gave me a smile.

"Who organizes the fair, Mrs. Norton?" I asked curiously. "Lord Bradford?"

"Oh no. The rector's wife, Mrs. Thornton, does most of the organization while the women from Wakefield village do the actual work. Lord Bradford only provides some of the entertainment."

By this time, everyone had finished eating, and Lord Bradford asked if we were ready to return to Wakefield Manor.

"If you don't mind, I would like to show Deb the south side of the island, Bernard," Reeve said. "We can follow you home later."

Lord Bradford hesitated, then he looked at Mama. "It is all right with me if it is all right with Mrs. Woodly."

"Of course you may show Deborah the rest of the island, Reeve," Mama said quietly.

Lord Bradford nodded. Even he could scarcely object to an engaged couple riding by themselves for a short period of time.

So it was that while the rest of the party headed toward the causeway and the mainland, Reeve and I went in the opposite direction. We rode along in silence under the hot sun, and I noticed how the landscape began to change as we approached the south shore of the island. The beach became much narrower, and the horses walked more carefully as the sand underfoot turned into pebbles and small rocks. Gradually the trees gave way to a growing wall of stone, and, after a few more minutes of walking, there was only about six feet of pebbled beach left between the cliff wall and the lapping water.

I thought that at high tide there must be no beach on this shore at all.

"There's Rupert's Cave now," Reeve said with satisfaction. "This is what I wanted you to see."

I looked ahead of me and saw a great arched opening in the cliff wall to our left. "Rupert's Cave?" I asked.

"I have no idea how it got that name," Reeve said cheerfully, "but it's been called Rupert's Cave forever. It probably should have been named Smuggler's Cave because that's what it's famous for."

I looked from the cave to the waterline six feet away. At the moment the tide was almost at its lowest point. "Doesn't the cave flood at high tide?" I asked. "I shouldn't think it would be much use to smugglers if everything they hid inside it got soaking wet."

"It does flood at high tide," Reeve replied. "In fact,

the water gets almost halfway up the entrance. But the cave goes surprisingly deep, and there are a few high spots way inside that always stay dry."

I shivered at the thought of crawling so far away from the light of day. I have never liked small, dark places.

"Let's get down," Reeve said

We both swung down from our saddles and walked over to stand in the entrance of the cave. It was actually high enough for the horses to enter if they had to. The ground inside was very wet, as the sun never got at it to dry it fully.

I stepped back out into the sun and squinted as the midday brightness struck my eyes.

"Let's sit down for a few minutes before we go back," Reeve said. "We need to talk."

I looked around for someplace dry, and Reeve motioned me to follow him. A moment later, we had come to a place where the cliff descended toward the sea, and there was a flat rock that we could climb up to with relative ease.

We sat down and I took off my jacket.

Reeve looked at my bare arms. "You'll get a sunburn, Deb, if you're not careful."

"Do you mind?" I said.

"No, but sunburn can hurt, and your skin is very fair. The sun is hot today. Be careful."

"It's too hot for that wretched jacket. Why don't you take off yours?"

He slid his arms out of his jacket and took off his neckcloth as well. Then he lay back on the rock, his hands clasped behind his head, his eyes closed against the sun. In his shirtsleeves, with his open collar, he looked very strong. All that boxing with Gentleman Jackson, I presumed.

He said, "I told you this visit was going to be a horror."

"Your cousin Harry is nice," I said. "The Nortons seem pleasant. It's Lady Sophia who is the ogre."

"She's not so bad, really. You just have to know how to handle her."

I looked down into his face. His lashes were absurdly long for a man. *Good thing Amanda and her friends can't see him now*, I thought.

"Well she certainly hasn't been pleasant to me or to Mama. I don't care about me; I can take care of myself. But I don't want her upsetting Mama."

I told him about the conversation in the drawing room.

When I had finished, he sat up, frowning. "I'm sorry, Deb. She has always been like that, you know. She says what she thinks." His frown deepened and his voice became gruff. "She has always been pretty decent to me. After the accident where my mother died, she took after my father pretty fiercely for the way he treated me." He stared bleakly out to sea. "I have to confess, I've always had a bit of a weakness for the old girl."

I felt a constriction in my chest. Reeve almost never talked about his mother. I, too, looked out at the shimmering water and conceded, "Well, perhaps she is not as bad as she seems. But you will have to explain to her about Mama and me, because I am not going to say a word."

"Don't worry, I will."

A comfortable silence descended between us. I propped my chin on my updrawn knees and gazed at the sea. From where we sat, there was no land in sight anywhere.

Reeve picked up a pebble that lay on the rock's surface, and threw it into the water. Circles rippled around it as it sank.

"Deb?"

I turned my face to look at him.

He said, "We have to come up with a plan to force Bernard to turn over my money."

I sighed. "I know."

"Thanks to you, he has paid my Derby debts. But I want more than that. I'm sick to death of being Bernard's pensioner. I want to be my own master!"

"I know you do, Reeve." The hot sun had brought beads of perspiration to my upper lip and I licked them away. My lip tasted like salt. "I have come up with an idea," I confessed, "but it will depend upon how much Lord Bradford wants you to marry me. If he would prefer that you find another girl, then my idea isn't going to work."

His eyes were fixed on the lip that I had just licked. "What's your idea?" he asked.

"I thought I might tell Lord Bradford that I want to live at Ambersley after we get married. You will say that you refuse to live there unless you are its real master. Then I will say that I have decided not to agree to the marriage unless he turns over your money to you," I lifted my braid off my hot neck. "But this isn't going to work, Reeve, unless he really wants to see us married."

"Hmm." He picked up another stone and threw it casually into the water. It amazed me how far out it went. After a minute, he said thoughtfully, "I can tell you this, Deb, the last thing Bernard will want is a broken engagement. It is such bad form. Scandalous, really. All the things that horrify his conventional little Lambeth heart." He narrowed his eyes against the sun. "Under the ultimatum you have just outlined, I think Bernard will agree to turn over my inheritance to me." He threw another stone, this one with force. It must have gone halfway to America, I thought.

He turned to look at me again and smiled approvingly. A few damp patches had come out on the back of his shirt from the heat. "It's a grand idea, Deb."

I thought about what he had just said. "Is it really so scandalous?" I asked nervously. "What is going to happen when we *do* break our engagement?"

He waved his hand dismissively. "It is only scandalous if one or the other party cries off. Since you and I will make a mutual decision, there can be no scandal attached to the severing of our relationship."

"Oh," I said.

"Bernard will have a fit, of course," Reeve said. He did not look as if this prospect bothered him in the least.

"Well," I said heroically, "the important thing is for you to get your money."

"You're a great girl, Deb," Reeve said. "I don't know what I would have done without you."

"I agree. In fact, I'm beginning to think you might owe me something—like a horse of my very own," I said, shooting him a sideways look to gauge his reaction to this piece of blackmail.

"If we pull this off, I will buy you one of Lady Weston's hunters," Reeve said.

My heart stopped. "Oh Reeve," I said. "Do you mean it?"

"I do. You will deserve it."

I would, of course.

"Come along now," he said. "We had better be heading back before Bernard sends a rescue party after us."

I laughed and followed him to reclaim our horses.

CHAPTER
seven

TWO DAYS WENT BY UNEVENTFULLY. ON THE FIRST day I rode with Reeve in the morning, then walked sedately in the gardens with Mama and Mrs. Norton in the afternoon. The following morning it rained, but by afternoon the clouds had blown away, and we paid a visit to the small village of Wakefield, which lay to the west of the manor, to meet Mr. and Mrs. Thornton, the local rector and his wife.

Lord Bradford and Lady Sophia had arranged a garden party for the afternoon of the third day of our visit.

"We've invited a few friends from the immediate neighborhood to meet you and your mother, Miss Woodly," Lord Bradford told me as we rode back from our visit to the rector. "Now that the London Season is over, most of the local people are in residence once again."

I was not overly pleased to hear this. Considering the fact that our engagement was a sham, I thought that the fewer people Reeve and I met together, the better. However, I could hardly say this to Lord Bradford.

I turned my head to look at him. We were riding side by side along the narrow country road and as his steady gray eyes met mine, he smiled. "Allow me to take this opportunity to tell you how pleased I am with Reeve's engagement," he said.

I could not keep my surprise from showing on my face.

Lord Bradford interpreted my expression. "Reeve does not need to marry a young lady with money, Miss Woodly," he said. "He has a great deal of money himself."

You have Reeve's money, not Reeve, I thought. But I held my tongue.

Lord Bradford was going on, "Nor does he need to marry a young lady who thinks he is a hero out of a poem."

I stared at him in astonishment. "Don't tell me you have heard of *The Corsair*?"

"I have a seventeen-year-old daughter, Miss Woodly," Lord Bradford replied in a dry voice. "Of course I have heard of Lord Byron. It was not until I got to London, however, that I realized that Reeve was actually being compared to that idiotic corsair fellow."

"It *was* a little revolting," I admitted.

Lord Bradford's mouth set in a straight line that made him appear very stern. "Reeve has many faults, but I will say this for him. He is not vain."

"I think Reeve has fewer faults than you credit him with, Lord Bradford," I said evenly.

Once more that shrewd gray gaze swung my way. "Perhaps he is finally growing up. He is certainly less restless than I have ever seen him, but then he has only been here for four days."

I gave him the faintest suggestion of a smile. "Might I suggest, Lord Bradford, that if you wish to keep Reeve in good temper you find more for him to do than to attend garden parties—delightful as I'm sure tomorrow's entertainment will be."

Suddenly Lord Bradford grinned. The smile transformed his blunt-featured face, making him look almost handsome. He said, "I told you I liked this engagement of Reeve's, Miss Woodly. I think he's got himself a girl who understands him." The smile died away. "As much as anyone can understand Reeve."

The lane widened, and at his suggestion we moved our horses forward to join Reeve and Sally, who were just ahead of us.

"Papa," Sally said. "What do you think about an expedition to Minchester Abbey?"

As Lord Bradford talked to his daughter, Reeve and I rode in silence, and I thought about my conversation with his trustee.

Lord Bradford's approval of me as a wife for Reeve was both good and bad, I decided. The good part was that Lord Bradford sounded as if he would want to do whatever he could to promote our marriage. This would make it easier for Reeve to extract his inheritance before our vows were actually said.

The bad part, of course, was that Lord Bradford would be livid when he learned that he had been duped.

Oh well, I thought for perhaps the hundredth time since I had agreed to this imposture, it was his own fault for being so rotten to poor Reeve for all these years.

It would make me feel better, though, if he would not be so nice to me.

*   *   *

The following morning was sunny and clear, but as the day progressed toward noon the clouds began to sweep in from the Channel. Lady Sophia was furious. She would not have her garden party ruined.

"It is not as if we've invited hundreds of people, Cousin Sophia," Lord Bradford said reasonably. "There is plenty of room in the house if we have to move inside."

"I won't have it," Lady Sophia said. She thumped her cane. "Do you hear me, Bernard? I planned a garden party, and a garden party I will have."

"I hear you, Cousin," Lord Bradford said resignedly.

We all heard her. She had not raised her voice, but it could have cut through crystal it was so sharp.

"I am sure the rain will hold off," Mrs. Norton said cheerfully.

Lady Sophia glared at her. "How can you be sure?"

"I just have a feeling," Mrs. Norton replied in that same cheerful voice.

Lady Sophia gave her a scathing look.

We were all gathered in the garden, which did look exceptionally lovely. Food was being laid out on a long, linen-covered table, and two liveried footmen presided over a punch bowl and several icy tubs of champagne.

I said mildly, "It will not be as nice indoors as out, but Mama and I will still have a chance to meet your neighbors and isn't that the whole point of the party, Lady Sophia?"

I seemed to have said the right thing, for her face

cleared as if by magic. "That's right, Missy," she cackled.

I saw Reeve shoot her a suspicious look. "Who exactly is coming, Aunt Sophia?" he asked.

"I imagine you will know all of them, Reeve," she replied innocently. "You used to visit at Wakefield quite frequently when you were young. Do you remember Geoffrey Henley?"

Reeve's face brightened. "Of course I remember Geoff. Is he coming? I thought he was in the army."

"He was wounded in the Peninsula and invalided home," Lord Bradford said. "He will be here. And his sister as well, with her new fiancé."

"Gad, Charlotte can't be much older than Sally," Reeve said. "Is she really getting married?"

"I will be making my own come out next Season, Reeve," Sally said in an injured voice. "At this time next year I may very well be engaged myself."

Reeve looked at his cousin and realized that he had hurt her feelings. He shook his head mournfully. "You make me feel like an old man, Sal."

Her face cleared, and she giggled.

The sky was even darker now than it had been fifteen minutes before.

"Oh dear," Mama said, looking up at the rolling clouds. "I hope everyone arrives before the rain comes."

Lady Sophia glared at poor Mama. "It will *not* rain."

Half an hour later, just before the guests were due to arrive, the sky began to brighten. Reeve and I had been walking through the garden together, talking idly of this and that, when the first ray of sunshine peeped through.

The garden at Wakefield Manor covered almost five acres. Its centerpiece was an ornamental fountain surrounded by clipped yew and round beds planted for summer color. Clumps of sweet peas, clematis, phlox, roses, hydrangeas and other soft-colored plants flowered in purple, white, blue, and pink. To the south, beyond the fountain, was a yew arch which led one into a small wood, which was crisscrossed with shady walks. An old walled orchard lay at the edge of the woods.

It was a pretty, comfortable sort of garden that in no way resembled the miles and miles of stretching parkland and formal flower beds at Ambersley.

We were walking back from the fountain toward the house when Reeve looked up at the sun breaking through the clouds, and laughed. "By God, I believe Aunt Sophia must be a witch. She commands the elements."

"The wind changed," I said practically. "There was no witchcraft about it."

At that moment, the French doors leading from the morning room into the garden opened and a group of people came out onto the stone terrace.

"Who are these people?" I asked Reeve. "Can you see?"

"It looks like the Martins. They own Coverdale, which is about four miles to the east of here. Sir Timothy has been a friend of Bernard's forever."

"This is going to be awful," I said gloomily.

"You can't say I didn't warn you, Deb."

I thought about trying to explain to him that it

wasn't meeting these people that was bothering me, it was meeting them under false pretenses. But I said nothing. The last thing I wanted to do was to try to make Reeve feel guilty.

A few minutes later we arrived on the terrace, which was lined with stone pots filled with the same flowers that grew around the fountain. Lady Sophia introduced Mother and me to the Martins.

Sir Timothy, who had the high-colored face of someone who spends a great deal of time outdoors, gave me a look of approval. I was wearing a white-muslin dress with a scooped neck and short sleeves trimmed with fine white embroidery. My hair was braided with a blue ribbon and woven into some kind of fancy knot at the back of my head.

Sir Timothy took my hand and bowed over it with surprising grace. "Glad to see you've got a girl who looks as if she can stand up to you, boy," he said to Reeve. "Not an itty-bitty thing who's afraid of her own shadow."

Lady Martin said, "How do you do, Miss Woodly. Please excuse my husband's bluntness. I've been trying to civilize him for years, but to no avail."

Lady Martin had humorous hazel eyes and hair that was going gray, and I liked her immediately. "How do you do, Lady Martin," I said. "I am so pleased to meet you."

The Martins were introduced to Mama, and we all stood talking for perhaps five minutes until the next guests, the Reverend and Mrs. Thornton, arrived. Then the doctor from Fair Haven and his wife and daughters came out to the terrace.

"I wonder where Geoff is," Reeve was saying to me, when the French doors once more opened and another group of people came out to the garden.

This was the largest party of guests so far, consisting of a man in his late forties, a woman who was obviously his wife, a young man Reeve's age who walked with a slight limp, another young man of about Reeve's age, and a girl who looked to be about eighteen.

The Henleys, I thought. *The young man with the limp must be Geoffrey, the girl must be his sister Charlotte, and the tall, elegant-looking young man with her must be her fiancé.*

"There's Geoff now," Reeve said eagerly, and he began to walk in the direction of the door.

I stayed behind a moment to finish what I was saying to Mrs. Calder, the doctor's wife, and then I followed him.

Lady Sophia was waiting for me at the top of the terrace stairs. "I have a surprise for you, Miss Woodly," she said. "There is someone here I particularly want you to meet."

I shot her a suspicious glance. She was looking far too pleased with herself, I thought.

Reeve was talking to the young man with the limp.

Slowly, escorted by Lady Sophia, I approached the group.

"Swale," Lady Sophia said, "Allow me to present my nephew's fiancée, Miss Deborah Woodly."

Behind me I could hear someone's breath catch audibly.

Lady Sophia continued, "Miss Woodly, this is Viscount Swale."

I allowed Lord Swale to bend over my hand. Next I smiled and greeted Lady Swale, who introduced me to Geoffrey and Charlotte.

Charlotte said with an impish smile, "Reeve, you must allow me to introduce you and your fiancée to *my* fiancé, Lord Lynly."

Lord Lynly!

It took a moment for those two words to register. Then I felt all the blood drain away from my face.

Oh my God, I thought, *that horrible horrible woman. She did this. She did it on purpose.* My stomach churned and I could feel myself beginning to shake.

I lifted my eyes and looked into the face of my brother.

He was as pale as I was.

"Hello, Deborah," he said in a strangled voice. "I did not expect to see you here."

I opened my mouth, but no words came out. I felt Reeve step close and then his arm came around my shoulders.

"Steady, Deb," he said.

His words and his presence did steady me. I inhaled air deeply into my lungs, trying to overcome the sick feeling in my stomach.

Charlotte said in a bewildered voice, "What is going on, Richard?"

He replied in the same strangled voice in which he had spoken earlier, "Deborah is my half sister."

"Good God," Geoffrey said.

"I thought it was time you two met," said Lady

Sophia. She was watching us with bright, curious eyes. "I don't like the idea of my nephew marrying a girl who is an outcast from her family."

Reeve had not dropped his arm from my shoulders, and now he turned to look at his aunt. "You have gone too far, Aunt Sophia," he said coldly. "This was neither the time nor the place for such an introduction. Now that we are here, however, I suggest we move inside, where we can be private." He glared at his aunt. "You can stay out here."

She looked furious. "I will not."

"Oh yes you will." He looked very grim. He sounded absolutely furious. He was so intimidating, in fact, that Lady Sophia actually gave way.

"You are overreacting to this, Reeve," she said huffily. "It was necessary that they meet."

"Not like this," Reeve said implacably. He made a shooing motion. "Come along, Lynly. And you, too Charlotte. We had better talk this out before we face the others."

"I would like to know what is going on here also," said Lord Swale in a measured tone of voice.

I shut my eyes.

Reeve's arm tightened around my shoulders. "You will know, sir, but for the moment I think it is necessary for Deb and Lynly to talk privately."

Lady Swale said, "Come along with me and have something to eat, Max. We will hear all about this in due time, I'm sure."

Thank God, I thought. I did not need people staring at me, trying to decipher what I was feeling. "What about Mama?" I said to Reeve.

He looked at Geoffrey. "That is Mrs. Woodly over there, in the blue dress. Will you ask her to join Deb and me in the drawing room, Geoff?"

"Of course," Geoff said soberly, and went off to do Reeve's bidding.

Without speaking, the four of us went into the house and entered the white-and-gold drawing room. No one sat. For the first time I really looked at my brother.

He was several inches over six feet, like Reeve, but he was thinner. His hair was a soft brown brushed in the latest mode, and his eyes were hazel. He looked at me, and said, "I had no idea you were engaged to Cambridge, Deborah."

For some reason the sound of my name on his lips was like a blow to my stomach.

He has no right to say my name, I thought to myself furiously.

My voice, when I replied, was even. "Why should you? You have never concerned yourself with us, have you?"

The faintest flush came into his pale cheeks. "Over the years your mother has made it perfectly plain that neither of you wanted anything to do with *me*."

"You have no right to say that, just because we would not condescend to beg," I said hotly.

He looked confused. "Beg? What do you mean? Why should you need to beg?"

My laugh was not pleasant.

My brother looked at Reeve. "What is going on here, Cambridge?"

Reeve replied promptly, "Deb is talking about the

fact that for the last eighteen years, she and her mother have been left to live in poverty."

Either my brother hadn't known this, or he was a consummate actor. Probably the latter. "That can't be true," he said. He looked back at me. "My uncle has always seen to your welfare."

"Is that what he told you?" I asked scornfully. "Well let me tell you, my lord, a cottage and fifty pounds a year to live on hardly constitutes what I consider a decent living."

His hazel eyes widened in shock. "He gave you more than that!"

Reeve said grimly. "No he did not."

At this moment, the door to the drawing room opened and Mama came in. "Did you want to see me, darling?" she said, coming forward to join me.

I took her hand in mine and held it tightly.

"Yes, I did, Mama. I wish to introduce you to your stepson, Richard Woodly, Lord Lynly."

Mama's eyes flew to the tall young man standing next to Charlotte. Bright color flushed into her cheeks. "Is it true?" she asked. "Is this really Richard?"

"Yes, ma'am." He was looking at her with a strange mixture of hurt and longing. He said a little wistfully. "You look just like I remember you."

Mama gave him her sweetest smile. "And you look just like your father."

"So people tell me," he said.

Charlotte said in a bewildered voice, "I don't understand any of this, Richard. Will you explain?"

Richard hesitated, seeming not to understand everything himself.

With Mama's hand still in mine, I said in a harsh voice, "I will be very happy to explain, Lady Charlotte. My mother was Richard's father's second wife and Richard's stepmother. I was born when Richard was five, but my father neglected to provide for my mother and me in his will. My father died when I was three, and Richard's trustee, my uncle, evicted us from Lynly Manor. We were allotted a small cottage near Cambridge with a pittance to live upon, and that is how we have been existing ever since." I gave my brother a hard, unfriendly look. "This is the first time Richard and I have met since we were very young children."

Charlotte looked horrified.

Richard looked appalled.

Mama said, "I am sure that Richard did not know how straitened were our circumstances, Deborah."

I said, "Well he certainly never bothered to check on us, did he?"

By now Richard was starting to look angry, too. "You might have let me know how you were faring! I'm not a mind reader, after all!"

"No, you're just a self-involved, miserly bastard," I said hotly.

"Deborah!" Mother said in horror.

"Really, Miss Woodly," Lady Charlotte said in outrage.

"Good for you, Deb," Reeve said in stout support.

At this moment, the door opened and Lord Bradford came into the room.

"Several new guests have arrived whom I'd like Mrs. and Miss Woodly to meet," he said.

Mama smiled at him. "Deborah and I will join you in the garden in just one moment, Lord Bradford."

He gave her a shrewd look, then his eyes swung to me. I was sure my cheeks were flushed with anger.

Lord Bradford didn't say anything, however, he just nodded and left.

Mama said to me, "Deborah, we must return to the party."

I met her clear blue eyes. I drew in one deep breath and then another. My stomach was still in a knot. I nodded, and said tightly, "All right."

I started toward the door with Reeve behind me.

"Cambridge," I heard my brother say. "Will you stay for a moment? I have a few questions I would like to ask you."

"I have a few things I would like to say to you as well," Reeve replied grimly.

I walked out the door and followed Mama back to the garden.

Later that night, when everyone had gone home, and the last of summer's light was lingering in the sky, Reeve and I went for a walk.

"What an afternoon," he said feelingly. "I had no idea that Charlotte's fiancé was your brother. It's true they were both in London during this past Season, but our paths never crossed. Apparently Lynly isn't much of a gambling man."

"He probably doesn't want to spend his money," I said scornfully.

Reeve was silent. The sound of water tumbling in the fountain came softly to our ears, and I could smell both the summer flowers and the salt from the sea. Two nightingales were singing in the woods.

Reeve said, "According to Geoff, Lynly seems to be a good sort. In fact, the family were very pleased with Charlotte's engagement—and not just because Lynly has money, either."

"Obviously they don't know him very well," I said contemptuously.

"Come and sit for a minute," he said.

I followed him to one of two stone garden benches that flanked the yew arch into the woods. We sat down.

Reeve said, "Lynly wanted me to remain in the drawing room so he could ask me about what your life had been like since your father died. I told him about it. In detail."

I smoothed the soft muslin fabric that covered my lap. "And what did he say?"

"He was truly horrified, Deb. You see, his uncle had told him that it was your mother's decision to leave Lynly Manor. Mr. Woodly told Lynly that he had bought a comfortable establishment for your mother and was making her a substantial yearly allowance. He told Lynly that it was your mother's wish not to be disturbed by any member of the Woodly family. That was why Lynly never tried to get in touch with you."

I looked up into his face in disbelief. "How could he believe such a fairy tale? Why on earth would Mama do such a peculiar thing as that?"

We were sitting so close that I could feel the warmth of his skin. He said, "You have to remember that Lynly was only eight when your father died, Deb, and his uncle was his guardian and his trustee."

I was finding all of this hard to accept. I had hated my brother for so long. It was not easy to let such angry feelings go.

I said stubbornly, "He should have looked for us anyway."

"He should have," Reeve agreed. "But by the time he came of age, a stepmother and a half sister from his distant past probably didn't seem that important to him. Not when he thought you were taken care of."

"But didn't he look at his account books?" I demanded. "Didn't he see that we weren't getting any money?"

Reeve said drily, "I gather that Uncle John still keeps the books."

"Oh God, Reeve," I said. I punched the fist of one hand into the palm of the other. "Oh God."

"Lynly was right," he said soberly. "Your mother should have gotten in contact with him when he turned twenty-one. He would have done something about the injustice his uncle had perpetrated."

I said fiercely, "Mama wouldn't stoop to that."

"She should have," Reeve said.

"He probably wouldn't have done a thing," I said. "He was probably saying all of this just to impress Charlotte."

"Listen to me, Deb," Reeve said. "I know it's hard to let go of a grudge, but sometimes it just has to be done." He put his hands on my shoulders and made me turn to face him. "For both your sakes, I think you're going to have to forgive Lynly for his neglect."

"I do not have to," I said. I added with angry honesty, "I don't *want* to."

"I know you don't." He bent his head and rested his lips on the top of my head. He said gently, "But it will be best for everyone if you do."

I was very close to him. I had been close to him many times before, but for some reason this time it felt different. The night, the scent of the flowers and the sea, the sound of the fountain, the call of the nightingales. The touch of his lips on my hair.

I had the oddest feeling that I wanted to lean against him, to feel the strength of his body pressed against mine.

I frowned and tried to straighten away from him.

His hands remained on my shoulders, holding me where I was. "What do you say?" he asked.

I said curtly, "I will never forgive him, but I suppose I can be civil to him for the duration of this visit."

"That's my girl," he said. He released my shoulders and tipped my chin up and kissed my forehead. His lips lingered for a minute on my skin and made me feel very strange.

What is the matter with me? I thought.

He straightened away from me, and said briskly, "It's time we were getting back to the house."

I rose from the bench with alacrity. I wasn't sure what had just taken place between Reeve and me, but it made me feel definitely uncomfortable. I looked up at him, but could read nothing in the shuttered gravity of his face.

I said lightly, "What about an early-morning ride out to Charles Island?"

"Fine." He sounded preoccupied, as if he were

thinking of something else. There was a line between his brows.

I walked beside him in silence until we reached the house, where we rejoined the others in the drawing room for tea.

CHAPTER
eight

THE FOLLOWING MORNING MRS. THORNTON, THE rector's wife, fell down her front stairs and broke her leg. This news produced immediate consternation at Wakefield Manor.

"Of course, I feel sorry for the poor woman," Lord Bradford said in frustration, "but now who is going to head up the summer fair?"

"Surely Mrs. Thornton didn't undertake so massive an enterprise without help?" I asked in surprise.

Reeve and I had just come back from our ride to find Lord Bradford and Harry sitting over the breakfast table, conferring about what they obviously considered a minor catastrophe. Mama was sitting with them, having her usual frugal breakfast of toast and tea.

"She had help, of course, but she is the one who always pulled all the threads together." Lord Bradford frowned. "I do not see how we are going to manage without her."

"The summer fair must go forward, Papa," Harry said. The expression on his square, blunt-featured face was determined. "The local people will feel cheated if it doesn't."

"I know that, Harry," Lord Bradford said crossly.

Reeve finished helping himself to a huge plate of

eggs and ham from the sideboard and came to join the rest of us at the table. With his perfectly chiseled features and tall, graceful body it didn't seem possible that he could share the same blood as the other two men sitting there.

He asked, "When did this accident happen? We saw Mrs. Thornton only yesterday afternoon, and she was perfectly all right then."

Lord Bradford puffed out his lips. "Apparently it happened early, as she was going out to her garden before breakfast. Dr. Calder stopped by half an hour ago to give me the bad news."

Mama said, "Don't any of the other ladies in the neighborhood assist in the preparation for this fair?"

I seconded her. "Yes, what about all those ladies we met yesterday?"

Harry pushed his plate away from him and looked at me. "You must understand, Deborah, that people like Lord Swale always hold a summer fete for their own servants and tenants. They will put in an obligatory appearance at the village summer fair, but they do not participate in putting it on."

"*Noblesse oblige*," I muttered nastily.

Mama shot me a reproving look. "So the bulk of the work is left to the rector's wife," she said.

Lord Bradford poured himself another cup of coffee. "Mrs. Thornton has always done a splendid job."

He looked distinctly gloomy.

Reeve had been steadily eating his way through the food on his plate, seeming to pay no attention to what was being discussed. He had evidently heard something, however, for now he said, "Well, someone will just have to step in and take Mrs. Thornton's place."

"Easier said than done," Lord Bradford said. "There are certainly many capable women who work with Mrs. Thornton, but none of them would accept one of their own being put in authority over the rest of them. Mrs. Thornton is above them in class, and so they do not object to following her orders. But let me try to put Lizzie Melbourne or Mary Brownley in charge, and there will be a rebellion."

Mama's gentle voice said, "Cannot they all simply keep going on doing the jobs they have been doing for years without Mrs. Thornton to direct them?"

I shook my head decisively. "People are like horses, Mama. They must have a leader."

Lord Bradford gave me an interested look. "You are right, Miss Woodly. They must."

Mama said with a soft laugh. "Deborah and her horses."

Lord Bradford looked at Mama's plate. "Surely you are going to eat more than that, Mrs. Woodly? Why, a cat couldn't subsist on two pieces of toast and a cup of tea for breakfast."

He had noticed exactly how much Mama had eaten.

She gave him her lovely, serene smile. "I assure you, that is all I have eaten for breakfast for years, Lord Bradford, and I have not wasted away to nothing yet."

"Well, there certainly isn't much of you," Lord Bradford said gruffly.

I gave him a sharp look. It seemed to me that Reeve's noxious cousin was entirely too interested in my mother.

Reeve finished chewing a slice of ham. "What precisely goes on at this fair, Bernard?"

"There is dancing on the green in town. There are jugglers for the children. There is an archery contest and a rowing contest, and this year I have arranged for an equestrian exhibition. There is a horse race out to Charles Island and back, in which most of the local gentry participate. There is a huge amount of food set up in tents on the turf near the village. There are traveling singers, and the youngsters play hide-and-seek and other games of that ilk."

"It sounds like fun," Reeve said.

I looked at him in surprise.

He went on easily, "I have an idea. Why doesn't Deb visit Mrs. Thornton and find out all her secrets? Then Deb can run the fair in Mrs. Thornton's place."

I was stunned. I glared at him. How dare he volunteer me for such a task?

"Are you mad, Reeve?" I demanded. "I don't know any of these people! Nor have I ever attended this fair. I couldn't possibly attempt to organize it."

"Your mother will help you." He turned to Mama and gave her his most beguiling smile. "Won't you, Mrs. Woodly?"

"I don't know about that, Reeve," Mama said worriedly. "Deborah is right. She and I are strangers here. Why should any of the local folk listen to us?"

"Because Deb is my fiancée, and I am Bernard's cousin," Reeve replied promptly. "And because they desperately want this fair to go forward."

Lord Bradford gave me a dubious look. "I think you are asking too much of Miss Woodly, Reeve. As she herself said, she has no knowledge of how things are run here."

"She will find out from Mrs. Thornton," Reeve said.

"Oh I will, will I?" I said sarcastically. "And what about you, Reeve? Will you help as well?"

"Yes," he said surprisingly, "I will."

The shock of surprise that ran around the room kept us all silent.

"I like the idea of the horse race," Reeve said blandly. "It sounds like fun."

I frowned, and repeated, "I cannot ask women I do not know to work for me."

"Nonsense," Reeve said. "You're a born general, Deb."

I stared at him uncertainly.

He gave me an encouraging grin.

Just think how impressed Bernard will be if you pull this off.

I could read him like a book. He wanted me to do everything in my power to encourage Lord Bradford to hand over his money.

"Well . . ." I said reluctantly. "I suppose I could at least go to visit Mrs. Thornton and see if she thought such a plan was feasible."

"You're a great girl, Deb," Reeve said.

I was starting to get a little sick of hearing those words.

I waited another day before I went to see Mrs. Thornton. After all, I thought, it was only fair to give the poor woman a chance to recover from her injuries. I did not want to admit to myself how daunting I found the thought of taking on the running of a fair that was apparently so important to hundreds of people.

Damn Reeve for getting me into this, I thought. I didn't know why I put up with him.

My interview with Mrs. Thornton did not go as badly as I had feared it might. She was delighted to have someone take charge of the affair, and after so many years of running it she was so well organized that it seemed all Mama and I were going to have to do were to act as the messengers to carry out Mrs. Thornton's orders.

Even the ladies of the town were cordial when Mrs. Thornton called a meeting and introduced Mama and me. It was evident that everyone was anxious to see the affair come off, and they appeared perfectly amenable to taking suggestions from the Earl of Cambridge's intended bride and her mother.

After the garden party, the next thing on Lord Bradford's agenda to entertain Reeve and Mama and me was a dance. For this grand endeavor Lord Bradford had invited a larger assortment of guests than those who lived only within the immediate neighborhood. In fact, a number of people would be coming from a great enough distance that it would require their staying overnight at Wakefield Manor.

Sally and Mary Ann were in a state of high excitement and could talk of nothing else. Neither of them had yet made their official comeouts into society, and a dance such as this one, where they could actually wear ball gowns, was an occasion of great magnitude in their lives.

Once again I felt the familiar qualm of conscience as Lord Bradford described his plans to us, and the girls chattered on with undisguised delight. Every day it seemed to me that Reeve and I were becoming more deeply entangled in this pretend engagement of ours. Every day it seemed as if it was going to be harder and harder to extricate ourselves from the web of our own making.

Then, on the day before the dance was due to be held, Robert came home.

I had been in the village, conferring with a group of ladies in regard to the entertainment for the fair. The day was hot, and I had chosen to drive Lord Bradford's trap so that I could wear a lightweight dress instead of a riding jacket and boots. I was by myself, as Mama had gone to pay a neighborhood visit with Mrs. Norton.

When I returned to Wakefield Manor, I drove directly to the stables to leave off the trap and as I pulled into the cobblestoned stable yard a powerful-looking young man with light brown hair stepped out of the shadow of the redbrick stable building and into the sunlight. He stood stock-still and watched me as I stopped my mare and waited for one of the grooms to come to her head.

I shook off a groom's assistance and climbed down from the trap myself. When I turned, I was surprised to see the brown-haired stranger standing next to me. He stared into my face, and said in a hard voice, with a distinctly unpleasant edge, "So you are the girl who is engaged to my dear cousin, Reeve."

I could feel hostility radiating out from him. Hostility, and something else I couldn't name.

I knew immediately that this must be Robert.

I lifted my chin, and replied coolly, "Yes, I am Deborah Woodly."

His eyes flicked over me, going from the top of my head to the tips of my feet. Hot color flushed into my face. I can honestly say that no man had ever looked at me like that before. I felt as if he had stripped me naked.

I wished that I were wearing my riding habit and not a thin muslin dress. I wished that I had a whip in my hand, so I could cut him across his outrageously rude face.

His eyes were blue-gray and not quite two inches above mine. I stared into them, and said in a frigid voice, "You must be Robert."

He bared his teeth at me in a parody of a smile. "How clever of you, Deborah. I am indeed Reeve's cousin, Robert." He bowed and held out his arm. "May I escort you back to the house?"

"I am perfectly capable of walking without assistance, thank you," I returned sharply. I didn't want him to touch me.

He laughed. It was not a nice sound.

I decided instantly that he was, without a doubt, the most thoroughly unpleasant man I had ever met. No wonder Reeve couldn't abide him.

Unfortunately, I couldn't forbid him to walk beside me, and we began to go together along the path that led toward the house.

He stepped close to me and deliberately brushed his shoulder against mine.

I leaped away from him onto the grass verge and turned to give him a furious look.

He said, "I have been wondering why my beloved cousin decided to get married. I have always thought it would be many years before Reeve was ready to settle down." Once more he stripped me naked with his look. "You're a little skinny for my taste, but your eyes and hair are very good."

I said through my teeth, "Look at me like that one more time, and I will hit you."

I saw a spark of violence in his eyes, and immediately I regretted my words. "Try it, darling," he said softly. "Please do try it."

My heart began to hammer in my chest.

There was something not quite right about this man, I thought. Why should he hate me so intensely when he didn't even know me? For it was hatred that was fueling his interest in me; of that I was suddenly certain.

At last we reached the house, and I went in through the back door, trying not to look as if I were hurrying. It was five-thirty, and the rest of the house party had returned from their various afternoon activities and were getting ready for dinner. Gratefully, I turned my back on Robert and ran up the stairs to my room to change my clothes.

The house party always gathered in the rear drawing room at six-thirty before we went in to dinner. This evening, as Mama and I entered the elegant white-and-gold room, with its crystal chandelier, white-satin-covered furniture and gilt wall mirrors, the atmosphere was very different from what it had been for the last week or so.

Reeve and Robert stood on opposite sides of the

room from each other, but the antagonism between them was so powerful that it shivered through the air.

Lady Sophia looked angry.

Harry looked resigned.

Sally looked distressed.

Lord Bradford looked stoic.

The Nortons were trying to look as if they noticed nothing out of the ordinary.

I felt Mama glance nervously at me.

As soon as he saw us, Lord Bradford stepped forward. "Miss Woodly, Mrs. Woodly, allow me to present my eldest son, Mr. Robert Lambeth."

Robert came across the room to bow over our hands.

"How do you do," I said woodenly, as he took my fingers into his large, powerful grip. Neither of us said anything about our earlier meeting at the stable.

Robert might not be overly tall, but everything about him was powerful. Menacing, almost.

Once more I saw that glint of violence in his eyes.

Across the room, I could see Reeve scowl ferociously.

Now that all of us were present, we went into the dining room.

Everyone kept up a good pretense that all was normal during dinner. I noticed that Lady Sophia had put Robert and Reeve as far away from each other as was possible, and Robert conversed with Mary Ann Norton with at least a semblance of politeness. After dinner was over, and the ladies retired to the drawing room leaving the gentlemen to themselves, I was afraid that things would get more dangerous, but when the men joined us in the drawing room, tense courtesy reigned, at least on the surface.

It didn't take long for Reeve to snag me for a walk in the garden. I went with alacrity, feeling Robert's gaze burn into my back as we left the drawing room to go along to the morning room and thence out the French doors into the garden.

We walked for a while in silence until we reached the stone bench on the side of the yew arch, where, with wordless communication, we sat down side by side. I turned to Reeve and said forcefully, "What a thoroughly unpleasant man your cousin is!"

"He hates me," Reeve replied.

"Why?" I demanded.

He sighed. "I rather think it's because he thinks I am standing in the way of what he regards as being rightfully his. You see, Deb, Bernard is my heir. And after Bernard, of course, comes Robert."

I frowned, trying to make sense of this statement. At last I said in bewilderment, "But surely Robert cannot be so foolish as to think that you will not marry and have sons of your own to inherit the title?"

Reeve picked up a yellow rose that someone had dropped next to the bench and began to strip the petals off it one by one. The rich scent of the mutilated flower drifted through the summer air. He said, "You see, after the . . . accident . . . I think Robert actually convinced himself that I never *would* marry, that one day he would really be the Earl of Cambridge."

My heart cramped at his mention of the accident but I managed to say steadily, "That's a ridiculous assumption, of course, but even if it were true, Reeve, you and Robert are the same age. Why should he think that he would live to succeed you?"

Reeve stripped another few petals off the unfortunate rose. He did not meet my eyes as he said, "Accidents happen, Deb, and I have suspected for a while that Robert might be planning an accident for me. Of course, now that he thinks I am going to marry, and will perhaps have a son to displace him, his incentive to do away with me will only be increased."

I stared at him in horror. "My God, Reeve. Haven't you done anything about this?"

He threw the rose to the ground. "What can I do, Deb? Tell Bernard that I suspect his son of wishing to arrange my death?" He shrugged. "And who knows? Perhaps I deserve whatever Robert has in mind."

And so we were back to it again.

The accident.

The never-ending guilt.

"Your mother would not think that way," I said positively.

"No. Mother was an angel. She would never think ill of me, no matter what I did." His voice was sad and bitter all at once.

I did not know how to answer him. The corrosive guilt he had lived with for so many years had become so much a part of him that words alone would never free him from it.

What had happened to Reeve was this. At the age of fifteen, he had been driving with his mother from London to Ambersley in the Cambridge town chaise. Being young and enthusiastic, Reeve had begged Lady Cambridge to allow him to take the reins of the chaise, which was a much larger and heavier vehicle than the phaetons he was used to driving around the Ambersley estate.

Lady Cambridge, a loving and far too indulgent parent, had agreed.

The coachman, who knew Reeve had never before driven on the road, had objected, but he had not been able to gainsay his employer.

Reeve was going too fast when he met a cart on a blind turn. He pulled his horses too far to the right in order to avoid it, and overturned the chaise in a ditch. It was an ugly accident, as the carriage had turned over several times before coming to rest at the bottom. Lady Cambridge and the coachman had been thrown from the vehicle. Lady Cambridge's neck had been broken, and she had died instantly, while the coachman had suffered internal injuries and lived for another few days.

Reeve had broken his arm.

It was a tragedy, of course. A tragedy for Lady Cambridge, a beautiful and loving woman who had been cut down in the middle of her thirties; a tragedy for the coachman, who had left a wife and two small children. And it had been a tragedy for Reeve, who had been left to bear the guilt of it all.

The fact that Lord Cambridge had never forgiven Reeve had not helped Reeve to be able to forgive himself. His father blamed him for the death of the wife he had loved, and Reeve blamed himself for the death of his mother.

I had often thought that if Reeve's father had shown him any sort of compassion, if he had admitted to Reeve that part of the blame for the accident had lain with Lady

Cambridge's folly in permitting a half-grown boy to drive a vehicle he should never have been allowed to touch, then the accident would not have had so destructive an effect on Reeve's character.

But Lord Cambridge had labeled his son as reckless and irresponsible, and Reeve had done his damnedest to live up to his father's image of him. The result, of course, had been that wretched will and the extension of Reeve's minor status five years beyond what was the ordinary age.

I sat next to him now and looked at his hand, which was lying palm up on his thigh, and impulsively I reached over and laid my hand over it. His fingers closed around my wrist and he turned to look at me.

For some reason, my heartbeat increased.

I said fiercely, "Don't you dare let that horrible man do anything to you."

A faint smile glimmered in his eyes. His fingers increased their pressure on my wrist, and he pulled me closer to him. He said, "Would you really miss me that much, Deb?"

My heartbeat grew faster and louder. I was acutely conscious of his thigh so close to mine.

The smell of the crushed rose was strong in my nostrils.

This is all wrong, I thought in confusion. *I should not be feeling like this about Reeve.*

His fingers were on my wrist, and I was afraid that he would feel the hammering of my pulse. I tried to pull my hand away, but he held on to it.

The sound of voices came to us through the summer night. Reeve lifted my hand to his lips and kissed the inside of my wrist, where my pulse beat, before he stood to greet Sally and Edmund Norton.

The four of us stood talking for a while and then we all returned to the house for evening tea.

CHAPTER

nine

I USUALLY SLEPT LIKE A BABY, BUT THAT NIGHT I lay awake for a long time before I went to sleep.

What was happening between Reeve and me? It was as if this pretend engagement had knocked our old friendship out of its comfortable path and pushed us onto a new road that I was not at all sure that I liked.

I had never in my life felt uncertain with Reeve. His dark, romantic splendor had been a fact in my life for so long that I never thought it could exercise a pull on my senses.

In short, I was thoroughly upset by my reaction to him in the garden. And he had only held my hand!

At last I drifted off to sleep to dream a disturbing dream where I was riding through a dark, enclosing forest. Something evil was pursuing me, but I didn't know what it was. I awoke in a sweat and couldn't get back to sleep again.

I lay awake thinking gloomily that I would make a beautiful sight with dark circles under my eyes for the dance that evening.

When finally morning crawled around and I went down to breakfast, it was to find that Harry had taken Reeve into Chichester to look at a horse Harry was purportedly thinking of buying.

I thought the purpose of the trip was more likely to keep Reeve separated from Robert for the day.

After breakfast, Lady Sophia ensconced herself in the morning room, from whence she issued orders about readying the house for the influx of guests that were expected for the evening's dance. Mrs. Norton, Mama, and I were her minions, and the three of us worked like Trojans to make sure that the guest bedrooms were prepared properly, the cook was ready to serve twenty persons at dinner and forty more at supper, that there would be tea and coffee served at supper as well as lemonade and champagne, that card tables were set up in the rear drawing room, that the furniture in the long gallery was removed so that there could be dancing, and that chairs were set up along the walls for those who wished to watch.

Mary Ann and Sally were given the job of looking for the arrival of the musicians.

Acting upon Lady Sophia's orders, all of the men made themselves scarce for the duration of the day.

"Most useless things in the world, men," she muttered as she sent her female slaves scurrying here and there. "They only get in one's way whenever anything important needs to be done."

"Come now, ma'am," Mrs. Norton said good-humoredly, "they must have some uses."

"Not when it comes to putting on a dance," Lady Sophia snapped.

By three o'clock, the house was in order, and by five o'clock the first of the guests who had been invited to remain overnight at Wakefield began to appear. Lord

Bradford and Lady Sophia greeted them, while Mama and I remained upstairs to get ready for the great occasion.

I wore one of my London dresses, a high-waisted, white-satin ball dress with a strand of pearls, which Reeve had bought me, clasped around my throat. Susan did my hair in a twist with white roses tucked into it. Mama wore blue and looked like an angel.

My brother would be coming this evening with the Swales, and though I tried to tell myself that I didn't care one iota about seeing him again, I knew it wasn't true.

All of the relationships that had been the basis of my life for so long—my friendship with Reeve, my hatred of my brother—were changing, and I didn't like it. It made me feel as if I were losing a grip on my world.

I wished fervently that I had never agreed to this pretend engagement in the first place.

When Mama and I both were ready we went down the carved-oak staircase to the rear drawing room, where we found the guests who were to spend the night at Wakefield gathered, along with the family and the Nortons. As we came into the room, my eyes instinctively looked for Reeve.

He was standing in front of the fireplace talking to a red-haired woman I didn't know. He wore a dark coat, an intricately tied cravat and satin knee breeches that fairly molded themselves to his slim hips and long legs.

Across the width of the drawing room, his eyes met mine.

His eyebrows lifted in a gesture of resignation.

I smiled.

Then I looked for Robert.

He was standing along the left wall of the room, with his back to the door, talking to a black-haired young lady who seemed extremely vivacious.

Lady Sophia, attired in purple satin and wearing a formidable array of diamonds on her withered bosom, was standing directly under the crystal chandelier talking to an elderly gentleman with a startlingly bald head, which glistened in the light of the many candles above it.

"My dear Lady Sophia," said the bald-pated man in the loud tone of those who are partially deaf, "who is the beauty in the doorway?"

As she turned to look at me, the expression on Lady Sophia's face was exceedingly sour. "That is Miss Woodly, my nephew Cambridge's intended bride," she replied.

I saw Lord Bradford crossing the room toward us. "Miss Woodly, Mrs. Woodly," he said. "You must allow me to introduce you to some of our friends."

We made the rounds of the drawing room, smiling and greeting a collection of people whose names and faces I worked hard to commit to memory. While we were doing this, the guests who lived in the immediate neighborhood began to arrive.

One of these guests was my brother.

I looked at him out of the corner of my eyes as I stood talking to two of the overnight visitors, Viscount Morley and his wife. In his formal evening dress, Richard looked handsome and elegant and well-bred; just the sort of young man, in fact, that every parent hoped his daughter would bring home.

Familiar, cleansing anger swept through me at the thought.

I know I didn't make a sound, but something must have showed on my face, for Viscount Morley gave me a startled look, and asked, "Is anything wrong, Miss Woodly?"

I forced a smile and assured him that everything was perfectly fine.

Shortly after that it was time to go in to dinner.

Ordinarily Mama and I, as the widow and daughter of a baron, would not command the escort of either of the two earls (one of whom was Reeve) or the two viscounts who were present. However, as this evening was in effect being held in our honor, our status was elevated, and I found myself being escorted by the Earl of Merivale while Reeve took in Mama.

Dinner seemed to go on for a very long time. Robert, who was at the other end of the table from Reeve, conversed with grim-faced politeness with Charlotte Henley.

Once or twice I caught Lord Bradford shooting a worried glance in Robert's direction, and I thought that it must severely tax the patience of his family to have to treat him continually like a dog they were afraid was going to bite.

As we slowly ate our way through the turtle soup, salmon, roasted capon, ham, a haunch of venison, plus a huge assortment of side dishes, I made conversation with Lord Bradford, who sat on one side of me, and with the amiable Lord Austin, who was seated on my other side.

After the ice cream and fruit had been served, the ladies retired to the long gallery. It did not take long before we were joined by the gentlemen, and shortly after that the musicians struck up the first dance.

Ordinarily the honor of leading off the first dance would fall to the Countess of Merivale, but tonight Reeve bowed before me, took my hand, and led me out to the floor. The rest of the party formed up after us, and, when the set was filled, the gentlemen bowed, the ladies curtsied, and the dance officially began.

As the evening progressed, I danced with a succession of smiling, good-natured men, both young and middle-aged, and about halfway through the dance I realized that this party was not at all unlike the local dances I had attended with Mama at home. The clothing was much more elegant, of course, and the social status of the guests more elevated, but the same kind of friendliness and good humor prevailed.

I was actually enjoying myself.

Then my brother asked me to dance.

I did not want to dance with him, but I could not say so in front of all these people. So I gave him my hand in silence and allowed him to lead me to the floor.

The top of my head only came up to his mouth. He was as tall as Reeve.

"Well it's clear to see that they're brother and sister."

The words came, loud and clear, from the deaf bald-headed man who was sitting next to Lady Sophia on one of the gilt chairs that lined the walls of the long gallery.

My fingers, which were clasped within Richard's, stiffened.

He looked down into my face, and said gravely, "My uncle will be coming to visit the Swales within the next few days, and I want you to know, Deborah, that I am going to demand that he give me an explanation for his treatment of you and your mother."

The music began and we bowed to each other.

I said, "No explanation can erase eighteen years of injustice."

"I realize . . ." Before he could complete his sentence, however, the dance swept him away from me.

"I would like to talk to you after I have seen him," Richard said, when the motions of the dance had brought us back together once more.

"I have nothing to talk to you about," I returned contemptuously.

The dance separated us again.

"I think you owe it to your mother to see me," he said when we were once more joined together. "You are right when you say that injustice cannot be erased, but it can be rectified."

I didn't want to talk to him. I didn't want to take anything from him. But he was right. If he was willing to give Mama a more substantial allowance, I had no right to do anything that would stand in the way of her receiving it.

I clenched my teeth. "All right," I said just before the steps of the dance separated us again.

After the dance was over, he walked me back to where Mama was standing with Lord Bradford. "I will call upon you after I have spoken to my uncle," he said. A touch of steel came into his voice. "I can assure you, Deborah, that I am very interested in hearing what he has to say about all of this."

He could not be more interested than I, I thought, as

I watched him bow to Mama and ask her to dance. She accepted with a warm smile.

It seemed to me that Mama was far too pleased to see her negligent stepson again.

"Are you enjoying yourself, Miss Woodly?" Lord Bradford asked me genially.

"Yes, my lord," I replied. "Everyone has been very kind."

The music was starting for the next dance, and I heard someone come up on my other side.

"May I have the pleasure of this dance, Miss Woodly?" Robert Lambeth asked.

I glanced quickly at Lord Bradford to see if he would rescue me by claiming that he had asked me first.

He looked at his eldest son, frowned, and said nothing.

I said woodenly, "Of course, Mr. Lambeth," and allowed Robert to lead me to the floor.

It was a country dance, not a quadrille, thank God, and to all intents and purposes we were just another couple going up and down the line, hands joined, smiles on our lips. The only difference was that Lord Bradford stood on one side of the room watching us, and Reeve stood, shoulders against the wall, arms crossed, on the other.

Robert knew he was being watched.

He laughed when we came together for a minute, and said, "Do you feel like one of the Sabine women, Deborah?"

I didn't know who the Sabine women were, but I could deduce that their fate had not been a happy one.

I looked him straight in the eyes. "I don't know what you're talking about."

The shutters that veiled his eyes with the semblance of civilization lifted for a minute, and I could see into the violence that lurked beneath. "Ask Reeve," he said. "He'll tell you."

I went in to supper with Reeve and Harry and Mary Ann Norton. There had been one long table set up in the center of the front drawing room, and around it were placed several smaller tables. The four of us filled our plates from the lavish display of food along the wall and took one of the smaller tables.

It had become very evident over the course of my stay at Wakefield Manor that Mary Ann and Harry had grown up as friends much the way Reeve and I had. They were very comfortable together, with dozens of shared memories and similiar tastes.

Mary Ann was all in favor of Harry's becoming a doctor and as we discussed Harry's future, she waxed indignant over Lord Bradford's refusal to let his son go to London to get the proper training.

"Harry is the sort of person who *should* be a doctor," she declared vigorously as she paused between bites of lobster patties. "He has always cared about people."

Harry put his hand over his breast. "Thank you, Mary Ann."

"It's very important that you get the proper training," she said, giving him an impish smile. "Remember those noxious brews you used to mix up when we were children?" She turned to me. "He would actually try to get me to drink them. He called them tonics!"

Harry said in a mock injured tone, "You would have been much stronger if you had taken them."

"Hah," Mary Ann said. "I would probably have been dead."

I listened to them, and smiled, and wondered how two brothers could be as different as Robert and Harry.

Suddenly I remembered what Robert had said while we were dancing and turned to Reeve to ask, "Who were the Sabine women?"

Reeve choked on his lobster patty.

"Who was talking to you about the Sabine women?" he asked when he had swallowed some champagne and got his breath back.

"Never mind," I said. "Who were they?"

Reeve glanced at Harry.

"She asked you, not me," Harry replied.

Reeve patted his lips with his napkin. "The Sabines were a tribe of people who lived on the outskirts of Rome in the early days of the empire. They were eventually conquered by Rome and lost their national identity," he said.

Mary Ann was interested now. "But what happened to their women?"

Reeve took another swallow of champagne. "I believe that when the battle that defeated the Sabines was over, their women suffered what one would call a 'fate worse than death' at the hands of the Roman soldiers."

The two men looked at each other.

"In other words, they were raped," I said.

Reeve sighed. "In other words, they were raped."

Mary Ann and I glared at our two escorts.

"Men are so disgusting," Mary Ann said.

"Wait a minute," Harry protested. "Just a minute ago, I was someone who cared about people."

A dimple dented Mary Ann's cheek and her large brown eyes softened. "I didn't mean you, Harry."

"I should think not," Harry said huffily. "Nor do I think it is proper to be discussing such a matter with young ladies."

"Be careful, Harry," I warned. "You're beginning to sound like your father."

Reeve gave me a penetrating look. "I still wonder who mentioned the subject to you, Deb."

"Oh, it's just something I came upon in a book," I said airily.

He did not look as if he believed me, but he held his tongue.

The rest of the dance went by very pleasantly. Mama danced as much as I did—twice with Lord Bradford, I noticed. She looked like a girl and was obviously having such a wonderful time that I didn't have the heart to mention to her that Lord Bradford's preference for her might lead to gossip.

After the musicians had played the last dance, and the guests who had traveled to the ball were awaiting their chaises, Reeve and I stood in the front hall to bid them farewell.

"I will call upon you as soon as I have heard from my uncle," my brother repeated as he prepared to leave with the Swales, and this time I found within myself less resistance to seeing him again.

"Very well," I said. "Just send word so that I will be sure to be at home."

"Richard," Charlotte called, "are you coming?"

"Yes," he returned. Then he reached out, took my hand, and gave it a brief squeeze. "I would very much like to have a sister, Deborah," he said. "Try not to think too ill of me, will you?"

He was gone, leaving me with all sorts of conflicting emotions churning around in my heart.

I felt Reeve looming beside me.

"It was Robert, wasn't it?" he said.

I stared at him in bewilderment.

"It was Robert who mentioned the Sabine women."

I sighed. "Yes."

"Stay away from him, Deb. I don't want his hatred of me to spill over onto you."

I thought that it was already too late for that, but I refrained from saying so. I smiled. "Don't worry, Reeve. I have no intention of coming within ten feet of your cousin if I can help it. I think there's something wrong with him."

Reeve said, "His temper is volatile. Even as a child, he was subject to fits of blind, unreasoning rage. But Bernard could usually control him then. As he has gotten older he has gotten more and more out of hand."

"It is hard to believe that he and Harry are brothers," I said. "One is so gentle and the other is so violent."

Lady Sophia was approaching us with her bald-headed friend, and Reeve heaved an impatient sigh.

I said politely, "The dance was a huge success, Lady Sophia. Everyone had a wonderful time."

She actually smiled at me. "If there's one thing I know how to do, gel, it's put on a dance. Now, Crumly, it's time you were seeking your bed. You're too old to be up past midnight."

The old man took my hand in his age-spotted one and patted it a half a dozen times. He looked at Reeve. "Beautiful girl you've got yourself, boy. I've always liked 'em tall and willowy, myself."

Mr. Crumly was short, and his stomach was that of a woman six months pregnant.

"Thank you, sir," Reeve said gravely.

With difficulty, I refrained from rolling my eyes.

"Good night, Lady Sophia," I said sweetly. "Good night, Mr. Crumly."

The two old people moved off, and five minutes later I followed them upstairs. I had had little rest the night before, and I was tired. Within ten minutes, I was fast asleep.

CHAPTER
ten

I SLEPT LATE AND SO MISSED BREAKFAST THE FOL-
lowing morning, which I learned later had been attended
only by the gentlemen in the house. By the time I arrived
downstairs at eleven most of the other ladies were beginning to make their belated appearances as well, and by
one o'clock all of the ball guests had departed, leaving
only the house party to gather in the dining room for luncheon.

Lady Sophia was in fine fettle, reliving the tri-
umphs of the previous evening's dance, for which she
took all the credit. The rest of us were content to listen to
her and make noises of agreement when they were called
for.

When luncheon was over, Lord Bradford asked
Reeve and me if he could speak to us privately in the library. Reeve quirked an eyebrow at me, and I nodded
that I understood the time had come for us to present
Lord Bradford with our demand for him to relinquish
his hold on Reeve's inheritance.

The library at Wakefield Manor was paneled in
warm chestnut wood and, like the rest of the rooms in
the charming old house, it was lovely without being
overwhelming. There were a few occasional chairs set

in front of the large carved fireplace, and Lord Bradford gestured Reeve and me to take a seat.

"I thought it was time for the three of us to have a talk about your upcoming marriage," Lord Bradford began pleasantly once we were all sitting facing each other. "I have told the both of you separately how pleased I am with your choice, Reeve, but don't you think it is time that you set a date for your nuptials? There was a good deal of curiosity expressed upon that subject last night. I'm sure you were questioned about it as well as I."

"We would very much like to set a date, sir," Reeve returned in an equally pleasant tone. "There is just one small detail that is holding us up."

I had my hands clasped together tightly in my lap. The idea that I tell Lord Bradford that I wouldn't marry Reeve unless he had control of his money suddenly seemed far less brilliant to me than it had originally. There was something about sitting in this charming library and confronting the man himself with such a demand that was rather daunting.

I shot Reeve a look that was a blatant plea for help.

He nodded faintly, turned to his cousin, and said in a steady voice, "You see, Bernard, Deb wants to live at Ambersley. Well, you can hardly blame her, can you? She grew up in the neighborhood there. All her friends are there. She's comfortable there." The line of Reeve's mouth became very grim, and suddenly he looked older than his twenty-four years. "But I won't live there if I'm not the master. I haven't lived there since my father died, and I won't live there now. Not under the humiliating conditions imposed upon me by that blasted will.

So, unless you see fit to give me control of my money, Bernard, Deb and I are likely to remain unmarried until I turn twenty-six."

I was impressed. Reeve had done an excellent job of stating the case, I thought. I flashed him a quick, approving smile.

Lord Bradford looked surprised. "But I thought I told you that I would turn over half your money to you upon your marriage, Reeve. Did you perhaps misunderstand me? There will be no problem with your living at Ambersley as your own master."

Some of Reeve's dignity deserted him as he ran agitated fingers through his hair, causing it to fall across his forehead in a most Corsair-like way. He scowled. "Why do I have to wait until we get married, Bernard? Why can't I have my money now? That way I can get Ambersley ready for Deb."

"To my knowledge, Ambersley is in perfect repair, Reeve," Lord Bradford said in a measured tone.

Once more Reeve and I exchanged glances. This interview was definitely not going the way we had planned it.

Well, I thought, it was my turn to weigh in. I raised my chin and said bravely, "Lord Bradford, I have decided that I am not going to marry Reeve unless he has control of his inheritance first."

He looked at me with interest. "And why is that, Miss Woodly?"

I replied promptly, "Because I think it was terribly unfair of his father to make such a will in the first place. I think Reeve would be a wonderful landlord, and it has been deeply humiliating for him not to have charge of his own inheritance." I had a brilliant idea and sat up straighter in my chair. "I have no dowry to bring to Reeve, and this is going to be my contribution to our union. I want him to have his inheritance."

"But he will have it," Lord Bradford repeated. "As soon as you are married."

The two of us glared at him.

"Damn it, Bernard," Reeve said. "Why are you being so obstinate?"

Lord Bradford folded his arms across his chest and looked from one of us to the other. "For how long have you two known each other?" he asked.

This change of subject bewildered me. "I came to live at Hawthorne Cottage when I was three," I said. "Reeve was seven."

"And you played together as children?" Lord Bradford asked.

Reeve shrugged. "We did when Deb got a little older. She was always a game 'un, even when she was a babe."

"Hmmm," said Lord Bradford.

Reeve and I exchanged uncertain looks. What was going on here?

Then Lord Bradford said in a soft, dangerous-sounding voice, "Is it at all possible that the two of you are trying to fool me with a mock engagement?"

My eyes and Reeve's met in sharp alarm.

"Aha," said Lord Bradford. "So that is it."

"That's not it at all, Bernard," Reeve said forcefully. "Deb and I love each other. Don't we, Deb?"

I nodded vigorously.

"Perhaps you do," Lord Bradford said. "I hope you

do. For one thing is very certain, Reeve. You are going to marry each other."

My mouth dropped open.

"This engagement has gone too far for you to cry off now," Lord Bradford continued grimly. "It has been published in the papers. Deborah has been introduced in London as your fiancée, and she has been visiting here in the same capacity. The scandal should either of you cry off would be enormous. I will not have the Lambeth name subjected to such a public disgrace."

My brain was in a whirl. This was not at all what we had expected to happen.

I blurted out, "But what if we both said that we had discovered we would not suit?"

Implacably, Lord Bradford shook his head. "It's too late for that." He turned to Reeve. "I will hold to my side of the bargain, Reeve. I will turn over to you half of your money once the marriage is accomplished. But if you cry off, you will not get one single farthing out of me over your allowance until you are twenty-six. Is that perfectly clear?"

Reeve's dark eyes were shooting black fire. "Yes, Bernard, it is perfectly clear."

"I will be happy to hold the marriage here at Wakefield," Bernard said. "Shall we say in two weeks' time?"

"Damn it, Bernard," Reeve shouted. "I am sick to death of you running my life for me!"

"Marry Deborah and you may run your own life," Bernard said pleasantly. "Think about that, Reeve." He stood up. "Now, if you will excuse me, I have some work to do. I'm sure the two of you have things to talk about."

"Come on, Deb," Reeve muttered, and stalked to the door with me trailing behind him. We went out into the hall and stood looking at each other, neither of us knowing what to say.

"Let's ride out to Charles Island," Reeve said. "Bernard is right. We need to talk."

"I'll change my dress," I said, and ran upstairs to my room.

My mind was in a whirl. What were we going to do? Neither of us had ever dreamed that Bernard would call our bluff.

It was blackmail, I thought indignantly as I put on my riding dress. Blackmail, pure and simple.

My temper was as hot as Reeve's as I went down to the stable to meet him. Bernard was a thoroughly horrible man, I thought. How dare he issue us such an ultimatum?

It was also extremely humiliating that he had seen through our scheme so easily.

What in the name of God were Reeve and I going to do?

The sky was dark and overcast when I met Reeve in the stable, and the head groom warned us not to go out, that a storm was blowing in from the Channel. Neither Reeve nor I was in a mood to listen to advice, however, and we rode out under the heavy clouds, along the road that led south to the village of Fair Haven and the sand causeway that would take us to Charles Island.

"God damn Bernard," Reeve said viciously as we started off together along the road. "He always manages to put me in the wrong."

It was true. Once more Lord Bradford had put Reeve into a position where his back was to the wall.

I said unhappily, "I suppose we should have foreseen that he would suspect something when we demanded the money before the marriage."

"But why the bloody hell is he so intent on getting me married?" Reeve said explosively.

"I don't know," I said. "It is some quirk he has gotten into his brain, I suppose."

The wind blew stronger as we approached the Channel, but neither of us was in a mood to return to the manor. We were halfway over the causeway when the first drops of rain began to fall. A minute later, the heavens opened. Thunder rolled and lightning flashed farther out over the water.

"Wonderful," Reeve said through his teeth. "This is just what we need."

I raised my voice to be heard above the pelting rain. "We've got to get out of the lightning, Reeve!"

"It's low tide; let's head for Rupert's Cave," he shouted back. He put his horse into a gallop, and I followed close behind. Within a few minutes we had come to the stony, south side of the island, with its high rocky cliff towering above the water. By this time I was drenched through to my skin and the thunder and lightning were coming uncomfortably close to shore.

Rupert's Cave was high enough to accommodate the horses as well as us, and we were all under cover by the time the thunderstorm broke over the island. The rain had been warm but it was cool within the cave and I shivered with the chill of my wet clothes.

We moved up against the wall of the cave, away

from the small rivulet of water that ran down its middle, and Reeve took off his jacket and hung it across my shoulders. "It's wet, but it's better than nothing," he said.

Outside the cave the thunder crashed.

Reeve looked down at me. His face was wet with rain, and drops clung to his lashes. He said, "Do you know, I've been thinking, Deb, that perhaps our getting married wouldn't be so terrible a thing after all."

I stared at him in astonishment.

"Think about it yourself," he urged. "I would get my money and you"—he gave me a charming, crooked smile—"you would get all the horses you wanted to ride."

I pulled his wet jacket more closely around me, and said impatiently, "Reeve, there is more to marriage than that."

"I know there is." We were standing just within the entrance to the cave, with the horses behind us. Between the rolls of thunder, the sound of the rain beating on the rocks of the shore was very loud. Reeve took out his damp handkerchief, took my chin in his hand and carefully dried my upturned face. Then, still holding my chin with his long fingers, he said coaxingly, "I think you and I would deal together very well in other ways, too, Deb."

Then he bent his head and his mouth came down on mine.

I was totally unprepared for such an action on his part, and I went perfectly still with the shock of it. A crack of thunder split the heavens just outside the cave, and I jumped. His mouth did not release mine, but his hands spread themselves on my back and pulled me closer to him. We were both soaked to the skin, and as our bodies pressed together and I felt the heat of his skin scorching into mine, it was as if we had no clothes on at all. His lips on mine hardened, exerted pressure, and opened my mouth. Then his tongue entered between my teeth.

I had never felt anything remotely like this before in my life. My knees buckled, and I put my arms around him to keep myself from falling down. The muscles in his back under his soaked shirt were hard and defined under my outstretched hands.

His lips left my mouth and trailed a train of kisses along my cheek to my ear. He said huskily. "Deb, darling, you are definitely not a little girl anymore."

I couldn't say a word.

He held me away from him and looked down into my face.

"Say yes, Deb. Please say yes."

Outside the thunder boomed. One of the horses whinnied nervously and pawed the wet, pebbly ground. The other shifted his hindquarters in sympathy.

"I don't think this is a good idea," I whispered. "Suppose in a few years time you find someone you really love?"

He said positively, "I will never care for another girl as much as I care for you." He bent his head to kiss me again, and this time his hand came up between us to touch my breast. My breath ratcheted in my throat, and my nipple stood up hard against his palm.

Lightning flashed and he looked down at me, a

dark angel momentarily illuminated against the gloom of the cave. His eyes were glittering.

"Say yes," he commanded me again.

"All right," I heard myself saying. "I'll do it."

As we waited out the rest of the storm in Rupert's Cave, Reeve talked cheerfully, making plans for our immediate future. I struggled to answer in a normal voice, scarcely hearing what either of us said.

All I wanted was to get back to the privacy of my own room so I could think about what had just happened between us.

Eventually the storm blew over, and we mounted our horses to head back to the manor.

Reeve was silent as he rode next to me. The horses splashed through the puddles left by the heavy rain, and Reeve's face disclosed nothing as he watched the path in front of him.

For the first time in my life, I felt awkward with him. For the first time, I didn't know what to say.

We were almost at the house when he said, "I'll find Bernard and tell him what we have decided."

I wet my lips. "You're certain you want to do this?"

He nodded his dark head decisively.

"I want to take charge of my own life, and if this is the way I have to do it, then this is what I'll do."

I said, "I think two weeks is too short a time. It doesn't even give us time to call the banns, for heaven's sake."

"We can always get a special license," Reeve said

a trifle impatiently. "Bernard is right, Deb. If we're going to do this, there's no point in dragging it out."

We parted in the front hall, Reeve to go in search of his cousin and me to run upstairs, to change my clothes and to clear my brain so I could think about what had just happened out at the cave.

Susan lay in wait for me, and I let her help me out of my drenched riding clothes and into a muslin afternoon dress. Then I dismissed her and went to sit in the window seat of my bedroom and stare out at the drenched turf. The sun had come out and the leftover raindrops on the thick green grass sparkled like a field of diamonds.

I shut my eyes and once more felt Reeve's lips on mine, felt the heat and hardness of his long body pressed against me. I drew a deep, uneven breath into my lungs. I felt that my life had been steered into a new path without my consent, and I was frightened.

I had always felt safe in my friendship with Reeve. Since his father's death he had come to Ambersley eight or nine times a year, for a few days at a time, and it had been enough for me to see him for those short periods of time. We had ridden together, laughed together, even gone out shooting together.

We had been friends.

Then this afternoon he had kissed me in the cave, and suddenly everything was different.

I had had admirers before. As I had once told Reeve, it was true that I was tall and had no money, but I had had admirers. I had never encouraged them because they had always seemed to me to be uniformly colorless and boring.

It had never before occurred to me that for years I had unconsciously compared all the men I met to Reeve.

I was terribly terribly afraid that I was falling in love with him.

I was falling in love with him, and I was going to marry him.

I said out loud, "*God, what a disaster.*"

Reeve was not marrying me because he loved me. He was marrying me to get control of his inheritance. He had made that perfectly plain.

The kiss in the cave, which had been so earth-shattering for me, had probably meant very little to him. I knew very well that Reeve must have kissed dozens of women in his life. He liked kissing women—as he had liked kissing me.

Deb, darling, you are definitely not a little girl anymore.

He was right. I wasn't a little girl anymore. I was a woman who was finally aware of her own emotions. And those emotions had me terrified.

I would not have been so frightened if I had thought that Reeve loved me back. In fact, if I thought that, I would probably be feeling quite glorious right now.

But he didn't love me back. He thought I was a "great girl." He would never like any girl better than me.

I remembered my words to him. What would he do if he ever met a girl whom he really loved?

I went and flung myself on the bed, my arm over my forehead to shade my eyes. There was no point in torturing myself like this, I thought sensibly. The deed was done. I was going to marry Reeve, and I would have to deal with the situation as best I could.

We both would.

Oh well, I thought resolutely, *now Reeve will definitely be able to afford to buy me one of Lady Weston's hunters.*

Somehow, the thought was not as comforting as I had hoped it would be.

CHAPTER
eleven

I CAME DOWNSTAIRS HALF AN HOUR LATER TO LOOK for Reeve to discover if he had had a chance to talk to Lord Bradford. When I asked the butler for my fiancé's direction, he told me that he was in the long gallery with Robert.

The long gallery was the place where the dance had been held the previous evening, and I hurried along the hallway, terrified at the thought of Robert and Reeve alone in the same room together.

The sound of men's voices reached my ears as I approached the door.

"Such a sporting fellow as you are, Cousin, must be up to all the rig in fencing," Robert's voice said.

"I have been known to take a turn or two at Angelo's," Reeve returned smoothly.

"Why don't we try out the blades, then, and see which of us is the better? The rugs and the furniture have not yet been restored to their proper places."

I remembered that one of the short walls of the long gallery was hung with a selection of crossed fencing swords, and at these words I increased my pace to almost a run. At this point I heard Harry's voice and realized that, mercifully, he was in the room with Reeve and Robert.

Harry objected, "I say, I don't think that is such a good idea, Robert. *You* haven't had the opportunity to fence with Angelo, and you know how annoyed you get when you lose at anything."

As I reached the door to the room Robert was spinning around to glower at his brother. "Oh yes, I have fenced with Angelo, and I can tell you, Harry, that I have no intention of losing to Reeve!"

Reeve said, "Oh, you'll lose to me, Robert. I grant you're a good shot and a bruising boxer, but you'll lose to me at swordplay."

Robert's face turned a dark red. "We'll see about that, Cousin," he snarled.

Reeve was standing next to the short wall to my right, with a sword already in his hand. He gestured now to the array of fencing swords that decorated the wall of the gallery, and said to Robert, "Choose your weapon, and we'll see who is the better of us two."

As Robert strode to the wall and selected a sword, Reeve began to peel off his coat.

Harry, who was standing in front of a picture of one of his ancestors, halfway between the door and the sword wall, said urgently, "Reeve, I don't think this is a good idea."

I stepped into the room and spoke up firmly. "I agree with Harry. I don't like swords. Someone is liable to get hurt."

Reeve spared me a glance. "Oh, are you here, Deb? The foils have tips on them. There's no need to get into a pelter."

He moved away from the wall to the center of the polished-wood floor as he spoke and waited while

Robert flung off his coat. The dull red of Robert's face had been replaced by a set white look that made me feel extremely nervous.

I thought a duel was a disastrous idea, but short of flinging myself between Reeve and his cousin, I didn't know what I could do to halt it.

"Do something," I appealed to Harry.

He shrugged, his eyes glued to the two men in the middle of the floor. "Nothing to be done now, Deborah. It will be all right. The foils have buttons."

At this moment the two men raised their swords, saluted each other, and the fight began.

To my great relief, it soon became obvious that Reeve was by far the better swordsman. Robert attacked with an almost animal-like ferocity, but Reeve fought with a calm pace and a dexterity that constantly kept Robert from breaking through his guard. Every attack Robert launched was baffled by a return thrust.

I stood beside Harry and watched tensely. Even though Reeve was clearly in control, I didn't trust Robert and couldn't rid my mind of the fear that Reeve was in danger.

As the two men moved up and down the gallery, Reeve's breathing remained normal, but Robert was panting, and sweat was beginning to soak his shirt. He was obviously growing more infuriated by the minute at not being able to break through Reeve's guard, especially since Reeve did not even appear to be exerting himself very much. Robert was forced to acknowledge a number of hits, and as he did so his fury kept steadily rising.

Finally Reeve said, "Had enough, Robert?"

"No, damn you," Robert snarled. He wiped the sweat from his forehead with his forearm. "I'll beat you yet. I'm out of practice is all!"

Reeve laughed.

The laugh triggered an almost maniacal reaction in Robert, and he launched himself upon his cousin like a madman.

It was then that I saw that the button had become detached from Robert's sword.

Robert saw it, too, and instead of pulling back, he increased the ferocity of his attack.

"*Reeve! Look out!*" I screamed in terror.

But Reeve had seen. Faced with the full extent of Robert's violent fury, his own sword came to life in a way it had not before. In a matter of thirty or so seconds, Robert found the length of his sword grasped tightly in Reeve's left hand and the button of Reeve's own foil pointed directly at Robert's throat.

He was disarmed.

He stood there in the center of the room, his chest heaving. "Damn you!" he said. "Damn you to hell, Reeve!"

"It's about time someone taught you a lesson, Robert," Reeve said coldly. "Your family has made excuses for your behavior for far too long."

The blood hatred between the two men was so strong it could almost be smelled in the denuded long gallery.

Harry said, "Reeve's right, Robert. That was unpardonable."

Robert threw the hilt of his sword in Reeve's direction. "You'll be sorry for this," he snarled, and rushed out of the room. So blinded by rage was he that he almost crashed into me as he went by.

I looked from Reeve to Harry.

"Is he insane?" I said incredulously. "He saw that the button had come off his foil."

Harry looked uncomfortable. "It was very bad of him, Deborah, but Robert sometimes has these fits of blind rage. There is no real harm in him. He just . . . does not think, sometimes."

"No real harm in him?" I echoed. "He just tried to kill Reeve!"

"He didn't mean it," Harry insisted. He moved forward to take the foils from Reeve, so that Reeve could go to retrieve his jacket.

As Reeve came back toward Harry, sliding his arms into his sleeves, he said, "Well, he looked bloody serious to me."

Harry sighed. "He's jealous of you, Reeve. He's been jealous of you ever since we were children."

Reeve had been straightening his neckcloth with long, careless fingers, but at Harry's words his fingers stilled. He frowned. "Why on earth should Robert have been jealous of me when we were children?"

Harry replied soberly, "You were always my father's favorite, and Robert has never forgiven you for that."

At these words, Reeve's mouth dropped open in astonishment. "Your father's *favorite*? Have you taken leave of your senses, Harry? Bernard thinks I am the most irresponsible, worthless jackanapes of his acquaintance. Look how he has kept an iron grip on my purse strings for all these years. He never even trusted me to run my own properties!"

This last sentence was said with a great deal of wounded pride, and I found myself walking to Reeve's side in wordless sympathy.

Harry looked at me, then his eyes slowly returned to Reeve. He said, "Perhaps he has been a little too zealous in discharging his obligation as your trustee, but you know how Papa is. Give him a responsibility, and he is absolutely fanatical about carrying it through."

I frowned. "But what did you mean earlier, Harry, when you said that Reeve was always your father's favorite? Do you mean he favored Reeve above his own children?"

Harry rubbed his chin. "I don't know if you've noticed how Papa is about the Lambeths, Deborah, but in his mind there is our family, and then there is the rest of the world. Reeve was destined to be the Head of the House of Lambeth, you see, and as such, Papa considered him as the sun that shone in the firmament of our world." Harry gave Reeve a crooked grin. "From the time I first remember your coming to visit, when I was five years old, Papa would give us a long lecture about the importance of your future position. He drummed it into our heads that you were to have precedence over us in every single thing we did. He made that very very clear. And he did it every single time you came to visit."

Reeve stared at his cousin in horror.

"Are you serious, Harry?"

"Perfectly serious," Harry returned.

"Good God," Reeve said. He was clearly appalled. "No wonder Robert hates me."

"Robert's sort of temperament did not react at all well to this sort of thing," Harry agreed. "It didn't help, either, that you were taller than he was, and a better athlete."

A little silence fell. I looked at Reeve. He was staring blankly at a picture on the far wall of a dark-haired woman in a green dress with two little girls gathered in front of her full silk skirts.

Reeve returned his gaze to his cousin, and asked grimly, "And how did your kind of temperament react, Harry?"

"Oh, it didn't take me long at all to discredit all of Papa's nonsense," Harry said blithely. "You were so oblivious to it yourself that it was hard for me to take your great position too seriously."

"I am very glad to hear that," Reeve said. He shook his head in slow disbelief. "What in the name of God could Bernard have been thinking?"

"He can't help it," Harry said simply. "He just has this exaggerated notion of the importance of the House of Lambeth. It's why he doesn't want me to be a doctor. He's afraid it would demean our name to have a simple doctor in the family."

I said to Harry indignantly, "Your father is positively Gothic."

"I know," Harry replied with a smile. "But he would die for any of us, truly he would."

Reeve said grimly, "It would be more useful if he simply trusted us to know our own business, Harry."

"True, but that is not the way Papa's brain works."

I heard steps on the bare floor of the long gallery, and we all turned to see who had just come in. It was Mary Ann Norton. She looked at the two swords in Harry's hands and a faint frown puckered her brow.

"Were you and Lord Cambridge having a duel, Harry?" she asked lightly.

"You know me better than that, Mary Ann," Harry returned. "Swordplay is not in my repertoire of tricks."

She hesitated. Then, "I saw Robert rushing out the front door a few moments ago," she said. "He looked . . . upset."

Harry sighed. "Yes, well, as you have probably guessed, it was Robert who was dueling with Reeve. He lost, and you know how he is when he loses."

She gave the exact sort of sigh Harry had. "I know," she said. Her large brown eyes turned to me, and her expression changed to a radiant smile. "I have just learned from Lord Bradford that you will be getting married here at Wakefield in two weeks' time. How exciting, Miss Woodly." Her gaze moved to Reeve. An adorable dimple appeared in her right cheek. "I suppose Lord Cambridge just couldn't wait."

"That's right," Reeve said with a notable lack of enthusiasm.

I swung around to stare at Reeve. "Is that true?" I demanded. "Did you and Lord Bradford really decide upon two weeks?"

"Bernard said he will get a special license," Reeve said. "There's no point in delaying matters, is there, Deb?"

"But we can't return to Ambersley until after this

dratted fair I am running, Reeve, and that is not for another three weeks."

He shrugged. "So we'll get married and remain here at Wakefield for a week before we go back to Ambersley. I don't see any reason we can't do that. Do you?"

I chewed my lip. "Well . . . I suppose not. I just don't understand why your cousin is in such a hurry for us to say our vows."

The two of us had been speaking as if we were alone, and now Harry cut in, "Good God, Reeve, did you and Papa really decide upon the wedding date without even consulting Deborah?"

Reeve said a little impatiently, "If Deb doesn't like the date, she has only to say so."

"I have said that the date is fine," I snapped.

Mary Ann said hesitantly, "Excuse me, but I wonder if you have thought about your wedding clothes, Miss Woodly? Or have you brought your dress and the rest of your garments with you to Wakefield?"

Of course I had done no such thing. I had not anticipated needing a wedding dress at all.

Reeve frowned. "You can get a dress and whatever else you need in Brighton. That's where all the *ton* goes for the summer. There are bound to be some good shops there."

I nodded absently. Clothing was the last thing on my mind at the moment. What I was trying to figure out was why Reeve suddenly seemed to be in as much of a rush to get us married as Bernard was.

A thought suddenly struck me. "Good grief, I have

not yet spoken to Mama, Reeve. She does not know anything about this new . . . development."

The two of us looked at each other as we realized that my mother was still under the illusion that our engagement was only a sham.

"You had better find her, Deb," Reeve recommended. "This is not the sort of thing you want her finding out from someone else."

Certainly not! I thought as I hurried from the room. Then, *What in the name of God is Mama going to say?*

I found my mother walking with Mrs. Norton in the garden, enjoying the sunshine after the rain and talking over the ball. I joined them with a smile and after a few minutes, sensing that I wanted to talk to Mama alone, Mrs. Norton tactfully removed herself back to the house.

I would have liked to ask Mama to sit down, but the garden benches were all wet from the rain, so we continued to stroll up and down the paths that led away from the central fountain.

"I have something to tell you, Mama, that I am sure will surprise you very much," I said.

My mother said serenely, "And what is that, Deborah?"

I said in a rush, "Reeve and I have decided to really get married, and we are going to do it in two weeks' time."

My mother stopped walking and looked up at me. "You and Reeve are going to be married?" she repeated.

"Yes."

She searched my face with eyes that were as blue as the rain-washed sky. "What happened, Deborah?"

I sighed and began to walk forward again. "I'm afraid things just got out of hand, Mama, and now we are in too deep to back out."

She said in distress, "Oh, darling, I was afraid this would happen."

One of the hedges beside the path dripped a few leftover raindrops onto my dress, and I brushed them away. "I know you were, Mama. But I truly think everything would still be all right if it weren't for Lord Bradford."

Once more Mama stopped walking. "What has Lord Bradford done?"

I said hotly, "He is the one who is forcing us to get married. He is so stuffy, Mama! He has this notion in his head that the Lambeths are more important than the King! Do you know what he said to us?" I imitated Lord Bradford's deep, measured tones: *"I will not have the Lambeth name subjected to a public disgrace."*

Mama bit her lip and said nothing.

"Is that not positively Gothic?" I demanded. "He would rather see his nephew forced into an unhappy marriage than risk the chance that a scandal might touch the sacred name of Lambeth."

"Will it be an unhappy marriage, Deborah?" Mama asked very soberly.

I could feel color flood my face as I tried to evade her question. "Oh, I don't suppose either Reeve or I will be *un*happy, Mama. We have known each other too long and like each other too well to be actively un-happy married to each other."

A distinct frown appeared between Mama's delicate fair brows. "I like Reeve very much," she said. "I have always thought him to be a fine young man. But I do not want you to marry him if you do not wish to, Deborah. Believe me, nothing but misery can result from such a union."

The hint of suppressed passion in the way she spoke shook me out of my own anger and made me look at her sharply.

"Misery?" I said.

"Marital relations between a man and a woman are very . . . intimate," she said. Faint color stained her cheeks but she continued staunchly. "To be blunt, Deborah, when you marry a man, you must share his bed as well as his name. I do not want you to feel that you are being forced into a marriage you do not want. If you want to cry off, I will stand behind you."

I stared at my gentle mother in astonishment.

"Lord Bradford would be furious," I said.

"I don't care one jot about Lord Bradford's opinion," Mama said. "Lord Bradford is not the one who is marrying Reeve."

I tugged at the tendril of hair that Susan had left loose around my ear. This was the last kind of reaction I had expected from my mother.

I said tentatively, "At least my marrying Reeve would solve our financial difficulties."

Mama said sharply, "I hope you are not thinking that your union with Reeve will take care of me, Deborah. I have managed to live very well for all these years

on the allowance allotted to me by the Lynly estate. I
don't need any more money."

"You may be getting more money anyway," I said.
"Richard told me last night that when his uncle comes
to visit the Swales, he is going to demand an explanation for why we have been so poorly treated for all this
time. I have a feeling that your stepson has intentions
of making restitution for his years of neglect."

Mama's small hand closed around my wrist. Hard.
"Did you say that John Woodly is coming to visit the
Swales?"

I looked down at the hand that was holding my
arm so tightly. Mama's knuckles were white with pressure.

"Yes," I said slowly. "That is what Richard told
me last night."

All of the color had drained from Mama's face.

"There is no mystery as to why we were treated so
poorly," she said tightly. "The Woodlys did not want
me to marry your papa, and when he died they got rid
of me. It is as simple as that."

I looked at my mother's face, and for the first time
I wondered if her relationship with the Woodlys wasn't,
in fact, far more complicated than she had led me to
believe for all these years.

Her hand on my arm relaxed, and she made a visible effort to pull herself together. "It was nice to see
Richard, but I want nothing to do with the rest of the
Woodlys, Deborah. If you see your brother again, I
would appreciate your telling him that."

"All right, Mama," I said very slowly.

"And I meant what I said about your marriage to

Reeve," she said. "Do not feel that you are obligated to do anything that you do not wish to do, Deborah."

"Reeve is desperate to get control of his money, Mama," I said. "In truth, I think if he has to go on the way he has been going for another two years, he may not make it to his twenty-sixth birthday. He desperately needs a purpose in his life, and I know he will take his responsibilities as a landlord seriously. I can't back out on him."

My mother's eyes searched my face.

"Are you sure, darling? Marriage is for life, you know."

I took a deep breath. I looked straight into her eyes. "I'm sure," I lied.

She nodded slowly. "Very well. It is your decision to make, Deborah. Have you and Reeve decided upon a date?"

"Lord Bradford is going to get a special license so that we can be married in two weeks."

"No," Mama said. "That I will not allow."

I stared at her in amazement. "Why not?"

"Rushing the wedding is not the way to avoid a scandal," my mother said. "There will be all kinds of gossip if you get married without a proper calling of the banns."

I asked bluntly, "Do you mean that people will be counting on their fingers?"

Once more the delicate color flushed into her cheeks. "Yes, that is precisely what I mean."

"Well, the counting won't add up to anything," I said.

"I am sure that it won't," Mama said stoutly. "But

if Lord Bradford wants to avoid gossip, this is not the
way to go about it."

"I'll tell you what, Mama," I said. "Why don't you
talk to Lord Bradford about this? I am quite sure that
he will listen to you better than he will listen to either
Reeve or to me."

"Very well," my mother said. She put her delicate
chin into the air. "I will."

CHAPTER
twelve

THE REST OF THE AFTERNOON WAS QUIET. SALLY and Mary Ann walked in the garden, no doubt feeling a little letdown after the excitement of the ball. Lady Sophia and Mama and Mrs. Norton disappeared upstairs to take naps. Harry went out with a gun, and Lord Bradford and Robert were nowhere to be seen. I was sitting in the library, idly looking through a book about the Italian Renaissance, when Reeve came in and suggested that we go out for a drive.

I agreed. After my conversation with Mama, it seemed to me that we had a few things we ought to discuss.

Reeve went to order the horses put to, and I went upstairs to get a hat. I was waiting at the front door when Reeve pulled up, driving Lord Bradford's curricle with a pair of his own carriage horses pulling it.

We drove eastward, along a path that went through the beech woods of the Downs, to a place called Oldtimber Hill. I had not been there before, and Reeve said he wanted to show it to me. The beeches that climbed the north side of the hill provided a shady walk to the top, and Reeve halted the curricle and left the groom we had brought holding the horses at the bottom while we took the long, winding path upward through the trees.

There was a wide expanse of turf along the top of the hill, and the views were well worth the climb. I feasted my eyes on an outstanding panorama of the Channel as well as views of the surrounding valleys and large downland estates of the local gentry.

Reeve and I stood side by side in the wind that was blowing off the Channel, while he pointed out the various local landmarks to me.

"And that is Crendon Abbey, the home of Lord Swale," he said, pointing to a great rambling stone house that lay about three miles from the place where we were standing.

I looked down at the immense building, the many outbuildings, and the sprawling park. "It looks almost as impressive as Ambersley," I said.

"Swale is plump in the pocket, no doubt about that," Reeve said. "Your brother made a good catch when he landed Charlotte."

"A lot better catch than you will have made," I returned a little grimly.

He made an impatient noise. "I thought we had covered that ground, Deb. I don't need a wife with money."

I stared down at Crendon Abbey and did not look at him. "Perhaps you don't. But I had a talk with Mama, Reeve, and she pointed out a few other things that I don't think either of us have taken into account."

He swung around to face me. "Such as?"

I bit my lip and continued to look at Crendon Abbey while I tried to find a way to say what had to be said delicately. "You can't deny that there was a great deal of gossip in London when you produced me as your fiancée," I began.

I shot a glance at him out of the side of my eyes and found him looking at me speculatively. The wind at the top of the hill was blowing strongly, and I had to hold on to my fashionable little straw hat to keep it from sailing away. Reeve motioned to the path that led down the hill and said, "Let's walk a little way until we can get out of the wind."

"All right," I said, and followed him back down the path. In a few minutes we had found a small grassy nook that was sheltered by the beginning of the wood.

Once we had established ourselves on the grass, he took up the conversation again. "You shouldn't be disturbed by gossip, Deb. There is always gossip about me." His voice took on a bitter note. "Ever since Byron wrote that damn poem, every time I hiccup someone is sure to write it up in the newspaper."

I plucked a wild daisy and nervously began to pull out the petals one by one. "You have to admit that this gossip had some basis, Reeve. When a man as notorious as you suddenly produces a fiancée out of nowhere . . . well, you really can't blame people for gossiping."

"It's nobody's damn business if I choose to marry," he said shortly.

He was reclining on the grass next to me, propped up on one elbow, his long legs stretched in front of him. The wind was much less forceful down here below the hilltop. It only stirred his hair lightly as he plucked a blade of grass and put it between his teeth.

I said, "Reeve, I am not trying to back out of our marriage, but this scheme of Lord Bradford's to marry us so quickly is a mistake. Mama saw that immediately. I cannot understand how a man as sensitive to scandal as Lord Bradford is did not see it as well."

I was sitting next to him, my legs folded under me, my sprigged-muslin skirt decorously spread over my feet in their light summer shoes. He looked up at me, squinting a little as the sun slanting through the trees shone into his eyes.

He said, "I suppose I'm as stupid as Bernard, but I don't see it either, Deb."

I gave up on delicacy, and said baldly, "People will think that you got me with child and then had to marry me."

Silence. Nothing in his face changed.

I ticked it off on my fingers for him in case he still hadn't understood.

"One: I am not your equal in either rank or fortune.

"Two: You unveiled me in London like a conjurer producing a rabbit out of a hat, took me to a few parties, then rushed me down here to Sussex to your cousin's house.

"Three: We will not be in Sussex above a few weeks before you marry me."

I leaned a little closer, anxious to make my point. "Now, you tell me, Reeve. If you had heard these things about someone else, what would *you* think?"

He was looking up into my face, the stalk of grass still between his teeth, his eyes still narrowed against the sun.

I said very firmly, "You must speak to your cousin and get him to give up this insane idea of forcing us to marry in two weeks' time."

Very slowly Reeve removed the blade of grass from between his teeth and threw it away. Then he reached up and put his hand on my arm. It took me a second to understand the fact that he was levering me down to the grass beside him.

Just for a moment, I resisted.

Useless. He was very strong.

In another second he had me where he wanted me, lying on the grass next to him. I looked up into his face, and what I saw there caused my heart to begin to hammer loudly in my chest.

I ran my tongue around my suddenly dry lips. "Reeve?" I said.

He didn't answer. He just removed my hat.

I tried again. "W-what are you going to do?"

His eyes were black and glittering between his narrowed lids. His face was hard. He said, "I'm going to kiss you, Deb." And he put his hands on either side of my shoulders and lowered his mouth to mine.

It was like the other time, only even more intense. He kissed me hard, and I shuddered with the violence of my own feelings. I opened my lips and kissed him back. He had been balancing himself over me, holding most of his weight on his hands, but now he lowered himself to the ground beside me, turned me and pulled me toward him. I felt his hard body against mine, felt his warmth, inhaled the special scent that was Reeve.

The blood was pounding through my veins, and I was dizzy with desire.

His tongue explored the inside of my mouth.

This went on for quite a while. Then his hand

reached into the scooped neck of my dress and found my breast.

I whimpered.

"Oh God, Deb," he said. I scarcely recognized his voice, it was so hoarse. "Oh God. We have to stop this."

"Yes," I panted. "We do."

He turned me on my back and inserted his leg between mine. I could feel him pressing up against me. His mouth was devouring mine. My arms were wound under his arms, clutching his back, holding him close to me. I arched upward, to get even closer.

His hand went down to my leg and began to push up my skirt.

I summoned up all the willpower I had left, and said strongly, *"Reeve."*

He shuddered. Then, with what appeared to be a superhuman effort of his own will, he flung himself away from me, jumped to his feet, and went to stand on the far side of the clearing, his head bent, his breath ratcheting audibly in the soft summer air as he tried to get himself under control.

I was not in a much better case. I sat up and rested my forehead on my updrawn knees.

I was profoundly shaken by what had just occurred between us.

Finally he spoke to me over his shoulder. "You wanted to know why I agreed to Bernard's wish that we be married in two weeks time. Well, that is the reason."

I sat in silence while I digested this comment.

Finally I said, "You want to sleep with me."

At that he turned to face me. His face was still taut, but a faint touch of humor glinted in his narrowed eyes.

"Jesus Christ, Deb," he said fervently "I desperately want to sleep with you."

"Don't blaspheme," I said automatically.

He made an impatient gesture with his right hand.

I rubbed my forehead. "I am so confused," I said.

His voice softened. "I understand, sweetheart. But I have a lot more experience than you have, and you can believe me when I tell you that you and I will deal very well together."

I was not altogether happy to hear about all his previous experience. What I wanted to hear was that he loved me.

He didn't say it.

What he said was, "Let's go along with Bernard, shall we, and let the marriage take place within two weeks." He unleashed on me the full power of his smile, seemingly fully recovered from the storm of passion that had overtaken him not ten minutes earlier. "I really don't think I can wait much longer than that."

He wanted my body, I thought. He was a young man, with a young man's appetites, and he had probably been celibate for a longer time than he was accustomed to. I supposed I should be grateful that he was waiting for me and not looking for relief with some doxy in Chichester or Brighton.

"Mama is going to talk to Lord Bradford," I said. "What if he changes his mind?"

"You can be certain that Bernard has already weighed all the possibilities and has come to the conclusion that it is more important to get me married than it is to have people speculating behind our backs for a few months' time. There may be some talk when we first are wed, but when a baby doesn't appear in an untimely fashion, he knows the gossip will die down."

He crossed the clearing and held out his hand to help me to my feet. Once I was standing in front of him, he looked down into my face. The smile had left his face, and it was grave. "Do *you* have any objections, Deb? If you do, now is the time to speak up."

I didn't meet his eyes but instead looked straight ahead of me, directly at his mouth.

This was not a good idea, as the stab of desire that pierced through my body indicated.

I lowered my eyes to fix on his chin, which was as beautiful as his mouth but not so explosive. "I suppose I don't if you don't," I said.

"Good." He bent down to retrieve my hat from the grass.

"It's too bad that we can't go directly to Ambersley after the wedding," he said as he perched the hat back on my head. "I am not particularly enamored of the idea of hanging around Wakefield Manor for another week, being skewered by the curious eyes of a houseful of people."

"Well, Reeve," I said spiritedly, "If you had not volunteered me to organize this bloody summer fair, then we would not have to remain at Wakefield Manor at all."

"I know, I know," he said gloomily. "It's all my fault."

"Well, it is."

He jammed the hat more firmly on my head and bent his head to kiss my bare neck where it joined with my shoulder. "I'll manage," he said. "Don't worry about that."

I felt the fire of that kiss all the way back to Wakefield.

I went into my mother's room when we returned and found she had arisen from her nap and was having a cup of tea. She poured me a cup also, and the two of us sat in front of the unused fireplace, with the soft wind blowing in through the open window, and I told her about my talk with Reeve.

I did not tell her about anything else that had happened on the top of Oldtimber Hill.

Mama said, "Deborah, I really do not want you subjected to unnecessary gossip."

"I don't care a jot about what other people think, Mama," I returned. "And neither does Reeve. Besides, as Reeve said, once it becomes clear that we did not have to get married because a baby was on the way, the gossip will die."

My mother put down her Wedgwood teacup and said with quiet determination, "If you really are determined to marry, Deborah, then I think it is important for you and I to have a talk."

I gave her a surprised look. "A talk about what, Mama?"

"A talk about what goes on between a man and a woman when they are married," she said.

Mama had a pale, set expression on her face. I had the distinct feeling that she was not finding this topic of conversation pleasant, and I said soothingly, "You don't have to do this, Mama. Reeve will tell me all that I need to know about that part of marriage."

He certainly knew all about it, I thought a little indignantly, remembering his comment on Oldtimber Hill.

Mama shook her head in disagreement. "Reeve is a man, Deborah, and while it is true that he is a very nice young man, *no* man has any idea about how a woman feels about this matter."

I frowned, not understanding what she was trying to tell me.

My mother laced her fingers together in her lap and looked at her hands, avoiding my eyes. She said, "I know you like Reeve, Deborah, and that is a good thing. And anyone can see that he is fond of you as well. But once you get into bed together . . . things will change."

My eyebrows drew together. I returned my teacup to the small circular table next to my chair, and said, "What do you mean, change?"

Mama's breath was coming quicker than usual. She said, her eyes on the wedding band that she still wore on her left hand, "Deborah, do you know what a man . . . looks like?"

I did, actually. Reeve and I used to swim naked in the river when we were children.

I didn't think it would be a good idea to tell this to Mama right now.

"Yes," I said.

My mother began to turn the ring nervously around her finger in a gesture that was unconsciously revealing. "Well then," she said. "Men are so much larger than we are. Even you, Deborah—you might have height, but Reeve is far bigger and stronger than you. I am quite sure that he will not mean to hurt you, but in the throes of passion, he inevitably will." She gave a helpless shrug of her shoulders. "It just happens, and the only thing a woman can do is pretend that it is all right."

I was appalled.

"Mama," I said in a constricted voice, "is this what your own marriage was like?"

Dark shadows had appeared beneath her eyes, and she struggled to find the words she wanted. "I do not want you to think badly of your father, Deborah. He was unfailingly kind to me, and I was always grateful to him for that. I am only speaking of a small part of marriage, but I feel it is my duty to prepare you for it. It is soon over, after all, and then you are free to enjoy the many bounties of the wedded state."

I thought of the bonfire of passion that had blazed up between Reeve and me earlier that afternoon. There was no doubt in my mind that making love with Reeve would not be the poor, maimed thing that Mama was describing.

I remembered now that, in the course of my growing up, there had been two men who had wanted to marry my mother. Both of them could have offered us a comfortable home and a life far easier than the one we were living.

She had rejected them both. Child that I was, I had thought it was because she was still in love with my father.

I did not think that now.

I said helplessly, "I do not think it will be like that with Reeve and me, Mama."

She did not look convinced.

"I love him," I said, voicing out loud for the first

time the frightening secret that I had been harboring in my heart. "Every time he kisses me, I go up in flames."

Mama's blue eyes widened. "He has kissed you?"

I gave her what I hoped was a reassuring smile. "He has kissed me very thoroughly, Mama, and I assure you that I liked it very much."

"Deborah . . ." Her voice was very tentative. She was still fiddling with her ring. "Do you know what happens when a man has . . . sex . . . with a woman?"

"Yes," I said. I had been raised in the country after all.

"And the thought of that does not frighten or disgust you?"

I thought of Reeve. Once again I felt the heat that had flooded through my lower body when he had pressed his hardness against me. "Perhaps it would if I were marrying some other man," I said. "But not with Reeve."

"Well," Mama said doubtfully, "that is good."

I got up, went over to her chair, bent down, and kissed her soft cheek. Her skin had the resilience of a young girl's. "Don't speak to Lord Bradford about us. Reeve is convinced that he has evaluated all the consequences and decided that the benefits of a quick marriage outweigh the drawbacks."

"But what are the benefits?" Mama asked in bewilderment.

"Lord Bradford has this fixed idea that marriage will settle Reeve down. And since Reeve is the head of the sacred Lambeth family, it is very important to Lord Bradford to see him settled and setting up his nursery. Also, for some reason, Lord Bradford likes me and thinks I will be good for Reeve. Consequently, he is pushing to consummate the marriage as quickly as possible."

Mama leaned back in her chair and sighed.

"Well there can be no doubt that this is a brilliant match for you, darling," she said. "If you are certain that you really want to go forward with it . . ."

"I am certain."

"And you really love Reeve? You aren't just saying that to make me feel better?"

"I really love him," I answered soberly. And to myself I added, "God help me."

CHAPTER
thirteen

Three days later, Lord Bradford escorted Mama and me into Brighton so that I could shop for a wedding dress. As the prospective bridegroom, Reeve was excluded from this particular outing, and I thought it was only fitting that Lord Bradford, who had instigated this whole hasty affair, should be the one put to the trouble of taking us.

The seaside town of Brighton, which stands on a slope under the South Downs, was originally a tiny fishing village called Brighthelmstone. In 1783 the Prince of Wales visited it and decided to make it the locale for his residence outside of London. Fashionable society followed the prince to the newly christened Brighton until now, in the summer of 1814, the former fishing village was filled with the elegant squares and terraces of the very rich.

Our shopping expedition went very well. Lord Bradford had never struck me as a patient man, and so I was pleasantly surprised by his tolerance of what could only have been a very tedious morning for him. He had brought a book and he sat in the outer room of all of the shops we went into, waiting without complaint while I tried on dress after dress and Mama and I discussed and compared the various choices.

In the end, when we could not decide between two dresses we particularly liked, I tried them both on for Lord Bradford's inspection. He voted for a white crepe over a blue-silk slip and that was the one we took.

After our shopping was concluded, Lord Bradford suggested that we go for a stroll along the Marine Parade before we headed for home. Mama and I agreed, and we made our way down the elegant Steyne in the direction of the pavilion the Prince Regent had built as his residence.

My mother and I spent at least half an hour walking around the Regent's pavilion and gawking. Lord Bradford was utterly scornful of the fantastic creation, which had domes, minarets, cupolas, and spires, all reaching upward toward the white-cloud-dotted sky.

"The whole thing is in dreadful taste, and what's more, it's an inexcusable waste of money," he said. "With the war over, and all these demobilized men being thrown on the economy, to be spending huge amounts of money on an atrocity like this is unforgivable."

I could not disagree with him about either the dreadful taste or the waste of money. But there was something undeniably fascinating about a creation so horrendously inappropriate to its surroundings.

We finally tore ourselves away from the pavilion and proceeded toward the water, where we turned left toward the Marine Parade. We had been having an unusually fine summer and the weather today was delightfully warm and sunny. The few clouds in the sky looked like wisps of white mist floating across a palette of clear blue.

The Marine Parade went along the edge of the slender bay upon which Brighton was built, and on this lovely summer day it was filled with well-dressed people taking a stroll in the pleasant sea air. The women wore light muslin dresses and an amazing array of wide-brimmed bonnets to protect their complexions from the sun, while the gentlemen wore the correct morning dress of blue or black superfine coat with fawn-colored pantaloons and Hessian boots. Numbers of children scampered along behind their governesses and their high-pitched laughter rang in counterpoint to the *caw caw caw* of the gulls.

I walked on one side of Lord Bradford, and Mama walked on the other. The two of them conversed easily about a variety of topics while I looked around and enjoyed the holiday sophistication of what had at one time been a simple fishing village.

Then someone from behind me called my name.

I turned my head and saw my brother approaching us. He had Charlotte on his arm and on his other side walked a tall, thin man whom I had never seen before.

Perhaps it was the man's height, but I had a sudden premonition that this was my much-hated Uncle John.

Richard waved to me to stop.

After a moment's hesitation, I did, and Lord Bradford and Mama, who had been deep in conversation, halted with me. We all turned around as Richard and his party came up to us.

Richard's handsome face was grave as he said, "Deborah, I would like to introduce you to your uncle, Mr. John Woodly."

It amazed me how normal Woodly appeared. In my

fantasies I had always imagined him as a vicious-looking ogre, but this man had ordinary brown hair and blue eyes and regular features. In fact, one might even say that he was rather nice-looking. None of the evil of his character appeared on his face.

I looked him directly in the eyes, my own narrow and unmistakably hostile. I gave a terse nod and said nothing.

John Woodly said nothing to me either. Instead his mouth set in an angry line, and he turned to Charlotte. "If you will excuse me, Lady Charlotte, I have an errand to attend to." His eyes swung next to Richard. "I will meet you at the carriage in an hour's time."

He turned on his heel and was gone.

Richard stared after him, anger clearly stamped on his face. Then he turned to my mother. "I apologize for my uncle's rudeness, Lady Lynly. . . ." His voice trailed off and he took a step forward. "Are you all right?" he asked.

Both Lord Bradford and I looked at my mother also. She was white as chalk and visibly trembling.

Before I could move, Lord Bradford took charge. "Come and sit on this bench, Mrs. Woodly," he said. He put his arm around her shoulders and half guided, half carried her to the wooden bench that had been placed so that people could have a good view of the sparkling sea.

Richard, Charlotte, and I crowded after the two of them. Once Mama was seated, with Lord Bradford sitting beside her holding her hand in a reassuring grip, he turned to me and said, "Do you have any smelling salts?"

I never carried such insipid things, and now I regretted it.

Charlotte said, "I have," and she dug in her reticule and produced a small vinaigrette.

Lord Bradford held the salts up to Mama's nose, and I sat on the other side of her on the bench and watched closely as the color came flooding back to her face.

"I am so sorry," she said faintly after Lord Bradford had withdrawn the vinaigrette. "I don't know what made me take such a turn. It must have been the sun."

It had not been the sun. It had been John Woodly, and we all knew it.

"Are you feeling better, Mama?" I asked worriedly.

She drew a long, unsteady breath. "Yes. I am perfectly fine now, darling."

Clearly, she was not.

Lord Bradford said authoritatively, "You are going to sit here for ten more minutes until I am satisfied that you won't faint if I allow you to get up."

Mama managed a wobbly smile. "Really, my lord, it was nothing. Only a small touch of the sun. I am all right now."

"Lord Bradford is right, Mama," I said. I looked at him in concern. "Is there anyplace where we could get her a cool drink?"

"I will fetch her a glass of lemonade from Currier's," Richard volunteered. He and Charlotte had been standing in front of us, shielding Mama from the curious eyes of the passersby. "It is not far from here. I can be back in five minutes."

I smiled up at him. "Thank you. That would be very kind."

He went off, his long legs covering ground quickly. After a moment, Charlotte sat on the bench on the other side of me.

Lord Bradford continued to hold Mama's hand, and I noticed that she made no attempt to withdraw from him. He began to talk to her of something entirely unrelated to what had just happened, and I realized that he was giving her a chance to pull herself together.

My opinion of his sensitivity went up.

Mama was turned toward Lord Bradford, listening to him, making it only polite for me to turn to Charlotte.

I started to make some idiotic comment about the weather, but she interrupted me. "I would like to take this opportunity to let you know that Richard is deeply upset about his family's neglect of you, Deborah."

Her voice was very quiet, but there was no mistaking her sincerity.

I opened my mouth to say *"he should be,"* but then I changed my mind. I was reluctantly coming to the conclusion that perhaps my brother wasn't such a bad person after all and that it would be only decent of me to meet him halfway in any attempt to establish a relationship between us.

I stared at a seagull that had perched on the bench opposite us on the Marine Parade, and said shortly, "I suppose it wasn't Richard's fault."

Charlotte leaned toward me in her earnestness. "Truly it wasn't. You must believe me when I say that he had no idea that you had been left in poverty. John Woodly has always acted as his steward, you see, and the books his uncle showed him listed a rather substantial sum of money going to you and your mother each quarter. That is why Richard was so shocked when he learned the truth. He had no way of knowing that the sum he had been seeing was false."

I removed my eyes from the seagull and turned to stare at Charlotte in amazement. "Do you mean to tell me that that wretched John Woodly was falsifying the books?"

Charlotte nodded, her green eyes somber.

"How the devil could my father have left such a man in charge of his estate?" I exclaimed, my voice louder than it had been.

"I have no idea," Charlotte said. "I *can* tell you, however, that Richard has hired a new steward to check all the estate's books to see if his uncle was embezzling on a larger scale than simply your allowance."

Enlightenment struck. I could feel my eyes widen. "You mean Woodly was keeping for himself the money he said was going to us?"

Once again Charlotte gave me that somber look. "Where else was the money going?"

"That bastard," I said.

Charlotte tried to look scandalized by my language. She didn't succeed.

I looked back at the bench across the way. The seagull had been joined by a mate, and they were perched on either side of it, like bookends. I said grimly, "If Richard is really having dear Uncle John investigated, then what was he doing strolling along the Marine Parade in Brighton with him as if you were all one big happy family?"

Charlotte shifted on the bench next to me, as if she was uncomfortable. "Mr. Woodly is a guest of my parents, Deborah. Richard and I are simply trying to keep up a semblance of courtesy."

I gave her a shrewd look. "Does Woodly know that Richard is having him investigated?"

Charlotte's eyes were on the reticule in her lap. She shook her head. "That is another reason for keeping up appearances. Richard doesn't want to alarm his uncle until he has found out the whole truth."

Lord Bradford's voice had fallen silent for the last few minutes, and I realized now that my conversation with Charlotte had attracted his and Mama's attention.

"What an utter scoundrel," Lord Bradford said with loathing.

Mama said in a stifled voice, "I am afraid that he is."

"Here comes Richard with your lemonade, Lady Lynly," Charlotte said. "I'm sure a cool drink will make you feel much better."

The three of us watched my brother making his way toward us through the crowd of strollers on the Marine Parade. I thought that both his height and his grace of movement made him a distinctive figure even in that elegant congregation. He handed a full glass of lemonade to Mama with a courtly bow and as she drank it, I spoke pleasantly to Charlotte and Richard about my wedding plans, impulsively inviting them to attend the ceremony.

Mama finished her lemonade and we said goodbye to my brother and his fiancée and walked back up the Steyne to where Lord Bradford had left the curricle.

Our drive home was far more subdued than the drive into Brighton had been. There was some very unpleasant history between my mother and John Woodly, that was obvious. I wanted very much to know what it was, but it was equally obvious that Mama wasn't about to confide in me.

Well, I thought optimistically, there was no reason for the two of them ever to meet in the future. Even if we established a relationship with Richard, and I was actually beginning to hope that we would, my brother was not going to be on good terms with his uncle now that he had found out that John was cheating him.

Mama would live at Ambersley with Reeve and me and perhaps Richard would give her an allowance so that she would feel she was not completely dependent upon Reeve. She could take up her old social life in the village, and there was no reason for her ever to see John Woodly again.

Having settled my mother's future to my own satisfaction, I leaned back in the curricle, looked at the scenery and idly wondered what Reeve would think when he saw me in my wedding dress.

We arrived home to find Reeve and Robert going at each other with their fists in the stable yard. They were surrounded by a circle of grooms, who looked to be urging them on with disgusting enthusiasm.

"Oh my God," Lord Bradford groaned, and he jumped down from the curricle, leaving Mama and me to alight by ourselves.

"Stay away, Papa," Robert snarled at his father, as Lord Bradford barked an order for the grooms to disperse. "It's a fair fight. There's no reason for you to get involved."

This was said as the two men circled around each other, bare fists raised, each one hungrily looking for an opening to attack the other. They had to have been at this for a while. Reeve's lip was bleeding copiously, and Robert's eye was beginning to swell. They had taken off both their coats and their shirts, and their bare upper bodies were shining with sweat.

Mama and I came up to stand beside Lord Bradford, and he said to us in his most authoritative tone, "Go back to the house. This is no place for ladies."

I had no intention of budging an inch, and so I told him.

"Miss Woodly," he said through his teeth. "*Ladies* do not watch boxing matches."

"That is my future husband out there with blood pouring down his chin," I snapped, "and I intend to stay right here and make sure that nothing terrible happens to him."

"I will monitor this fight," Lord Bradford said. "There is no reason for you to be here."

Mama said in a frightened voice, "Why don't you just stop it, Bernard?"

Bernard?

I turned to stare at my mother, whose beautiful blue eyes were fixed upon Lord Bradford.

Once more he put his arm around her shoulders and turned her toward the house. "Sometimes it is better to let boys get their frustrations out with their fists, Elizabeth. It releases tension and everyone is better off."

Elizabeth?

*What the hell is going on between my mother and
Lord Bradford?*

I crossed my arms, and said grimly, "Neither
Reeve nor Robert are boys any longer, Lord Bradford."

He ignored me and gave my mother a gentle push.
"Go along now. You will be upset if you remain here to
watch this."

Mama went.

I stayed.

The sound of a hard thump brought my attention
back to the violence that was occurring in broad daylight in the middle of the Wakefield stable yard.

Obeying the orders of Lord Bradford, all of the
grooms had disappeared. Now it was just Reeve and
Robert pummeling each other under the hot summer
sun.

Robert was shorter than Reeve, but he was built
like a bull and was clearly relying on the sheer power of
his punches to take Reeve down. As I watched, he
landed one on Reeve's brow bone that sent Reeve stag-
gering back. Reeve's eyebrow began to bleed copiously.

My nails dug into my palms. I felt sick to my
stomach.

Reeve grinned!

"Good one, Robert," he said as he held up his fists
and came in for more.

The two men circled each other again, then Reeve
ducked under Robert's guard with a quick uppercut that
caught Robert on his unprotected chin. Robert quickly
backed away, shaking his head as if to clear his brain.
His chin began to bleed.

I was beginning to think that Lord Bradford was

right and this was in fact no spectacle for a lady. I wanted to scream at them to stop.

Instead I stood in silence and watched the long smooth muscles sliding under Reeve's glistening bare skin as he danced gracefully around Robert. If Robert looked like a bull, I thought, Reeve looked like a thoroughbred.

The first thing any self-respecting thoroughbred would do if he was confronted by an angry bull would be to run. I thought furiously that Reeve didn't even have the sense of a horse.

At this point the match erupted into a storm of ferocious blows. Robert had evidently determined to end things quickly, and he swung his powerful arms with deadly intent, aiming for Reeve's stomach and his face.

But if Robert was more powerful, Reeve was faster. He jerked his head aside to avoid Robert's fist and, weaving back and forth, he came in with his own punch, connecting solidly with the point of Robert's already-bleeding jaw.

Robert went down heavily.

Reeve stood over him, hands on hips, while Robert tried slowly to pull himself to his knees.

Lord Bradford walked forward. "That's it, boys," he said. "The fight is now officially over."

Robert, who had made it to his hands and knees, panted, "No, it's not."

"You've been beaten, Robert," his father said. "Acknowledge it like a man."

Robert looked up at his father. "You always take his part." His slightly unfocused eyes moved slowly to Reeve. A look of sheer rage contorted his face. "I hate you," he said. And collapsed in the dirt of the stable yard.

I took Reeve back to the house with me so that I could attend to his cuts and bruises. I made him sit on the terrace while I went for water and salve. I didn't see any point in getting blood on the rugs or the furniture just because he was stupid enough to get into a fight.

His lip was bleeding, his eyebrow was bleeding, and his knuckles were skinned and bloody as well.

He was as happy as a clam.

"I've never been sure if I could take Robert in a fistfight," he confided in me as I picked up a cloth, dipped it in water, and began to clean the blood from his knuckles.

"These are disgusting," I said.

He winced. "Do you have to be quite so thorough?"

"Yes," I said. "Did you have to fight with Robert? You heard him. He hates you badly enough already. Was it necessary to exacerbate it?"

"Nothing I can do will ever make Robert cease to hate me," Reeve said. "And besides, it was he who forced the fight on me."

"You could have walked away from it," I said. I scrubbed even harder. "It takes two to make a fight."

"He called me a name," Reeve said.

I rolled my eyes. "Lord Bradford was right. You may have the bodies of men, but in some ways you are still little boys."

"Oh stop sounding like a grandmother, Deb," he

said impatiently. "Why do you think half of the men in London frequent Gentleman Jackson's boxing saloon?"

"I have no idea," I returned austerely.

"We like to hit each other," he said.

I rolled my eyes again.

I had finished washing his knuckles, and now I spread salve on the open scrapes and wound a bandage around them.

"Now let me see your lip," I said.

He held his face up to me. The lip had stopped bleeding, and I gently sponged the blood off his chin. His lip was split open but there was nothing I could do about that and so I left it alone. Then I looked at his eyebrow.

I frowned. "This is deep. I wonder if it needs to be sewn."

The cut eyebrow was on his right side, and I was standing on his left, tilting his face toward me. Now he rested the full weight of his head against my breast, closed his eyes, and said, "I'm sure it doesn't need stitches, Deb. Just clean it out and put some salve on it."

I hoped very much that he could not hear how my heart had accelerated under his cheek. I frowned down at the dark head that was resting so confidingly against me. "I think perhaps I should try to find Harry," I said.

Very slightly he shook his head. His eyes remained closed, his long lashes spread upon his hard, masculine cheekbones. "You take care of me," he said.

I looked at the cut that was just above his eyebrow. "It might scar."

"I don't care."

I gave in. "Well, we'll leave it for now. I'll clean it out good and put salve on it. Harry can look at it later."

"Mmm," he said. He made no attempt to lift his head.

"Are you feeling faint?" I asked sarcastically. "Perhaps I ought to send for Dr. Calder?"

He turned his head and buried his face in the hollow between my breasts.

I jumped. "Reeve! Someone may come along!"

He kissed me. "We'll tell them that I felt faint." His voice was muffled by my breasts.

My heart was hammering. I could feel the fire of his kiss right through my dress. I put my hands on his head and plucked him away from me.

"Behave yourself," I said severely.

His dark eyes glittered up at me. "You're no fun, Deb," he complained.

"And *you* have no sense of propriety."

He smiled at me, mischief as well as desire sparkling in his eyes. "Neither do you," he said. "That's why we get along so well."

We stared into each other's eyes.

A voice came from the door of the terrace. "Oh here you are, Reeve. Are you all right? I hear you got into a fight with Robert."

It was Harry.

Reeve and I straightened away from each other.

"Yes, it's true," I said, "and I wish you would have a look at this cut on Reeve's eyebrow, Harry. I think it may need to be sewn."

Harry looked pleased. "Well, I'm not a doctor yet, but I'll be happy to look at it."

Reeve said stubbornly, "You are not sticking a needle in me, Harry."

"Stop being such a baby and let Harry look at you," I said.

Reeve scowled, but he let his cousin look at his wound. Fortunately Harry gave his opinion that the eyebrow did not need to be sewn, and, after I had attended to the cut, the three of us returned to the house to get ready for dinner.

CHAPTER
fourteen

To MY GREAT RELIEF, ROBERT DID NOT APPEAR AT dinner. When Lord Bradford inquired as to his where-abouts, Harry said that he had told his valet that he was going into Fair Haven for the evening.

Lord Bradford frowned when he heard this.

Lady Sophia said with satisfaction, "He's probably going to that dreadful Golden Lion to drink himself into a stupor."

Lord Bradford's frown deepened. "I don't think that's a fair statement just because Robert has chosen to go into town."

"There's no other reason for him to go into that wretched little seaport, and you know it, Bernard," Lady Sophia said. She turned to Reeve, who was sitting next to her. Silence fell as she surveyed his beat-up face. One of his eyes was beginning to blacken nicely. "Got the better of him, eh Reeve?" she cackled.

Reeve winced as the hot oyster soup touched his cut lip. He put down his spoon and turned to his aunt. "Now what makes you think that I was the winner?"

Lady Sophia gave a very unladylike snort. "You're here at the dinner table and Robert's getting drunk in Fair Haven," she pronounced.

Reeve started to grin, then winced again as his cracked lip stretched.

Lady Sophia smirked, shook her head and looked at me. "Looks as if you won't be getting kisses for a while from this lad, Missy," she said with a wicked grin.

Across the table from me I could see how Mama's cheeks flushed pink with embarrassment.

I said calmly, "It doesn't look like it, does it, Lady Sophia?"

Lord Bradford said, "That is quite enough, Sophia. This is a very improper subject for the dinner table, as well you know."

"Oh pooh," the old lady said. "You're as starched up as the rest of your generation, Bernard. We weren't so mealymouthed when I was young."

"Things were different a thousand years ago, Aunt Sophia," Reeve said. He raised his eyebrows at her in mock horror. "And I, for one, would like to know how *you* know about the Golden Lion."

"Reeve," Lord Bradford said ominously.

But Lady Sophia was waving her arthritic, clawlike hand. "Leave the boy alone, Bernard. He's the only one left in the family with any spirit."

Clearly Lord Bradford did not agree, but just as clearly he did not wish to prolong this discussion. Instead he turned to Mr. Norton, who was seated on the far side of Mama, and asked him a question about his afternoon's shooting. Shortly conversation at the table became general, except for Lady Sophia, who kept Reeve's attention centered on herself.

After dinner was over, and the men had returned to

the drawing room after having their port, Reeve asked me to go for a walk with him in the garden.

Lady Sophia banged the floor with her cane as we went out, and shouted after us, "Remember his lip, Missy. No kissing."

"That woman is a menace," I muttered to Reeve, as we stepped off the patio stones and began to stroll along the walk that would take us to the fountain.

He chuckled. "She says what she thinks. You're two of a kind, Deb."

I stopped short. "Don't you dare compare me to that horrid old woman," I said hotly.

"Well, perhaps she is a trifle rude," he admitted.

"You don't mind her because she dotes on you," I said. "It's a very different thing with the rest of us."

"How did your shopping in Brighton go?" Reeve asked, prudently changing the subject. "Did you get your dress?"

"Yes, but after we finished shopping, the oddest thing happened." We had reached the garden benches that stood at the entrance to the wood, and Reeve took my arm and drew me to the seat beside him. The daylight had faded while the men had been drinking their port, and the three-quarter moon was very bright in the night sky. Reeve's hair looked as black as his evening coat in the white moonlight.

I said, "We ran into Richard, Charlotte, and John Woodly when we were walking along the Marine Parade," and I proceeded to tell him all about that strange meeting.

When I had finished, he said with a mixture of incredulity and anger, "Do you mean to tell me that that infamous Woodly has been embezzling your mother's money for all these years?"

"According to Charlotte, that is precisely what he has been doing," I replied.

"That bastard," Reeve said bitterly. "How can a man like that look at himself in the mirror in the morning?"

I looked up at the moon, as if I could find the answer there. "I don't know," I said.

Reeve squinted a little with his bruised eye, as if it were hurting him. "What is your brother going to do now that he knows the truth?" he asked.

I folded my hands in my blue-silk lap. "I don't know," I said again. "It was Charlotte I was speaking to, not Richard. But she said that Richard has hired a new steward to go over all of the account books to see if dear Uncle John was taking money out of the estate elsewhere as well."

"I'll lay you a monkey that he was," Reeve said instantly.

"I never bet against sure things," I returned.

Reeve laid one of his damaged hands briefly over mine, then withdrew it. "I'll make it my business to speak to Richard myself about this matter, Deb," he said. "Once I come into my money, you know that your mother will never want for anything, but, dammit, as your father's widow, she deserves the money that Richard thought his father's estate was paying to her for all these years."

I stared down at my hands, which looked forlorn now that they were no longer covered by his. "I agree with you, Reeve. I know you will always take care of

Mama, but I think she deserves some money from my father's estate as well."

He shifted his weight on the bench, moving his shoulder as if it ached. He really had absorbed some hard punches from Robert that afternoon.

Served him right, I thought stubbornly. He shouldn't have been fighting in the first place.

He said, "Your mother actually fainted when she saw John Woodly?"

I nodded somberly. "There is something between those two, Reeve. I can feel it. She turned as white as snow as soon as she saw him, and he couldn't get away from her fast enough."

Reeve shifted again. "Perhaps he was feeling guilty. After all, this was the woman he has been robbing for eighteen years."

I shook my head. "A man like that doesn't feel guilty. Nor does it explain Mama's reaction. She didn't know what John had done."

He didn't reply.

I turned around on the bench to face him fully. His face was pale, his features very clear cut in the moonlight. "I've observed before that Mama reacts violently to the mere mention of John Woodly's name."

"He was the one who condemned her to that tiny cottage in the first place, Deb," Reeve pointed out. "I don't think it's odd that she should react negatively to the mention of his name."

"I suppose that's true." I searched his moonlit face. "Did you mean it when you said that you would talk to Richard about securing Mama a pension?"

"Of course I meant it."

I smiled up at him. "I would talk to him myself, but I think you will do it better."

"Thank you," Reeve said, much moved.

I laughed at him. "You're welcome."

He watched me for a long moment, his eyes hooded, so that I could not read them. Finally he said, "Do you know what I have been thinking?"

I gave him a mystified look. "What have you been thinking, Reeve?"

"I was thinking that when necessity dictates, one must improvise, and that perhaps I could use my tongue instead of my lips."

"What?"

"Licking is good," he explained, "and I have noticed on other occasions that you taste delicious."

At this point he had moved his hands to my shoulders. I tried to pull away from him and get to my feet. "You are disgraceful, Reeve. And disgusting as well. There will be absolutely no licking. Do you hear me?"

"You don't know what you're missing," he said.

I folded my lips tightly to keep him away, thinking I was being very clever, but those resourceful hands of his moved like lightning. Before I realized what he was about he had pushed down the front of my low-cut blue-silk evening dress, thus exposing my breasts.

"Reeve!" I squeaked in horrified protest.

"Mmm?" His tongue was already on one exposed nipple.

He was right about the licking. The feeling it caused was sensational.

"Don't do that," I heard my voice say. But my body was saying otherwise. My back arched, and my hands came up to bury themselves in his hair, holding his head to me.

He moved his tongue to my other breast.

I said in a ragged voice, "This has got to be a sin. We aren't married yet."

"Nine more days," he said. "Jesus, Deb, I don't know if I can wait that long."

"You have to," I said. "And don't . . ."

"I know, I know, I know . . ." He drew a deep unsteady breath and raised his head as if he were straining against an invisible force that was holding him to me. "And don't blaspheme."

I pulled my dress up to cover my aroused nipples and moved away from him as far as I could get on the bench. I said with as much dignity as I could manage under the circumstances, "You are making this whole waiting business much worse by this kind of behavior, Reeve. If you conduct yourself in a gentleman-like way for the next nine days, we shall both be better off."

He reached over and pulled a ringlet that was dangling on the nape of my neck.

I said, "And if you *don't* behave, I'll punch you in the mouth. That will make you sorry."

He heaved an ostentatious sigh. "All right, all right, all right. I hear you, Deb."

I stared at him for a minute in the moonlight. He was looking very gloomy.

I said, "Cheer up. At least Harry didn't insist on shaving your eyebrow to sew up that cut."

"Hah. I have news for you, Deb. Harry is going to have to graduate from physician's school before I let him anywhere near me with a needle and thread," Reeve said. "You would probably do a better job than he would at present."

I thought of the pathetic unevenness of my mending and shook my head. "I don't think so."

He unfolded himself from the bench and got to his feet. "All right. I think I can go back to the drawing room now without mortifying myself."

"What do you mean?" I asked.

He said in a mystifying tone, "I'll show you in nine days' time."

The tea tray came in at ten-thirty, and after we had finished, the ladies and Lord Bradford and Mr. Norton retired to bed while Reeve and Harry and Edmund Norton went along to the billiard room for a game.

I was deeply asleep when some movement in the room must have alerted me enough to drag me up to consciousness. I opened my eyes and saw a shadow pass in front of the partially opened window, where a ray of moonlight spilled into the room.

I said sternly, "If that's you, Reeve, you can just remove yourself from this room immediately."

But I knew, even before the answer came, that it wasn't Reeve. I opened my mouth to scream, and a hand came down over my mouth.

"It's not Reeve, Deborah." Even thick and blurred with drink, I recognized Robert's voice. "I've come to pay you a visit in his place."

The moonlight from the window allowed me to see the wide bulk of Robert standing over my bed. His big hand was half-covering my nose as well as my mouth, suffocating me, and I reached my hands up to rip it away. He grabbed my wrists and pinned them both over my head with his free hand. I strained to release myself, but he held me seemingly without effort.

Then he laughed.

Fear struck me like a blow as I realized what it was that Robert had come to do. My legs were trapped under the covers so that I couldn't kick him, but I tried to roll away from him, desperately trying to free my mouth so I could scream.

His hand left my mouth for a fraction of a second and then his mouth came down on mine, grinding into me, shoving my head back into the pillow. I gritted my teeth but he pried my lips open with his own and thrust his tongue inside my mouth.

His breath stank of brandy.

I couldn't believe how powerless I was. I was young and strong and utterly and completely helpless beneath Robert's assault. I had never before fully realized the difference between a man's strength and a woman's.

With his free hand, Robert was ripping the covers away from my lower body. Then I felt the full weight of him on top of me and his knee came up to force apart my legs.

Blind, mindless panic ripped through me. I bucked and kicked and twisted under him, desperate to get away.

"I'm going to have you first, you beautiful bitch," Robert growled against my mouth. "Let's see how Reeve likes *that.*"

He had lifted his mouth slightly to taunt me, giving me a chance to croak out one weak, ineffectual cry for help. In a second his mouth was mashing mine into a pulp again.

I felt his hand pushing up my nightdress.

No, No, No, I screamed in my mind, and fought harder against the strength and the weight that were overpowering me.

Suddenly there was the sound of splintering glass.

Robert went limp on top of me.

I heard Mama's quavering voice say, "Deborah? Are you all right, Deborah? Oh God, did that man hurt you?"

I strained to roll Robert's heavy body off of me, not caring if he landed in a pile of broken glass. Mama was standing next to the bed with a broken vase still clutched in her hand. Her hand was trembling so badly that I was afraid the remainder of the vase was going to drop to the floor.

"Oh God, Mama. Thank God you came," I said. My own voice was trembling as badly as hers. "Robert was going to rape me."

"He didn't?" Her voice was urgent.

"No." My head was going back and forth like a metronome. "You came in time."

She shut her eyes. "Oh thank God," she said. "Thank God, thank God, thank God."

She dropped the remains of the shattered vase on the edge of the bed and held out her arms to me. I slid off the bed, away from the inert figure of Robert, and went into my mother's arms.

We clung together for a long, trembling minute.

"How did you know to come?" I finally managed to ask.

"I heard you call out," she said.

She was much smaller than I, but there was no doubt that it was her arms that were giving support and comfort to me. I said shakily, "I hardly made a sound. I can't believe you were able to hear me."

She held me closer. "Mothers have a sixth sense when their children are in trouble, darling."

Finally we separated and looked around the room. Robert was lying unconscious on the bed with blood seeping from a wound on the back of his head. The bed was filled with shards of Mama's heavy crystal weapon.

A thought came to my mind. I said urgently, "Reeve must never find out about this. He would kill Robert."

"Someone must be told, Deborah," Mama said somberly. "I think we had better get Lord Bradford."

After a minute, I nodded in agreement.

"I'll go," Mama said, and she went next door to her bedroom to get her robe. I waited in the room with Robert, the fireplace poker in my hand. I wasn't taking any chances if he should come around and try his tricks again.

It wasn't long before Mama returned with Lord Bradford, who was wearing a dressing gown over his nightshirt. I told him what had happened.

I don't believe I have ever seen a man's face look so bleak.

"I don't know what I can say to you, Deborah," he said. "There are no apologies possible for a thing like this. Thank God Robert was stopped before he interfered with you, but there is no doubt that you have had a very shocking and frightening experience."

"It was not pleasant," I agreed shakily.

"I don't know what is wrong with Robert," Lord Bradford said in real despair. All of his usual demeanor of a man in control of his world was gone. "I must have made some terrible mistake in the way I brought him up to account for his turning out like this. For years I have told myself that he was only sowing his wild oats, but this kind of thing goes beyond the bounds of civilized behavior. This is vicious."

"It was aimed against Reeve," I said. My head was beginning to throb and I rubbed the back of my neck. "That is what he told me. He wanted to be first with me to get even with Reeve."

Lord Bradford closed his eyes.

Mama went over to him and put her hand on his arm. "Don't blame yourself, Bernard," she said gently. "Harry is a very fine young man, and Sally is a lovely young lady, and they are your children, too. There is something fundamentally wrong with Robert, and I'll wager there was something wrong with him from the time that he was a small boy. It's not your fault."

The pain on Lord Bradford's face made me forget my own horrors for a moment and feel sympathy for him.

I said, "I don't think we had better tell Reeve about what happened tonight, Lord Bradford. I'm afraid of what he might do."

"He would call Robert out, and he would have every right to do so," Lord Bradford said.

"I don't want Reeve involved in a duel with Robert," I said firmly. "I'm afraid he would kill him, and I don't want Reeve to have to live with another death on his conscience."

Lord Bradford ran his hand through his disordered brown hair. "I must confess that I would be very grateful to you if you allowed us to keep this quiet, Deborah. And I promise you that Robert will be gone from this house as soon as he is fit to travel. I will not subject you to such a dreadful experience again."

The three of us turned to look at Robert's unconscious body. He was breathing stertorously.

"That wound on his head will have to be attended to," I said. I turned to my mother and managed a faint smile. "You gave him a good whack, Mama."

There were dark shadows under my mother's eyes, and her return smile was not a success. "I did not want to take any chances," she said.

Lord Bradford made up his mind. "I'll get Harry. He spends so much time with Dr. Calder that he is half a doctor already. He can patch Robert up and help me carry him back to his own room. Then I'll get my own valet in here to clean up the glass and change the sheets. He is totally trustworthy."

"All right," I said. The pain in my head was growing worse, and I felt quite incredibly weary.

Mama said, "Would you like to sleep in my room for the remainder of the night, Deborah?"

I realized that I would like that very much. It wasn't until I was safe in the big bed next to her that I began to shake. Mama put her arms around me and held me as if I were four years old, and eventually I drifted off to sleep.

CHAPTER
fifteen

THE FOLLOWING MORNING, LORD BRADFORD TOLD the rest of the house party that Robert had gotten into a fight in town, had been set upon by a group of drunken sailors and badly beaten. Harry told me privately that when Robert had not come back to consciousness within an hour, he had insisted that Dr. Calder be called in. Robert had eventually come around, but Dr. Calder had said that he should not be moved for two days.

Lord Bradford posted a footman outside Robert's door with instructions not to allow him to leave it. He told Reeve and the rest of the house party that this was to prevent Robert from trying to return to Fair Haven, where he would once more get into trouble by trying to get even with the men who had beaten him. In reality, of course, it was to keep Robert away from Reeve and me.

Two days after Robert's attempt to rape me, Lord Bradford had his eldest son removed to a small property he owned in Hampshire. His face was extremely bleak as he told me this.

I found myself trying to comfort him. "Mama is right, Lord Bradford. Robert's bad disposition cannot be laid at your door. From what Reeve has told me, Robert has always thought that he should be the center of the world. Surely this is not a normal state of mind for a

young man such as he. Harry doesn't feel that way. Nor
does Reeve, for that matter."

"You are very kind, Deborah," Lord Bradford said.
"And very generous. You have every reason in the world
to fear and despise my family."

"Nonsense," I said.

He gave me a wry look. "Lady Sophia is hardly a
credit to us either, I'm afraid."

"She has been good to Reeve, and that is all that really matters to me," I said stoutly.

He looked at me for a moment in silence. Then he
said, "I cannot tell you how thankful I am that Reeve has
found you. I have not seen the boy look this relaxed and
happy in years." He gave me the warmest smile I had
ever earned from him. "That's really why I pushed for
such a fast wedding, you know. I didn't want you to get
away from Reeve. You're good for him. I really do believe that, with you, he may settle down and lead a decent, useful life."

I didn't know what to say. I could feel my cheeks
grow warm, and I mumbled something about Reeve and
I knowing each other forever.

Lord Bradford's gray eyes looked amused. "He
loves you, Deborah. Didn't you know that? He watches
you all the time, and the look on his face is unmistak-
able."

My cheeks grew even hotter. Lord Bradford patted
my arm. "I have high hopes for this marriage, my dear,"
he said. "Very high hopes indeed."

Then he had mercy on my embarrassment and left
me alone.

We had been standing by ourselves on the terrace

outside the morning room during this conversation, and now I walked slowly down the stone terrace stairs and into the sweet-scented garden, my mind full of what Lord Bradford had said.

Was it true? Did Reeve truly love me?

I reminded myself that when it came to Reeve, I couldn't trust Lord Bradford's word. Lord Bradford didn't understand Reeve. If he had understood him, he would never have withheld Reeve's money from him for all these years.

How wonderful it would be if Lord Bradford were right, I thought. *How wonderful it would be if Reeve loved me.*

I fought to contain the elation that I felt bubbling up inside of me. I must be very careful not to pressure Reeve for more than he was willing, or able, to give, I cautioned myself. Reeve's emotional balance was very fragile. He had never gotten over the accident that had killed his mother, and over the years I had sometimes wondered if he would ever be able to trust himself to love again. It seemed to me that in his mind, love was dangerous—or, at least, his love was.

A line from Byron's poem slipped into my mind: *He knew himself a villain.*

Damn, I thought. *Reeve has more sense than that idiotic Corsair.*

At least I prayed that he did.

I spent a great deal of the time before my wedding day working on the town's summer fair. Almost every day Mama and I met with the Wakefield village ladies committee to organize and coordinate the great event.

In truth, after having been in existence for so many years, the Wakefield Summer Fair almost ran itself. The same people had been doing the same jobs forever, and none of the ladies needed any directions from either Mama or me as to what needed to be done in their area of command.

"I haven't the vaguest idea why it is so important for you and me to be at these meetings," I said to my mother one morning as we returned home from a meeting at Mrs. Clark's, the wife of the village apothecary. "These women are perfectly well aware of what needs to be done; they don't need us."

"They don't need us to give them direction," Mama agreed, "but they do need us to make them feel that what they are doing is important. And it *is* important, Deborah. An affair such as this brings the whole village, indeed the whole surrounding area, together."

It was a warm sunny day, and I was driving Lord Bradford's gig with Mama sitting beside me. It had rained the night before and I concentrated on negotiating a rather deep and muddy puddle in the middle of the road. Then I glanced at Mama and casually changed the subject. "Do you think that perhaps Lord Bradford might be altering his mind about Harry going to the Royal College of Physicians?" I asked. "He did call him in to take a look at Robert the other night."

Mama said primly, "I do not know Lord Bradford's mind on that subject, Deborah."

I let the bay gelding I was driving trot along the narrow country road for about two more minutes, then I said, "I think it would be a very great pity for Harry to be unable to fulfill his dream just because his father was too full of his own importance to let his son become a doctor."

Mama said disapprovingly, "I do not think it is your prerogative to make judgments on Lord Bradford, Deborah. He has been very kind to the both of us, and surely the way he deals with his children is his own business."

The horse was beginning to lag, and I clicked to him to trot on. I said, "I don't think Lord Bradford has any notion at all about how to deal with people. In my opinion, he did a great deal of harm to Reeve by not allowing him to have control of his inheritance, and now he is trying to force Harry to become a clergyman against his own inclination." I glanced at my mother's profile. "Really, Mama, that is the outside of enough. Would *you* like to have as rector of your parish a man who hated his job?"

There was a distinct trace of anger in Mama's voice as she returned, "You exaggerate, Deborah. There is nothing to suggest that Harry would hate being a clergyman."

I was sitting as straight as a ramrod on the seat of the gig. "He says he will hate it, and I believe him," I said stubbornly. "Furthermore, it would be just like Lord Bradford to force poor Sally to marry someone she doesn't like, just because he has the right bloodlines or something."

I didn't know what perverse imp was making me say these things to Mama, but I was growing more and more uncomfortable about the closeness that I had perceived to be developing between my mother and my host. While my attitude toward Lord Bradford might have softened a little since my coming to Wakefield

Manor, that did not mean I had forgotten his sins against Reeve.

"*Deborah,*" Mama said. "That is a dreadful thing to say. I am quite sure that Lord Bradford would never never force his daughter to marry someone whom she could not like!"

Her voice was so vehement that I was startled. When I turned to look at her, her face under the brim of her blue-trimmed straw hat was very white. Her breast was rising and falling quickly with her hurried breath. She was clearly very agitated.

What is going on here? I thought.

"I'm sorry, Mama," I said in a subdued voice. "I didn't mean to upset you."

I sensed that she was making a great effort to get her emotions under control. "I'm not upset," she lied. "It is just that I do not like to hear you say such things about a man such as Lord Bradford. They simply are not fair."

"I'm sorry," I said again.

"You saw how horrified Lord Bradford was by what Robert tried to do to you," she said. "He would never dream of forcing his own daughter into such a situation as that."

I had been talking about marriage, not rape.

I remembered my mother's words to me when she had talked to me about the physical aspects of marriage, and I realized that, in her mind, the two were inevitably linked.

This thought made me feel very bleak about the kind of man my father must have been.

Mama said brightly, "Oh look, darling. Do you see

that cloud formation above us? Doesn't it look just like a seagull?"

It didn't, but I agreed with her, and we talked of the fair for the rest of the way home.

While Mama and I planned the Wakefield Summer Fair, Lady Sophia planned my wedding. When Reeve and I first agreed to Lord Bradford's two-week stipulation, I had assumed that we would have a quiet little ceremony followed by a small wedding breakfast.

Reeve's aunt decreed otherwise.

"We don't want anything to suggest that this wedding is something we are ashamed of," she had announced in her usual dictatorial fashion as soon as the date had been firmly set. "Reeve is the Head of the House of Lambeth and, as such, his wedding must be held in style."

Her idea of "in style" meant inviting all of the neighboring gentry as well as relatives whom Reeve told me he had not seen since he was ten years old. The Wakefield parish church would be packed to the rafters, because naturally all of the regular parishioners would wish to be in attendance also for the most exciting nuptials that had occurred within anyone's memory.

"I don't mind marrying you, but I am beginning to think that it is going to be a royal pain in the neck being married to the Head of the House of Lambeth," I said to Reeve on the eve of the great day as we walked together in the garden after dinner.

It was growing quite dark but the moon was bright enough for me to see him smile. "The old lady is getting to you, is she?"

"She is impossible, Reeve," I said. "If she gives me one more piece of advice about how to comport myself as Lady Cambridge, I am going to hit her over the head with her own cane."

"Once the wedding is over, Bernard plans to pack her off home," Reeve assured me.

I sighed. "That will be very nice indeed."

We strolled down the pathway in the direction of the wood, side by side but not touching. I was carrying a painted fan that Mary Ann had given me this evening as a gift. The scene on it showed a group of men and women with powdered hair sitting in front of a summerhouse. It was extremely pretty.

From out of nowhere, Reeve said, "I wonder why Robert isn't coming home for the wedding."

An alarm sounded in my brain.

"Bernard is such a stickler for appearances," he was going on. "I was fully expecting Robert to turn up sometime today, but he hasn't. And apparently he isn't coming tomorrow either."

"How do you know that?" I asked cautiously.

"I asked Bernard."

We were walking slowly along the garden path, and I opened my fan and regarded the picture on it, even though there really wasn't enough light for me to see it clearly. I said, "Did you also ask Lord Bradford why Robert isn't coming home?"

Reeve's feet crunched on the gravel path. "Yes, I did. He said it was because he was afraid that Robert would get into trouble in Fair Haven again."

I was still looking at the fan, refusing to meet his

eyes. I knew from the tone of his voice that he didn't believe Lord Bradford's excuse.

He reached out, put a hand on my arm to make me
stop walking, and said, "After you went to bed last night,
Harry and I went into the Golden Lion." An insect flew
in front of my face and I swatted at it with my fan.
Reeve went on, "When I mentioned Robert's getting
beaten up by drunken sailors, no one in the pub knew
what I was talking about."

Damn, I thought. I did not want Reeve to know
about what Robert had tried to do to me.

"Perhaps the people you spoke to weren't there
when it happened," I said.

Somewhere in the woods a nightingale began to
sing.

Reeve said grimly, "Something as momentous as
Lord Bradford's eldest son getting beaten into a pulp
would have been common knowledge to every person in
that pub last night."

The nightingale had now launched into a full-
fledged aria.

I waved my fan again at an imaginary insect. "Oh, I
doubt that Robert got beaten into a pulp," I said. "It was
probably only a little round of fisticuffs, such as the two
of you indulged in."

"For God's sake, put down that fan and look at me,
Deb," Reeve said angrily. "Bernard had Robert barri-
caded in his room for two days!"

I closed my fan with a snap. "What did Harry say?"
I temporized.

"He claimed to know nothing about it, but I don't
believe him either."

The first nightingale had been joined by another and the double-throated beauty of their song was heartrendingly lovely.

"It has to do with you, doesn't it?" he demanded.

I opened the fan again. "Why do you say that?"

"Look at your face, Deb! It's a dead giveaway." He took the fan right out of my hand. "You'd better tell me what happened. You know that I'm going to find out, one way or another."

I thought gloomily that having a husband who could read one's face like a book could prove to be a definite drawback.

I bit my lip. "If I tell you, Reeve, you must promise me that you won't do anything rash."

"What did he do?" he asked grimly.

"You have to promise me, first."

The sky was growing dark enough for the stars to begin to appear. The nightingales sang on in perfect harmony. We faced each other on the graveled garden path, at odds for one of the few times in our lives.

He said, "I'm not promising anything until I hear what happened."

I folded my arms across my chest. "Then I won't tell you."

"*Deborah.*" He dropped my fan onto the walk, lifted his hands, and his fingers bit into my shoulders so hard that they were sure to leave bruise marks.

He never called me Deborah.

"Tell me," he commanded.

I took a deep, unsteady breath and told him what had happened the night Robert had come to my room.

When I had finished, I expected him to be furious,

to curse Robert, to vow vengeance. Instead he said nothing at all. His face looked frozen.

"I didn't want to tell you because I was afraid you would do something to Robert," I said. "Lord Bradford said you would call him out, and I didn't want that."

That frightening, ice-cold look was still on his face.

"Reeve?" I said.

His fingers were still digging into my shoulders.

"You're hurting me," I said.

That got through to him. He dropped his hands as if they had been burned. "Oh God, Deb, I'm sorry. I didn't mean . . ."

"I know. It's all right." I scanned his face, which was bleached as white as bone in the pale moonlight.

"I'm *all right*, Reeve. That's the main point, don't you see? Mama got there in time, and I'm all right."

"He tried to do it because of me, didn't he?" Reeve said.

I hesitated.

Reeve answered himself. "Of course he did."

"He was drunk," I said. "He didn't know what he was doing."

"Oh he knew what he was doing all right," Reeve said bitterly. "When it comes to me, Robert always knows what he is doing."

I bent to retrieve my fan from the pathway. When I had straightened up again, I said briskly, "Well, Lord Bradford has sent him away, and there's no reason for us ever to have to see him again."

He didn't reply, but began to walk forward again, his mind clearly taken up with what he had just learned. I waited until we were almost at the wood before I asked, as much to distract him as because I wanted to know, "Did you go over to Crendon this afternoon to see Richard like you said you would?"

He brought his attention back to me with a palpable effort. "Yes," he said. "I have news for you from that front, Deb. Apparently John Woodly has disappeared."

"Disappeared?" I echoed in confusion.

Reeve elaborated. "Richard doesn't know where he is. No one knows where he is. Richard has a suspicion that he has left the country."

We walked in silence while I digested this piece of information. "Then he *was* embezzling from Richard?"

"Almost certainly."

One of the nightingales had ceased to sing, but the other caroled on in solitary splendor.

Reeve continued, "One of the reasons it was so easy to do it was that Woodly was Richard's uncle, and Richard trusted him completely."

It struck me that Reeve himself was in a similar position with Lord Bradford. I also knew immediately that, when it came to Reeve's money, Lord Bradford was completely trustworthy.

I said as much.

"Bernard would not take a penny that did not belong to him. I have always known that," Reeve agreed. "It was not because I did not trust Bernard that I was so anxious to get control of my own property."

I rested my face briefly against his shoulder. His coat was warm against my cool cheek. "I know."

We turned away from the wood and began to walk back toward the fountain. He said, "I talked to Richard about his obligations to your mother, Deb."

I lifted my face. My fingers tightened on my closed fan. "Yes?"

"He is going to grant her a lifetime allowance of five thousand pounds a year."

A wave of relief swept through me. It was riches compared to what we had lived on for all of these years.

"That is very generous of him, Reeve." I laughed a little unsteadily. "It makes me feel dreadfully guilty about all of the terrible things I have thought about him over the years."

"It was a mistake not to approach him sooner, but you couldn't know that at the time," Reeve said gravely.

We had reached the fountain, and now we stopped in front of it. The moon was bright enough for us to see the bronze figures of cherubs that formed the centerpiece of the great stone bowl. The sound of the splashing water was cool and refreshing and the flowers that surrounded us gave up their fragrant scents to the evening air. I was acutely aware of the dark bulk of Reeve so close beside me in the night. He made no move to reach for me, however.

Instead he said, "Bernard had his solicitor out here today, Deb, and he signed over all of my estate to me."

I swung around to look up at him. "*All* of it?" I said incredulously. "I thought he was only going to give you half."

"He changed his mind," Reeve said. "He told me that I had matured greatly in the last few months. He said that our marriage will be the making of me."

He was staring at the fountain, refusing to meet my eyes. There was no expression on his face at all.

I said weakly, "I don't know what I have done to earn such an endorsement from Lord Bradford."

"He thinks you will make me happy," Reeve informed me.

He did not sound at all happy as he said this.

I didn't know how to answer him.

While he had made no physical motion to move away from me, I felt as if he had withdrawn. He said, "While the solicitor was here, I made a new will."

I looked up searchingly into his face, but all I could see was his immobile profile outlined against the dark, moonlit sky.

The nightingale was quiet.

"A new will?" I repeated.

"Yes. The property is entailed, of course, but I want you to know that if anything should happen to me, Deb, your future is secure. I put a hundred thousand pounds into a widow's jointure for you."

I felt as if a ghost had walked over my grave.

I tried to speak lightly, "Well, that is very generous of you, Reeve, but I don't expect to collect on that generosity for at least fifty more years."

A faint smile touched the corners of his lips, but he did not reply.

I folded my arms across my breast and tried not to shiver. *Don't be stupid*, I scolded myself. *Surely it is only normal for a man to make a new will when he is going to be married. There is no need for you to feel so uneasy.*

I closed the invisible gap that had opened between us and slid my arms around his waist, wanting to feel him solid and warm under my fingers. After a moment, his arms came around me as well, holding me close against him.

"Tomorrow night at this time . . ." he whispered, his lips against my temple.

I shivered, and this time it was in anticipation, not in fear.

CHAPTER
sixteen

CLOUDS MOVED IN AFTER MIDNIGHT, AND IT rained, but the day of my wedding dawned clear and cool. Mama and Mary Ann and Sally crowded into my bedroom to help me to get ready for the great event.

The two girls, who were my bridesmaids, were excited. Mama was nervous, and trying to hide it.

"Oh, Deborah, your dress is beautiful!" Sally cried as she walked around me, viewing my glory from all sides.

"I can't believe you found it in Brighton," Mary Ann agreed, following in Sally's footsteps. "It looks as if it must have come from one of the best dressmakers on Bond Street."

It was, in truth, an extremely lovely dress made of white crape over a blue-satin slip. The neckline was square and I wore the pearl necklace and pearl earrings that Reeve had bought me. Mama herself had done my hair, parting it down the center and pulling it smoothly to the back of my head, where she used the curling iron to turn it into a waterfall of ringlets. Small white roses adorned the top of my head like a crown.

"Don't forget your gloves," Sally said, handing me the long, white-kid gloves that went up to my elbows.

As I began to work them onto my fingers, the two

girls ran into the bedroom across the hall to look out a window that opened onto the front of the house.

"I think the men are leaving now!" Sally reported, rushing back into my room. "The phaeton and the curricle are both at the doorstep."

"They are! They are!" It was Mary Ann's voice from across the hallway. "Oh, Reeve looks magnificent, Deborah. You are so lucky!"

"How does Harry look?" I called back to her.

She came into the room, her cheeks pink. "Harry looks very nice."

I grinned at her.

"Oh Harry is not half as handsome as Reeve," Sally said carelessly.

Mary Ann's color deepened.

I winked at her.

She bit her lip.

Mama said, "Are you ready, Deborah? Have we forgotten anything?"

I glanced in the tall pier glass and blinked at the bridal image that was reflected back at me.

"I don't think so," I said.

"Girls," Mama said, "go and see if the carriages with the men have left. It would not do for Reeve to catch sight of Deborah before they meet in church."

Both girls ran across the room and returned to report breathlessly that the carriages were gone.

"The chaise should be arriving soon for us," Mama said then.

"Perhaps we should go down," I said.

Mama nodded.

I could feel the eyes of the servants on me as I walked down the stairs to the front hallway.

I was beginning to grow nervous.

Mama must have sensed my feelings, for she said, "Are you all right, darling?"

I looked into her anxious face. She looked beautiful today in an elegant sarcenet dress she had bought in the same shop where I had bought my wedding gown. The color of the gown was the same blue as her eyes.

I said honestly, "I am feeling a little nervous about being the center of so many people's attention. I will feel better after I see Reeve."

The chaise, pulled by Reeve's four beautiful bays, pulled up in front of the door, and footmen arrived from all over to set the stairs for us and to assist us into the carriage. Mary Ann and Sally rode with their backs to the coachman's seat while Mama and I faced front.

"Ready, ma'am?" the coachman called to Mama.

"Yes, thank you, Rogers," Mama called back through the open window next to her.

The chaise moved forward and we were on our way to the church.

Sally and Mary Ann talked the whole way. I did my best to enter into the spirit of their enthusiasm, but all I wanted was for the whole show to be over. Both Reeve and I would have been much happier with a quiet ceremony with only the immediate family in attendance.

Thank God we were getting away by ourselves for a few days! Reeve had taken a room at one of the nicest hotels in Brighton for the next three nights so that we would not have to spend the first few days of our marriage under the curious eyes of Sally and Mary Ann. After the ceremony, we would return to Wakefield Manor for the wedding breakfast, then drive into Brighton for our wedding night.

As we pulled into the village, I could see that the street was lined with people.

"They're the ones who couldn't fit into the church," Sally informed me. "You'd better wave to them, Deborah."

Obediently, I rolled down my window all the way and waved to my assembled well-wishers.

"God bless you, my lady!" a voice called.

"Ah, ain't she beautiful!" came another.

I smiled. "Thank you, thank you," I said.

Mercifully, the church came into sight, and the chaise rolled up to the front door. The footman jumped down from the front seat and came to set the steps for us. The four of us alighted and proceeded into the vestibule of the small, stone church.

Lord Bradford was waiting for us. He was to be the one to give me away.

I had a fleeting wish that I had asked Richard to do that office.

Lord Bradford smiled when he saw Mama. Then he looked at me.

"You look lovely, Deborah," he said.

"Thank you," I replied stiffly.

The organist was playing something by Mozart.

"Allow me to take you to your seat, Mrs. Woodly," Lord Bradford said.

Mama gave me an encouraging smile, laid her

hand on Lord Bradford's arm, and went with him down the aisle.

"Reeve and Harry are at the altar already," Mary Ann said, peering into the crowded church. "I can see the top of Reeve's head from here."

Lord Bradford came back into the vestibule. "Are you ready, girls?"

Sally smoothed her dress. "Ready, Papa!"

My young bridesmaids held their bouquets in front of them, assumed suitably grave expressions, and began to pace one after the other down the aisle.

Lord Bradford offered me his arm, and we followed.

Halfway down, I finally saw Reeve. We were both tall enough for our eyes to meet and hold over the rest of the congregation.

At last we reached the front of the church, and all of us in the wedding party turned to face the Reverend Mr. Thornton, who was standing on the bottom step of the altar. He raised his prayer book and, in a grave and dignified voice, began the service.

"Dearly beloved, we are gathered together here in the sight of God, and in the face of this congregation, to join together this Man and this Woman in holy Matrimony . . ."

I drew a deep, unsteady breath. The church was warm from all of the bodies that were crammed into it, and I felt the first dampness of perspiration under the crown of flowers that we had pinned so securely to the top of my head.

Mr. Thornton had finished reading the introduction to the service and now he looked sternly at Reeve and me, as he said, "I require and charge you both, as ye will answer at the dreadful day of judgment when the secrets of all hearts shall be disclosed, that if either of you know any impediment, why ye may not be lawfully joined together in Matrimony, ye do now confess it."

I glanced up at Reeve, as if I expected him to say something.

He was looking gravely back at Mr. Thornton and after a moment, I returned my eyes to the minister as well.

There was a pause. Then Mr. Thornton addressed Reeve and spoke the centuries-old words of the Church of England wedding ceremony: "Wilt thou have this Woman to thy wedded wife, to live together after God's ordinance in the holy estate of Matrimony? Wilt thou love her, comfort her, honor, and keep her in sickness and in health; and, forsaking all others, keep thee only unto her, so long as ye both shall live?"

Reeve looked at me, and said in a very low voice, "I will."

There was a white line around his nostrils.

Mr. Thornton next turned his attention to me. I heard him asking me if I would obey Reeve and serve him; if I would love, honor, and keep him—all the same things that he had asked Reeve about me. When he had finished, I said in a very firm and confident voice, "I will."

Reeve and I looked at each other. We continued to look at each other all the while the minister was asking "Who giveth this Woman to be married to this Man?" and Lord Bradford was stepping forward.

Then Reeve took my right hand into his, and we made our vows.

We knelt with bowed heads as the Reverend Thornton prayed over us and then he once more joined our right hands.

"Those whom God hath joined together let no man put asunder," he said.

Reeve and I were married.

The morning room was filled with white roses and people by the time Reeve and I got back to Wakefield Manor. The wedding cake was set up in front of one of the windows, a splendid array of food was laid out upon two long tables placed on the terrace that led into the garden, and the champagne was flowing.

My brother met us at the door, shook Reeve's hand, and congratulated him. Then he bent to kiss my cheek.

"I wish you very happy, Deborah," he said.

I smiled up at him. "Thank you, Richard."

The next hour was a constant repetition of congratulations and good wishes, and I smiled and smiled until I thought my cheeks would crack.

I cut the cake and had some food and two glasses of champagne and at last Reeve whispered in my ear, "Let's disappear now, shall we, Deb? You go first. I'll give you five minutes before I break away."

He didn't have to ask me twice. I began to thread my way toward the door, slipping between people who were talking as if they hadn't had a chance to socialize with each other in a million years. Finally I was in the hallway, where I lifted the skirt of my dress and ran for the stairs before anyone had the chance to stop me.

Susan was waiting to help me take off my wedding gown and put on my traveling dress of a light bisque-colored jaconet. While she was fastening me up the back, Mama came into the room.

"Are you almost ready to go, darling?" she asked.

"Just about," I replied. "My portmanteau is already in the chaise." I picked up my tan gloves from the small rosewood dressing table. "Reeve said he would come along to fetch me. We're going to slip down the back stairs and out by the side door."

As soon as I finished speaking, a light rap sounded on my door.

I went to open it, and Reeve stood framed in the doorway.

"Ready, Deb?" he asked.

He had changed from the evening dress he had worn for the wedding into his more familiar garb of morning coat, buff pantaloons, and Hessian boots.

"Ready," I said.

I turned to my mother. "I'll see you in three days' time, Mama."

She nodded. "Enjoy Brighton, darling," she returned, her voice only slightly constricted.

"Don't worry, Mrs. Woodly," Reeve said gently, "I'll take good care of Deb."

Mama gave him a shadowy smile.

Then Reeve had me by the hand, and we were sneaking down the back stairs like a pair of children escaping from the schoolroom. We walked around the side of the house and found the chaise waiting for us by the front steps.

Reeve handed me in, then he followed. The footman closed the door. The horses started forward.

The second part of my wedding day had begun.

We were registered at the Royal Crescent Hotel, which was located on the Steyne in the best part of Brighton. The hotel lobby was all carved walnut and satinwood, with a black-and-white-marble floor and green-marble pillars. Our suite consisted of a bedroom with a carved-rosewood bed, two dressing rooms, and a drawing room. My dressing room had a small alcove off of it where Susan could sleep, and Reeve's had the same for his valet.

"This hotel apartment is bigger than the house I lived in the whole time I was growing up," I said with some disapproval as I walked around the opulent quarters Reeve had deemed suitable for his wedding trip.

"Yes, it is, isn't it?" he agreed amiably. We were in the bedroom, and he was standing at the window, looking out on the green park of the Steyne.

I eyed his back. It was four o'clock in the afternoon, and I wondered what we could possibly find to do to fill in the hours until dinnertime. "Are you hungry, Reeve?" I asked him. "Would you like to have some tea?"

He turned to face me. The light from the window behind him lit his smoothly brushed hair and made it look like polished mahogany. He answered. "I'm hungry all right, but not for tea."

There was a hard, concentrated look on his chiseled face. His eyes swept all over me, and I could feel color rush into my cheeks. I said a little uncertainly, "Well, the earliest we can eat dinner is six o'clock."

He began to walk toward me. "I have no intention of waiting until dinner."

He reached me and put his hands on my shoulders. It was then that his meaning registered.

I was truly scandalized.

"*Reeve!* You cannot mean to go to bed in the middle of the afternoon!"

"I most certainly do," he replied. And before I could protest again, he bent his head and kissed me.

His mouth was hard and demanding, and it knocked the breath right out of my body. He wrapped his arms around me, bent me back so that my head was braced against his shoulder, and kissed me until I was so dizzy that I couldn't think.

When he finally lifted his head and stepped away from me, my knees were so wobbly I almost fell. Huge-eyed, I watched as he went silently to the doors that led into both our dressing rooms and locked them.

I swallowed.

Still in silence, he took off his coat and his neck-cloth and dropped them on the brown-velvet chaise longue that was positioned nearest to him. Then he was coming back across the carpet toward me.

I pulled myself together, and said severely, "This is not at all how I pictured things happening on my wedding day, Reeve. I always thought that I would be wearing my nightdress and waiting for you in bed. At night. In the dark. That is how it is supposed to be done, you know—not in the middle of the afternoon."

He raised an eyebrow at me. "Ah. So you have been picturing things, have you?"

"Not as much as you have, I'll wager," I retorted.

He stopped in front of me and grinned. "You're right about that."

He put his hands on either side of my head, his thumbs under my chin, and tipped my face up so that I had to look at him. He said, "You're not afraid of what is going to happen between us, are you, Deb?"

"No," I said truthfully.

With surprise, I realized that the expression in his dark eyes was worry. "It might hurt you at first. I would never want to hurt you, you know that, but I have to be honest and tell you that I've heard that a woman's first time can be painful."

I smiled up at him reassuringly. "I'm brave."

He smiled back. "You are. And I am incredibly lucky."

I turned my face and kissed his fingers which were cradling my cheek. His eyes turned black.

"Let's get you out of this damn dress," he said.

"You're going to have to undo the buttons, then, Reeve. I can't reach them."

"Turn around," he said tersely.

I presented him with my back and felt him fumbling with the small, covered buttons of my traveling dress.

"Damn," he grunted after a few minutes. "Couldn't you have picked a dress with bigger buttons? I can hardly get my fingers around these."

"I thought I was going to be wearing my nightdress," I retorted. "It's not my fault if you are in such a hurry that you have no decency."

"All right, all right, all right," he growled. "I think I've got enough of them undone for you to get out of it."

"I don't want to tear anything," I said, smothering a smile.

I had to admit that I was having fun.

"Will you take off the goddamn dress!" he roared.

"It's rude to shout," I said as I began to work the sleeves off my arms. I felt his eyes on me as I peeled the bisque-colored material away from my shoulders and breasts down to my waist. There was just enough room for me to slide it over my hips to the floor, where I stepped out of it. I bent to pick it up and went to put it on the brass-bound trunk that was placed at the foot of the bed. Then I turned to face Reeve.

The nipples of my breasts were easily visible through the thin cotton of my chemise. Reeve was staring at them, and for a moment the hardness of his face made him seem like a stranger. I had to restrain myself from folding my arms across my chest to hide myself.

He said in a hoarse voice, "You've changed from the little girl I used to go swimming with."

The reference to our mutual childhood restored my confidence; it reminded me that this was Reeve who was looking at me and not some stranger. I felt myself relax.

He said, his eyes still on my breasts, "I don't know why it took me so long to realize that you had grown up, but it wasn't until I saw you in London that I realized you weren't my little childhood friend any longer." He raised his eyes to my face. "You had turned into a beautiful woman right under my nose, and I hadn't even noticed."

I said a little unsteadily, "The same thing happened to me with you."

He started to approach me. "Did it, Deb?"

I nodded. "I realized it, I think, the first time you kissed me."

He bent a little and scooped me up in his arms.

"Reeve!" I said, breathless with surprise.

He began to walk me toward the bed. He carried me as if I weighed nothing—which I don't. He laid me down and bent to remove his boots. Then he joined me on top of the mattress.

"Now," he said, "let's get serious."

I looked up into his glittering eyes. "Show me," I said.

He kissed me again, and I opened my mouth willingly to the sweet invasion of his tongue. After a while his mouth moved away from mine to trail along my neck and down to my breasts. He pushed down my chemise and at the touch of his tongue on my nipple, ripples of sensation rolled down to my loins.

My breath caught in my throat.

"Do you like that, Deb?" Reeve murmured.

I swallowed. "Yes."

His mouth left my nipple and moved to the underside of my breast. "God," he said. "Your skin is so beautiful. It's like touching silk."

At this point, my hands were buried in his hair. My eyes were closed.

His mouth moved to my other breast.

Liquid sensation poured all through me.

I took my hands away from his head and began to pull his shirt away from his breeches. I wanted to touch his skin the way he was touching mine.

I slid my hands up his back and felt the strong muscles under the smooth skin. He felt wonderful.

He sat up for a moment and with one fluid motion he pulled the shirt over his head. Then he bent and ripped off his breeches.

I looked.

If I wasn't a little girl anymore, then he certainly wasn't a little boy.

"Good heavens, Reeve," I croaked. "You're simply not going to fit."

"I think we'll manage it," he said.

I wasn't so sure, but he was the one with the expertise in this area, so I didn't say anything else.

Besides, I didn't want him to stop what it was that he was doing.

He went back to kissing me, and now I felt his hands on my drawers, pushing them down. When he had got them to my ankles, I helped by kicking them fully out of our way.

"That's my girl," he said breathlessly, and then I felt his fingers come up between my legs.

I stiffened. I couldn't help it.

"It's all right, Deb," he said. "Relax. It will be all right."

Relax? I thought wildly. *How can I relax with him touching me like this?*

But after a minute I felt a paralyzingly sweet sensation begin to emanate from the touch of those long, clever fingers. He moved his body over mine. His tongue was deep within my mouth and now his fingers were also deep within my body.

I began to throb and, of its own volition, my lower body lifted itself upward toward Reeve.

"God Almighty, Deb," he groaned into my mouth. "God Almighty."

I didn't know what was happening. All I knew was that I was wet and hot, and the sensation that was sweeping through my loins was building toward some indescribable climax.

"All right," Reeve said hoarsely. When he spread my legs, I opened them willingly, and when he raised my knees, I let him. He positioned himself and his eyes met mine.

"All right?" he repeated.

The throbbing inside of me was crying out for him. "Yes," I said.

He moved into me slowly at first, but he didn't get very far before he stuck.

I almost cried with frustration.

He was sweating and breathing heavily as he said to me, "Hold on now, Deb."

Then he thrust. Hard.

My fingers bit into his shoulders.

He was in.

The two of us lay perfectly still, staring at each other, afraid to move. Reeve was sweating as if he had been out in the sun for hours.

After a while he panted, "Am I hurting you?"

"Only a little. It hurt at first, but it doesn't feel too bad now," I said cautiously.

I could see the muscles in his throat work as he

swallowed. He moved slowly back and forth inside of me.

"How does that feel?"

"It's not too bad," I said with the same caution as before.

He shut his eyes. Sweat was pouring off of him. "Dear God," he said.

"I'm fine, Reeve," I said. "You just go ahead and do what you have to do."

"I don't think I have any choice," he said hoarsely. And while my fingers gripped his shoulders tensely, he began to drive in and out of me, in and out, until finally he let out a noise that sounded like *Aahhhh!* and went still.

Then his weight dropped on me and I put my arms around him and held him while he struggled to recover his breath. Finally he lifted himself up a little without completely disconnecting us and looked down into my face.

"Are you all right, Deb?" he asked anxiously.

"I'm fine," I assured him. "It wasn't bad at all, Reeve. Really."

"Dear God," he groaned. "I feel like I've died and gone to heaven and she says it wasn't bad."

"It was actually quite nice for a while," I said with a laugh.

He rolled off me and gathered me into his arms. "It will always be quite nice from now on. I promise you."

"Mmm. I just think I need to stretch a bit more down there."

He cradled me close. "You will."

I closed my eyes and cuddled against him and thought that perhaps he was right.

We had dinner in the hotel dining room. Both of us were ravenous, and the dressed lamb, buttered prawns, asparagus, sole with white wine and mushrooms, and apple pie tasted exceedingly good. Reeve ordered a bottle of champagne, and I drank two glasses while he had the rest.

After dinner we went for a walk along the Marine Parade, where we watched the sun go down and the moon come up. By the time we got back to our hotel room, I was so sleepy I could scarcely keep my eyes open. Susan got me into the nightdress I was supposed to have been wearing for my first sexual encounter with my new husband, and I got into bed, told Reeve a firm good night, and was asleep in under five minutes.

I awoke the following morning with the sensation that someone was looking at me. I opened my eyes and saw Reeve lying on his stomach next to me. He was propped up on his elbows, his chin on his linked hands and his eyes on my face.

I smiled at him sleepily. "Good morning."

"Good morning." His face was grave. "Did you sleep well?"

I yawned. "I slept like the dead."

His lips smiled at me but his eyes remained grave. "Too much champagne," he said.

I looked at him. His hair was disheveled from sleep, his chin and cheeks unshaven. He looked wonderful.

But something was wrong.

I reached over and ran my fingers through his tangled hair. I said quietly, "Did I ever tell you that I loved you?"

"No." His voice was strange. "I don't believe you ever have."

"Well, I do."

He said a little desperately, "I would never want to do anything that would hurt you, Deb. You know that, don't you?"

I deliberately misunderstood him. "I thought you told me it would only hurt the first time."

He looked a little disconcerted.

"Let's try it and see if you're right."

He frowned. "Aren't you too sore?"

I said softly, "Kiss me, Reeve."

He shifted his weight until he was right next to me, then he lowered his mouth to cover mine. After a few minutes, his leg slid over mine as well.

All of the sensations I had experienced last night came back as we kissed and touched each other. Over and over he told me how beautiful I was, and deep within me the thrilling sensations of want and need climbed higher and higher. I closed my legs around his waist and this time, when he surged within me, there was no sharp pain to dissipate those wonderful feelings. This time there were only spasms of intense sensation, which intensified as he thrust back and forth within me, driving me to higher and higher peaks of excitement, until finally I exploded around him in an incredible climax of pleasure that rocked me to the very soul of my being.

Afterward we lay together, clutching each other

tightly, the sweat from both our bodies mingling intimately.

At last I croaked, in echo of his words yesterday, "I feel like I've died and gone to heaven."

His grip on me tightened. "I love you so much, Deb. God help us both, but I love you."

The desperate note was back in his voice again, and I buried my lips in his hair and said a prayer.

CHAPTER
seventeen

Reeve and I stayed three days in Brighton, and I blush to admit that we spent very little time outside our hotel room. We went to the dining room to eat and every evening after dinner we went for a walk along the Marine Parade. We also went shopping one afternoon, and Reeve insisted on buying me a pair of sapphire earrings, which he said exactly matched my eyes.

The rest of the time we spent in bed.

"It's a very good thing you had the idea to come to Brighton," I said to Reeve the morning that we were getting ready to return to Wakefield Manor. "We would have scandalized the entire Wakefield household by our behavior these last few days."

Reeve was lounging in a low chair in my dressing room, while I stood in front of the pier glass tying the pink ribbons of a straw bonnet under my chin. He lifted an eyebrow at me in the mirror. "Why do you think I insisted that we come to Brighton? I wanted to get you to myself."

I said regretfully, "Well, we are going to have to act like normal people once we return to Wakefield, Reeve. And that means getting up in the morning—not remaining in bed until two in the afternoon!"

He sighed gustily.

I turned away from the mirror and scanned the room to make sure I had not forgotten anything.

"Let's hope your dear Aunt Sophia is gone, at least," I said. "I wouldn't be at all shocked to have her ask me about my wedding night—in detail."

He chuckled wickedly. "You didn't have a wedding night, remember? You had a wedding afternoon. On your wedding night you passed out on me from too much champagne."

"Very amusing," I said.

"Ready?" he said, and, unfolding his length from the chair, he got to his feet.

I was ready, but I felt curiously reluctant to leave Brighton; and it was not just because I enjoyed the privacy that the hotel had afforded to newlyweds.

I felt safe here in Brighton.

No, it was more than that, I realized. I felt that Reeve was safe here in Brighton.

I had a horribly uneasy feeling that he might not be safe at Wakefield. Not from Robert. And perhaps not from himself.

"Ready," I said with a cheerful smile, and let him take my arm to escort me out of the room.

We were greeted like royalty upon our return to Wakefield. Lord Bradford and Mama, who had obviously been waiting for us, came into the hall the moment we stepped through the front door of the house.

"Deborah!" Mama cried, and flew to give me a hug.

I laughed as I felt the surprising strength of her slender arms as they clutched me close. "I've only been gone a few days, Mama," I said.

She stepped back and looked up into my face.

I knew I looked radiant. Even I had been able to see the glow that emanated from me when I regarded myself in the mirror.

The small frown that had been puckering my mother's brow smoothed out, and her expression changed into one of wonder.

Lord Bradford said pleasantly, "Did you enjoy Brighton, Deborah? You certainly had wonderful weather."

My eyes flew to Reeve, who was standing behind Lord Bradford. He winked at me.

I wondered what stuffy Lord Bradford would say if I told him that I had scarcely seen Brighton, that I had been otherwise occupied. I didn't say that, however. Instead I returned my gaze to Reeve's cousin's square, powerful face, and replied demurely, "It was very nice, my lord."

He said, "Surely it is time for you to call me Bernard, my dear. We are family now, after all."

I didn't want to call him Bernard.

"Thank you," I said.

He raised an admonishing eyebrow at me as if I were a child.

"Bernard," I said a little sulkily.

He nodded in grave approbation. Then he said, "I am certain that you must be anxious to freshen up after your journey." His eyes moved to Reeve. "I have put both you and Deborah in your room, Reeve."

Reeve nodded and took me by the arm. "Come along, Deb."

I went with him down the hall and up the center oak

staircase. Reeve's room was one of the first on the passageway in the left wing of the house and when he opened the door to let me in the first thing I saw was a magnificent green-velvet four-poster, whose hangings had been tied to the posts to allow for some movement of the summer air. The room's green-damask walls were hung with scenes of the Sussex countryside, there was a silk-covered chaise longue on the Persian carpet, a writing desk, a dressing table, two striped-silk chairs facing each other in a conversational grouping and two large, carved, black elephants, one on either side of the fireplace.

Reeve saw me staring at the elephants. "Some cousin of Bernard's wife sent them back from India," he explained.

I nodded and went to the satinwood dressing table to remove my hat and smooth my hair. Reeve went to look out the window, his hands clasped behind his back.

I stared unseeingly at my reflection in the dressing table mirror, deep in thought. "Reeve?" I said after a minute, "Have you ever suspected that your cousin might be interested in my mother?"

"Bernard?" Reeve said, swinging around to face me.

I looked at him. "Yes."

"I've never thought about it." He frowned, obviously thinking about it now. "I suppose it's possible, Deb," he said at last, slowly. "Your mother is still a very lovely woman."

I scowled. "Exactly how old is Bernard, anyway?"

Reeve said. "He's about fifty, I think."

"Fifty!" I replied scornfully. "That's ancient."

Reeve looked amused. "It's not that ancient, Deb, believe me. I can assure you that most fifty-year-old men are quite . . . er . . . capable."

I didn't want to think of Lord Bradford in such a way—particularly with my mother. It was disgusting.

I said quickly, "You won't mind if Mama lives with us at Ambersley, will you Reeve?"

"Of course I won't mind," he replied in surprise. "I have always assumed that she would do so."

I went to him, put my arms around his waist and rested my cheek on his shoulder. His arms came up to hold me close.

I kissed his chin because his neck was enclosed in a starched white neckcloth ànd I couldn't get to it. Even though he had shaved that morning, his beard pricked my lips.

He rested his mouth on the top of my head.

The summer sun streaming in the window bathed us both in warmth and light. I felt a familiar tightening in the lower part of my body, and I made myself step away from him.

"They will be expecting us back downstairs for tea," I said.

The hawklike look on Reeve's face told me that he was feeling the same way I was.

"Do we have to go?" he said.

I thought of my mother.

"Yes, we do."

"We should have stayed by ourselves in Brighton," he growled.

I glanced around the beautiful family bedchamber in which we stood, and knew that I, too, wished we had remained in the impersonal hotel apartment in which we had spent the first few days of our marriage.

"Yes," I said a little shakily, "I wish we could have."

It was a very strange feeling to meet once again all of the people with whom I had lived for the last few weeks. Reeve and I had been gone for only three days, but I was so changed in my own person, as well as my estate in life, that I needed to find new ways to relate to everyone else.

Lady Sophia, mercifully, had returned home to Bath, but her departure meant that I was put in her place at the head of the table, opposite to Lord Bradford. I tried very hard not to show how self-conscious I felt about this new honor.

Sally and Mary Ann regarded me surreptitiously but steadily during the whole of the meal.

Edmund Norton talked to Harry and Reeve about a boat he had been thinking of buying.

Mrs. Norton conversed calmly with Bernard and Mama, and Mr. Norton, who was seated on my right hand, talked to me.

"Did you have an opportunity to visit the Prince Regent's pavilion while you were in Brighton, Lady Cambridge?" Mr. Norton asked me kindly.

I wondered how long it would take me to grow accustomed to being addressed as *Lady Cambridge*.

"Not the inside," I replied. "But it is certainly an impressive piece of architecture from the outside."

He made some kind of response, and we continued

to converse as the salmon was succeeded by the venison which was succeeded by a roast of pork.

After a dessert of fruit and almonds had been served, the ladies retired to the drawing room for tea.

"Oh Deborah," Sally rhapsodized, "you look utterly beautiful. Marriage must be a very wonderful thing."

Mary Ann didn't say anything, but her eyes watched me closely.

I smiled at Reeve's young cousin. "It is perfectly splendid, Sally, as long as you marry the right man."

Sally heaved a loud sigh. "You got Reeve, you lucky thing. Where are the rest of us going to find a man to equal him?"

"Now girls," Mrs. Norton admonished sharply, "it is not at all proper of you to be asking Deborah about her marriage experiences."

Mary Ann's brown eyes dropped. "Yes, Mama," she said.

Sally wrinkled her nose at me.

My mother smoothed the already-smooth silk of her white evening dress.

I drank some of my tea, and said calmly, "How are the plans for the fair coming along?"

We talked of the fair until the men returned to the room. Then Mama and Bernard and Mr. and Mrs. Norton went to the whist table for a game and the rest of us went for a walk in the garden.

Sally and Edmund walked on ahead, absorbed in a conversation of their own. Sally's light voice and laughter floated back to us on the evening air. She was teasing Edmund about his passion for boats.

Reeve put his hand warningly over mine, which

was resting on his arm, and then he stopped walking to turn us to face Harry and Mary Ann. They halted also, and the four of us regarded each other across a three-foot expanse of graveled pathway.

Reeve said, "I have been wondering, Harry, if you have heard anything from Robert."

Harry gave Reeve a quick, sharp look. After a moment, he said tersely, "Actually, we don't know where he is."

My heart thumped once, hard.

Reeve's hand tightened on mine. "I thought he was in Hampshire."

Harry kicked at the gravel with his toe, refusing to meet Reeve's eyes. "He left there a few days ago, and no one has heard from him since."

The fading evening light showed us that Harry was continuing to stare at the ground in front of him. He kicked the gravel once again.

Reeve said in a very hard voice, "Deb told me what Robert tried to do to her, Harry, so there's no need to pull any punches here."

Harry's eyes flew to meet mine. I nodded.

Mary Ann asked in a hushed voice, "What did Robert try to do to you, Deborah?"

No one answered.

Then Harry said wearily, his eyes still locked on mine, "He tried to rape her, Mary Ann. There never was any drunken brawl in Fair Haven. Robert broke into Deborah's room and attacked her. Mrs. Woodly heard Deborah call for help and went in and hit Robert over the head with a vase. That's why my father sent him packing into Hampshire and refused to allow him to return for the wedding."

Mary Ann looked utterly horrified. "My God, Deborah. What a frightful experience!"

I swallowed. "Yes, it was."

Reeve's hand on mine was rigid.

I said to Harry in the most reasonable voice I could command, "Surely Robert will not attempt anything so outrageous again. Surely he must realize that he would be the first person to be suspected should something happen to Reeve or to me."

What I saw in Harry's face frightened me. He said in a hard voice, "Robert is out of control, Deborah. That became clear to me when he went so far as to try to rape you." He rubbed his hand across his eyes, as if he could chase away the sight that was lodged there behind them. He went on, "It's as if he's being eaten up inside by this violent hatred he has for Reeve. It's true that there was always a trace of brutality in Robert, but now . . ." He moved his eyes from me to Reeve and repeated somberly, "Now he's gone totally out of control."

Reeve stood beside me, his hand over mine on his sleeve, and said nothing.

"I don't understand," Mary Ann said distressfully. "Why should he hate you so much, Reeve?"

"I don't know," Reeve said.

"My father's only forty-six," Harry said. "Robert can't be fool enough to think that he would succeed as Earl of Cambridge for a very long time if you should die."

Shock ripped through me. *Forty-six!*, I thought. *Reeve told me the man was at least fifty.*

Reeve said soberly, "Perhaps your father should watch his step also, Harry."

Harry's mouth dropped open. "Surely you can't be serious, Reeve?"

"I don't know," Reeve said again. "Who knows what is on Robert's mind?"

There was a tense silence.

Then Reeve seemed to shake himself out of a reverie, and he turned to me. "We must take precautions," he said firmly, "and the chief precaution of all is that you are never to put yourself into a position where you are alone. Do you hear me, Deb? Robert has already tried to get to me through you. There is no reason to think he won't try it again."

I had never heard him sound so authoritative. Dictatorial, really.

"I hear you, Reeve," I said mildly.

The sound of Sally's voice was coming closer now, and Harry said hurriedly, "I don't want to say anything of this to my sister or Edmund."

Reeve nodded in agreement, and after a minute I began to talk cheerfully about how much I would like to return to Brighton one day so that I could see the inside of the prince's pavilion.

Upstairs, I used the dressing room to change into my nightdress and Reeve used the bedroom. His valet was gone when I walked into the green-damask-hung room, and Reeve was standing in front of the fireplace, staring contemplatively at one of the Indian elephants. He was wearing an elegant black-silk dressing gown, and I knew from past experience that he had nothing on under it.

He heard the dressing room door close behind me and turned.

I myself was wearing a white-lawn nightgown, and Susan had brushed my hair so that it fell in a loose waterfall of curls down my back.

Reeve looked at me, and his face was full of shadows. He said, "Your hair is the color of moonlight."

His loverlike words were so at odds with the somber expression on his face that I was disconcerted. I said a little uncertainly, "Do you think Robert will have the nerve to return here after what he has done?"

The expression on Reeve's face did not change. He said, "He may not return to the house, but there is nothing to stop him from returning to the neighborhood—in secrecy, if he so chooses."

I shivered even though the air in the bedroom was warm.

"I meant what I said earlier about you being careful not to go out alone," Reeve said.

I searched his face. "I think I am safe, Reeve. Robert said he only wanted to rape me because he wanted to have me before you did."

"Jesus Christ," Reeve said in despair. He shut his eyes.

I didn't even reprimand him for blasphemy.

"It's you I am worried about," I said.

Reeve opened his eyes and held out his arms and, thankfully, I went into them. He said as he rested his cheek on the top of my head, "Don't you see, Deb?

Robert wants to be Earl of Cambridge. Now that we are married, he will see you as his number one threat."

"I don't understand," I said.

He said grimly, "If you should have a son, then Robert would be knocked out of the direct line of succession completely."

He was so strung up with tension that I could fairly feel his body vibrating under my hands. I said, "For goodness sake, Reeve, we haven't even been married a week yet!"

"All it takes is once," he replied grimly.

I pressed my cheek into his shoulder. "We only have a few more days at Wakefield Manor, and I'll be careful," I promised, trying to reassure him.

There was no relaxation in his body as he said, "I shouldn't have married you. I've put you in danger by marrying you . . ."

"That's quite enough of that."

I pulled away from his arms and glared up at him furiously. "I don't ever want to hear you say that again, Reeve. Do you hear me?"

He looked down at me, and I didn't like the bleak look I saw in his eyes.

"Marrying you is the best thing that ever happened to me," I said. "I love you."

He did not look convinced.

I decided this might be a good time to distract him by changing the subject.

I folded my arms and said, "Another thing. You told me this afternoon that your cousin was fifty but, according to Harry, he is only forty-six."

Reeve looked utterly bewildered by this new topic. "Fifty—forty-six—what is the difference, Deb?"

"The difference is four years," I said austerely.

Enlightenment struck him. "Are we back to this business of Bernard and your mother?"

"Yes, we are," I informed him.

He put his hands in the pockets of his dressing gown and shrugged. "Well, what if Bernard *is* interested in your mother, Deb. What would be so bad about that?"

"Everything!" I retorted. "Good God, Reeve, look how he has treated you all these years."

He replied with misplaced patience, "He was trying to do the right thing by me, Deb. Bernard is not a bad man, you know."

"Perhaps not," I snapped, "but he most certainly is not the right kind of man for my mother."

A little silence fell between us. The folded silk collar of Reeve's silk dressing gown formed a V, leaving bare the strong column of his neck as well as his upper chest, where the crisp dark hairs began to grow.

He regarded me thoughtfully, and said, "Who is the right kind of man for your mother, Deb?"

I could feel my whole body stiffen. "Not your cousin, at any rate!"

There was a slight frown on Reeve's face as he continued to regard me. Then he said gently, "Your mother has a right to marry again if she should choose to do so. You can't expect her to spend the rest of her life just being your mother and nothing else."

My head snapped up as if he had hit me under the chin. I glared at him. "I never said I expected that!"

He didn't answer; he just looked at me with an expression in his eyes that I didn't like at all.

He said, "It's been only the two of you for so long that I realize you are closer than most mothers and daughters are . . ."

I interrupted him. "Stop! I am very sorry I brought the subject up if you are going to go on like this. I just don't happen to think that Lord Bradford and my mother are well suited. And that is all."

I turned my back on him and went to look out the window. The lanterns on the patio had been extinguished, and the garden was in complete darkness.

"Very well," he said quietly from behind me.

I inhaled the scent of the flowers that I could not see.

You are the last person in the world to talk about letting go of one's mother.

I thought the words, and as soon as they came into my head, I was horrified and ashamed.

I turned away from the window and smiled at him across the distance that separated us. "I'm sorry I snapped at you," I said. "I didn't mean it."

Once more he held out his arms. "Love me, Deb," he said in an aching voice. "Love me."

I flew across the room into his embrace.

He held me in a crushing grip, but even though he was hurting me, I didn't protest. After a long while something like a shudder went through his body.

Then he lifted me in his arms and carried me to the bed.

CHAPTER
eighteen

REEVE WOKE ME EARLY THE NEXT MORNING WITH a kiss. I opened my eyes and saw that he was leaning over me, dressed in riding clothes.

"Harry and I are going for a ride," he said. "Go back to sleep, Deb."

Considering that he had kept me awake for a good part of the night, I thought I did deserve a little more rest.

I gave him a sleepy smile in return and shut my eyes as he left the room.

I awoke again at nine-thirty, dressed, and went down to have breakfast in the morning room.

Mama and Lord Bradford were there already, sitting over their coffee in the bay window where the round oak breakfast table was set up. They were deep in conversation.

A frown came over my face.

It was *not* that I was too mean-spirited to want to share my mother, I told myself righteously, remembering Reeve's words of the night before. It was that I did not believe that Lord Bradford could ever be the right man for her.

But I did not like the softly glowing look that I detected in Mama's eyes every time she looked at the man.

"Good morning," I said ominously.

Mama turned her head and smiled at me. "Good morning, darling. Did you sleep well?"

I caught a glint of humor in Lord Bradford's eyes at this artless question, and I felt the telltale color stain my cheeks.

"Very well, Mama," I said.

"And where is Reeve this morning?" she asked next, looking over my shoulder as if she expected my husband to materialize there.

"He went for a ride with Harry," I said.

Lord Bradford said, "Doubtless Harry is anxious to tell Reeve that he will be going to London in September to attend the Royal College of Physicians."

My eyes flew to Harry's father's face.

"Is it true?" I asked. "You have changed your mind and said that Harry might attend the school?"

"I have changed my mind," Lord Bradford said with resignation.

He did not look at my mother, nor did she look at him, but there was something in the way that they studiously avoided eye contact that I found disturbingly revealing.

I said stiffly, "I am glad. It is what he has always wanted to do, and I think he will make an excellent doctor."

"So I have been made to understand," said Lord Bradford, with that same resigned expression still in his voice.

I glanced quickly at Mama, who was serenely drinking her coffee.

I walked over to the small oak sideboard and took

some ham cakes and eggs. All of this nocturnal exercise I was getting of late made me very hungry in the morning.

As I returned to the table carrying my plate, I said cautiously, "Harry told us last night that no one knows where Robert is."

A very bleak look came across Lord Bradford's face. His gray eyes suddenly looked so desolate that I felt an unwanted pang of sympathy for him.

"That is correct," he said. He made a gesture, as if he were brushing an ugly picture away from in front of his eyes. "I very much fear that I cannot guarantee your safety should he come within your vicinity, Deborah. Or Reeve's safety, either. It will be wise for you both to take precautions."

"Do you think he means to come back here?" I said.

Those bleak gray eyes met mine. "Yes," Lord Bradford said. "I do."

Sudden panic struck me. "Reeve!" I said. "He went for a ride with Harry. Suppose Robert is lying in wait for him somewhere? Suppose he shoots him or something?"

Mama's soothing, "Don't worry, darling," clashed with Bernard's, "Reeve will be all right, Deborah."

I glared at Lord Bradford in fear and outrage. "How can you say he will be all right when you have just admitted to me that Robert is a danger to him?"

"Robert may have gone beyond the boundaries of what any of us define as civilized behavior, but he is not stupid," his father said. "No matter how much he may wish to harm Reeve, he wishes even less to find himself in gaol on a murder charge."

Lord Bradford rubbed his forehead as if it ached.

I saw that there was pain reflected in Mama's face as she watched him.

"A murderer cannot inherit the title and lands of a man he has murdered," Lord Bradford continued starkly. "Robert will be careful about how he deals with Reeve."

After breakfast Mama and I decided to go into the village to attend one of the final meetings of the planning committee for the summer fair, which was to be held in three days' time. As it was another lovely summer day, we decided to walk down to the stables instead of having the trap brought to the front door for us.

Everything was well in hand for Saturday, Mama told me as we strolled along the gravel path that led to the stable block. The rich green turf of the Downs stretched all around us as we descended toward the pink brick stables, which were nestled in a curve of the hill that lay below the house.

We had almost arrived at our destination when we ran into Harry, who was charging up the path, head down, muttering what sounded to me like a litany of swear words under his breath.

He had his coat flung over his right shoulder, his neckcloth hung like a scarf around his neck, and his shirt and breeches were soaking wet. His boots squished as he walked.

"Harry!" I said, staring at him.

I looked over his shoulder, but he was alone.

"Where is Reeve?" I asked in terror.

Harry stopped and for the first time appeared to notice that someone was blocking his way.

He looked from me to Mama then back again to me.

"Where is Reeve?" he repeated sarcastically. "I have no idea where Reeve is, Deborah. He jumped on his horse as soon as we reached shore and galloped off like all the devils of hell were after him. I thought perhaps he might have come home, but they told me in the stables that he hasn't."

I stared at Harry's drenched condition.

"What happened?" I demanded. "Why are you soaking wet? Did the two of you decide to go swimming this morning in your clothes?"

Harry ran his fingers through his drying curls, which had fallen forward over his forehead. "We went swimming all right," he said. "It just did not turn out the way I thought it would."

I had a sick feeling in the pit of my stomach.

"Tell me," I said.

"Deborah," Mama said quietly, "perhaps Harry would like to put on some dry clothes first."

"No," I said adamantly. "I want to know now. What happened, Harry?"

Harry shifted his weight from one foot to the other, and his boots squished audibly.

"Last night, before we went to bed, I asked Reeve to come for a ride with me this morning," he began. "I had some good news that I wanted to share with him."

I nodded. "I know about that," I said.

"Well, we met as arranged at the stables at seven-thirty and we decided to go out to Charles Island as the tide was low and we could have a good gallop along the sands."

A little breeze came gusting up from the south, and Harry shivered as it blew against his wet garments. I had no intention of releasing him, however, until I found out what had happened. "Yes?" I said relentlessly.

"Well, that's what we did," he said. "We rode out to Charles Island. We had a splendid gallop along the beach, and then we dismounted and walked our horses while I told Reeve that I would be going to the Royal College of Physicians in the autumn."

"That is wonderful news indeed, Harry," I said automatically. "I am very happy for you."

"Thank you. Reeve was happy for me, too." Once more Harry ran his fingers through his disordered hair. "Then, as we walked along, Reeve said, 'Why don't we celebrate by going for a swim?' "

I was holding a soft leather reticule, and my fingers tightened their grip on its strings until they bit into my fingers even through my gloves.

"And you agreed?" I said.

Harry nodded. "It was a beautiful morning, and we had swum often off of Charles Island at low tide when we were boys. There was something reckless about Reeve that made me feel exhilarated, as if we really were boys again, so we stripped down to our breeches and went into the water."

Mama said quietly, "I assume that the both of you are competent swimmers."

"Yes," Harry said, "we can both swim. But it's been a very long time since either of us was in the water, and I had no intention of venturing too far from the shore."

My stomach was in a knot as I listened to him.

"What happened?" I asked fearfully.

Harry shook his head as if he still didn't believe what he was about to relate. "We were out off of Skull Rock, in a place where the water is deep but where it's easy to get back to shore in a hurry, when Reeve suddenly said to me, 'I'm going to try to make it to Fair Haven.' "

I stopped breathing.

"Fair Haven?" my mother said in horror. "Do you mean he was going to try to swim across the bay?"

"Yes," said Harry grimly. "That is what I mean."

Reeve isn't dead, I told myself. *Don't panic, Deborah. Harry said earlier that he isn't dead.*

Even so, my heart was hammering with terror.

Harry continued with his tale. "He struck out from the shore before I could stop him. I didn't know what to do. If I went after him, and tried to force him to turn around, I was afraid that the both of us might drown." He drew in a deep breath and let it out. "Finally I decided that I needed a boat."

"A boat?" Mama said faintly.

Once more Harry shifted feet. Once more I could hear the water in his boots squish.

He said, his eyes on my face, "I swam back to shore, flung myself on my horse, and galloped as fast as I could into Fair Haven. Once I was there I commandeered one of the fishing boats from the pier—I almost punched the old man who wouldn't let me have it at first—and I put out into the bay. I could see that Reeve was still swimming, but he was obviously getting tired."

"Oh my God," I said.

"I can tell you, I never rowed so fast in all my life," Harry said. "I pulled those oars as if my entire hope of salvation hung on every stroke. And when I finally reached him, and I could see him gasping for breath and barely managing to stay afloat, *he didn't want to get into the bloody boat.*"

"What?" Mama said.

Harry said grimly, "He told me to go away, that he was going to make it to Fair Haven on his own power."

One of my hands went to cover my mouth. "Oh my dear God," I said.

Harry said, "Well, it was perfectly obvious to me that if I left him to make it on his own power, he was going to drown, so I kept the boat alongside of him for the next few minutes while he struggled to stay afloat. When he was finally so exhausted that he was scarcely able to move his arms and legs, I hauled him in."

"Did he help you get him into the boat?" I asked in a voice that I scarcely recognized as belonging to me.

Harry looked at me, as if debating whether or not to tell me the truth.

"I need to know," I said. "It will make a difference as to how I deal with him. Did he help you to get him into the boat?"

"No," Harry said. "He didn't help me at all. In fact, he wanted me to leave him in the water."

I stared blindly at the stable buildings that were visible behind Harry's back. I didn't say anything.

Mama glanced at me, then she asked Harry quietly, "What happened after you got the boat to shore?"

"Reeve was furious with me," Harry said. "Once he had enough breath to speak at all, he cursed me up one side and down the other. Said that I was a sedentary old man with no sporting blood in me."

"He didn't mean it, Harry," I said wearily.

"I know," Harry said. His face was very bleak. "He was trying to kill himself, and he was angry with me because I stopped him. That's why he was so angry."

It was a terrible thing to have the words I feared the most spoken out loud.

A heavy silence lay between the three of us. At last I said to Harry, "What happened after that?"

"The rest of our clothes and Reeve's horse were still on Charles Island, so the two of us rode my horse back over the causeway. Reeve got dressed, jumped on his horse, and took off. I thought he would come back home, considering the fact that he was exhausted, as well as being drenched to the skin, but evidently he has not."

I said somberly, "Thank you, Harry. You saved Reeve's life."

Hot anger flared in Harry once more. "God Almighty, it seems as if my whole family has gone mad! My brother has run berserk, my favorite cousin is trying to drown himself . . . What the bloody hell is going on here?"

I thought of Reeve's words to me the previous night. *I never should have married you.*

"Don't you see?" I said tiredly. "Reeve thinks that by marrying me he has made me a target for Robert."

It took Harry a moment to understand, but when he did all of the anger drained from his face.

"He thinks that Robert will want to eliminate you before you can bear a child that will cut him out of the succession," he said flatly.

"Yes."

Harry cursed. Then he looked at Mama and apologized.

She shook her head to indicate that she didn't mind.

"We were all hoping that when Reeve married you he would be able to shake his demons," Harry said to me. "It seems, however, that that is not going to be the case."

I put my hands up, as if to shade my eyes from the sun. "So it seems."

"You have to do something, Deborah," Harry said urgently. "He was serious. I wouldn't trust him not to try something like this again."

"I will talk to him, Harry," I said.

"He seems to listen to you," Harry said doubtfully.

"I will talk to him," I repeated. "I doubt if he planned the episode this morning, you know. I rather think he just seized the moment."

"Well he sure scared the hell out of me," Harry said frankly.

"Yes," I said. "I can understand that he did."

Mama and I changed our minds about going into the village, and instead we accompanied Harry back to the house to wait for Reeve. Harry thought that it was fruitless to send men in search of him, as he was quite certain that Reeve had not kept to the roadways but was out somewhere on the Downs, hopefully not doing any harm to himself.

Unfortunately, Mama, Harry, and I met Lord Bradford as soon as we came in the back door of the house. He took one look at our faces, and at Harry's soaked condition, and demanded to know what had happened.

We all ended up going into the morning room, where Harry once more recounted his tale of what had transpired that morning out on Charles Island.

Predictably, Lord Bradford was furious.

"What is wrong with that boy?" he demanded. He was pacing up and down in front of the rosewood fireplace. "He has one of the best positions in the entire country. He has a wife he clearly loves. He has everything to live for." He stopped pacing and swung around to face the three of us, who were grouped in a semicircle around him, like spectators watching a dangerous bear. A muscle clenched along his jaw. "Obviously he is not nearly as stable as I had hoped he was."

I stepped forward to defend Reeve, but my mother surprised me by jumping in first.

"You are not being fair, Bernard," she said gently. "Reeve is only trying to protect Deborah. He is going about it in the wrong way, of course, but his motivation is honorable."

Lord Bradford's steely gray eyes met my mother's clear blue ones. "Anyone who tries to duck out of his responsibilities by killing himself is a coward, Elizabeth."

I clenched my fists and opened my mouth to answer him, but my mother shook her head at me. With difficulty, I shut my mouth again.

"Reeve is one of the bravest young men I have ever known," Mama said quietly but firmly. Her eyes maintained their unflinching contact with Lord Bradford's. "Do you realize that until his father died, he burdened Reeve with the full responsibility for his mother's death?" Mama's lips thinned with contempt. "Deborah sometimes told me about the things that Lord Cambridge said to Reeve, and I simply could not believe that any father could say such dreadful things to his son. It is nothing short of a miracle that Reeve has turned into the kind and caring young man that he is."

There was a deep line between Lord Bradford's level brows. "Reeve was only fifteen when he overturned that coach," he said gruffly. "It was a tragic accident and nothing more." His frown deepened. "I have always thought that Helen must have been insane to let him take the reins in the first place."

"Of course she was," Mama agreed. "But that is not what Reeve was made to think. He was made to think that he killed his mother. And now he thinks that he might be responsible for Robert's killing Deborah."

Silence fell as my mother and Lord Bradford continued to look at each other.

"I see," Lord Bradford said at last. "I see."

"He is not a coward," Mama said. "He is desperate."

I had tears in my eyes. My wonderful, wonderful mother. I had never before realized how well she understood Reeve.

The grim look had come back to Lord Bradford's face. He turned to me, and said, "It is my son who is the coward, Deborah. I apologize for what I said about Reeve."

I had such a lump in my throat that I couldn't talk. I nodded.

"What are we going to do now?" Lord Bradford said. "We can't let the boy kill himself!"

He was obviously horrified by the very thought, and it occurred to me that if something should happen to

Reeve, Lord Bradford would become the Earl of Cambridge. Under such circumstances, there were a lot of men who wouldn't be so anxious to preserve Reeve's life.

I cleared my throat and managed to speak at last.

"I will talk to him," I said. "But the best protection we can give Reeve is to do something about Robert."

A shutter came down over Lord Bradford's face. "There is nothing we can do about Robert. I cannot even cut off his money, as he has an inheritance from his mother."

I stared at the powerfully built man in front of me. "So he is to be left free to roam the countryside, an obvious danger to Reeve—and to me?"

"Deborah," Mama said, "if there were some way to safeguard you from Robert, you can be certain that Bernard would do it."

"We could tie him up and put him on a boat to Australia," I muttered.

"I do not think that is feasible," Lord Bradford said with grim disapproval. "At this moment, we do not even know where he is."

I knew I was being unreasonable, but I was frightened.

"I am going upstairs," I said. "When Reeve finally comes in, I will speak to him."

I could feel three sets of worried eyes boring into my back as I left the room.

CHAPTER
nineteen

Reeve did not return for another three hours, during which time I had almost worn a path in the Persian rug from my pacing. He was not expecting to see me when he came in the door of the bedroom, and he stopped in the doorway as if he had walked into glass.

"Oh," he said, with a feeble attempt at casualness. "You here, Deb?"

When the door had finally opened I had reached the fireplace in my pacing and I was standing in front of it now, my arms folded across my breast, facing him.

"Yes," I said. "I'm here. I've been waiting for you."

"There was no need for you to do that," he said, trying even harder to sound casual. "After I left Harry I decided that I would take Monarch for a ride along the Downs."

"So I heard," I returned. I took in his wrinkled and disheveled appearance. "I see that your clothes have dried."

He left the doorway and came into the room, approaching me as cautiously as one would a not fully tamed animal. "Yes. Did Harry tell you that we went for a swim?"

"Harry told me everything," I said.

He thrust his hand through his disordered hair. "Don't pay any attention to him, Deb. He convinced himself that I was on the verge of drowning, but I can assure you that I was perfectly all right. I would have made Fair Haven if he had not interfered."

He stopped when he had covered half of the distance between the door and the fireplace and we regarded each other now over the patch of luxurious carpet that I had been pacing for the last three hours.

I said grimly, "Harry said you had no breath left. He said you were hardly able to get your arms out of the water."

"He's exaggerating," Reeve said.

"I don't think he is, Reeve," I said. "I think Harry is telling the truth."

He scowled at me. "I can't stop you from thinking what you want to think. Now if you will excuse me, I am going to send for Hummond so that I can change my clothes."

"In a moment," I said implacably. "First, you and I are going to talk."

He shook his head. "I don't want to talk about this morning, Deb."

I walked behind him to the bedroom door and locked it. Then I turned back to face him, my shoulders braced against the heavy, white-painted, oak door. I said, "I'm not leaving, and the only way you are going to get out of this room is by knocking me down."

He was livid with fury. "You may be my wife, but you're not my keeper!" he shouted at me. "What I do is my own business, not yours! Now get out of my way!"

I'm not proud of what I did next, but I was desperate. I had to reach him somehow.

I let my eyes fill with tears. They slid slowly down my face, streaking my cheeks with wet.

The room went deadly quiet.

"Don't do that, Deb," Reeve said hoarsely. "Please don't do that."

"I can't help it," I said in a pitiful voice. "I love you so much, and you are trying to leave me."

"No," he said. "I'm not. You know I love you, too, Deb. *Please don't cry.*"

I had always sworn that I would never try to make Reeve feel guilty about anything, but now that my back was to the wall, I played that card for all that it was worth.

"If anything should happen to you, then I wouldn't want to live," I said.

The tears were still rolling down my face.

He looked positively anguished.

"I don't want anything to happen to *you*, Deb," he said. "Don't you see that?"

I sniffled. "I see it very clearly. I see that you still blame yourself for your mother's death and that you are afraid that by marrying me you have made me a target for Robert and therefore may be responsible for my death."

He was white around his mouth and nose. He stared at me out of haunted eyes and said nothing.

"You were fifteen years old when you overturned the coach that killed your mother, and the only person who blamed you for what happened was your father," I said. "Even Lord Bradford told me today that it was just a tragic accident and that he always thought that your mother must have been insane to allow you to take the reins."

He wet his lips as if he were going to say something, but I swept on.

"You have to put the accident behind you, Reeve. You can't continue to let it dictate what you do with your life. It wasn't your fault! The way your father treated you after the accident was disgraceful. Everyone thinks so."

He shook his head in disagreement.

"It's true," I insisted. "And in consequence, he made you feel so guilt-ridden and fearful of harming someone you love that you are ready to do something as drastic as making away with yourself, just to ensure my supposed safety."

A spark of anger had come back to Reeve's stricken eyes. "I am glad to know that you understand me so well," he said with an attempt at sarcasm.

"Well, I do," I replied.

My spurious tears had stopped by now.

"I also think that you are being incredibly stupid about all of this," I said.

The anger was now more than a spark. "Get away from that door, Deb," he said. "I'm leaving."

"Has it ever occurred to you, Reeve, that I am already carrying a child?" I asked.

His chin jerked infinitesimally, as if he had taken a blow.

"After all, you're the one who said it only took doing it once," I reminded him.

Silence.

"That would be a nice situation for me to find myself in, wouldn't it? To find myself bearing the heir to the earldom, with no husband, and Robert on the loose?"

More silence.

"Perhaps you ought to wait a few more weeks, Reeve, to find out how things stand with me, before you try to do away with yourself again."

He stood there in the middle of the floor, his long legs slightly spread, his wrinkled coat and shirt clinging to his strong body. His eyes were black with some emotion, but I did not know what it was.

I figured I had given him enough to think about for a while.

"You can call for Hummond now," I said. "I'm going downstairs to take a walk in the garden with Mama."

When I got back downstairs, however, it was to find that Charlotte and Richard had come to pay a visit. I sent a footman upstairs to tell Reeve that we had guests, and he joined us twenty minutes later, his dress immaculate, his neckcloth perfect, his face unreadable.

The four of us walked in the garden, and Richard told us what he had discovered of my uncle's perfidy.

For the eighteen years that John Woodly had been in charge of the Lynly estate, he had systematically embezzled money from it to line his own pockets.

"I feel like such a fool," Richard confided sheepishly. "It was just that Uncle John had taken care of the estate books ever since I was a small child and somehow it didn't seem . . . polite . . . to ask him any questions."

Charlotte patted his arm comfortingly. "It's not your fault, Richard."

I looked at her attractive, sharp-angled face and wide green eyes, and thought that I liked her very much.

"Did he do serious damage to the estate?" Reeve asked.

Richard sighed. "It will take me a few years to recoup from what he has stolen, but the damage is not irreparable. Fortunately, Charlotte's father has been very understanding. He is going to advance me the money I need immediately to pay the most recent bills that Uncle John ran up."

"What a thoroughgoing scoundrel the man is," Reeve growled. "When I think of how he left Deb and her mother to struggle for all those years!"

"I know." Richard turned to me, his face very grave. "That is the worst part of this whole nightmare, Deborah. The wrong that was done to you."

I sighed and repeated Charlotte's words, "It was not your fault, Richard."

We had come to a stop in front of the fountain, and my brother stood in front of the bronze cherubs, looking down at me, with the sun glinting off his light brown hair and the brass buttons of his riding coat. He said, "Did Reeve tell you that I am prepared to make an annuity to your mother?"

"Yes, he did." I looked directly back into his clear hazel eyes. "Can you afford it, Richard?"

He returned grimly, "I consider it my first priority. She was my father's wife, after all. And I myself have very happy memories of her from my childhood. She was so pretty and so much fun. I never knew my own mother, and I loved yours very much." His eyes were sad. "I missed her dreadfully when she left. I missed you, too, Deborah. I lost my father, my stepmother, and my little sister all at once." His well-cut lips tightened. "It was not an easy time."

I had never thought of how it might have been for him. Difficult as our life had been, I had had Mama. Poor Richard had been left with Uncle John.

Impulsively I reached up and kissed his cheek. "Well now that we have found each other, let's not lose each other again."

He gave me a wistful smile. "I would like that."

Reeve said, in that gruff voice men use when they are embarrassed to express sentiment, "If you run into any further problems, remember that you have a brother-in-law who will always be willing to help."

"Thank you, Reeve," Richard said in the same gruff tone that Reeve had used.

Charlotte and I exchanged tender, amused glances that said, *Men.*

There was the sound of feet crunching on the gravel, and we turned to see Harry approaching us from the house. He said that he had been sent to tell us that tea was being served in the morning room. As we walked back to the house, Reeve and Richard went first, deep in conversation with each other. Charlotte walked on Richard's other side and Harry fell into step next to me.

"Did you talk to him?" he asked in a low voice, his eyes on Reeve's broad back.

"Yes."

"And?"

I sighed. "I don't think he will try to do away with himself again, Harry. At least not for a while. But we simply must do something about Robert!"

"I know," Harry said gloomily. "But what? He hasn't committed a crime."

I felt like screaming. "But he's dangerous. We all know he's dangerous."

"I agree. But you can't arrest a man because you think he's dangerous, Deborah. He has to *do* something."

"He tried to rape me!"

"Do you really want to drag Robert into court and accuse him of that? Can you imagine what that would do to the family name?"

"The hell with the family name," I hissed, trying to keep my voice low enough so that I would not be overheard by the group in front of me.

"Be realistic, Deborah," Harry exhorted me. "Can you imagine Reeve allowing you to stand up in court and tell the world what had happened?"

I thought about it. "No," I said glumly.

Harry took my arm and slowed our pace so that Richard, Reeve, and Charlotte got farther ahead of us on the path. He said in a low voice, "Deborah, I have been thinking that perhaps you and Reeve ought to skip the summer fair and go directly home to Ambersley. The opportunities for exposure for the both of you at such an event are far too great for safety."

I have to confess that I had been worrying about the summer fair also. I just knew that Reeve would insist in taking part in the horse race, and perhaps the boat race as well. Hearing Harry voice my concerns out loud made them seem all the more valid.

"Perhaps you are right," I said.

"Talk to Reeve and see if you can get him to agree to leave Wakefield immediately," Harry urged.

I made up my mind. "All right," I said. "I will."

Richard and Charlotte went home after tea, and Reeve and Harry took guns out to try for some wood pigeons. While I hated to let Reeve out of my sight, I reasoned that he would be safe as long as he was with someone else, and I knew I could rely on Harry not to let him out of his sight.

While they were gone, I sought out Lord Bradford. I eventually found him in the kitchen garden with Mama.

They were discussing some of the herbs that Mama had grown at home that she thought Lord Bradford might like to try in his garden here at Wakefield.

Hah, I thought cynically. *As if Lord Bradford really cares about herbs.*

It occurred to me that another advantage of leaving Wakefield before the summer fair would be that I'd get my mother away from Lord Bradford.

I came up to the two of them with my sweetest smile and told them about Harry's recommendation. "I have to confess that I think it is a good idea myself," I said. "Robert has every reason to be in the vicinity of Wakefield but no reason to be at Ambersley. We will be far safer there than we are here."

Mama said immediately, "Of course you are right, darling. I shall be ready to leave whenever you wish."

There was a frown on Lord Bradford's face. "I

wonder if you would consider remaining for a few more days, Elizabeth," he said mildly. "I very much fear that the local ladies will be dreadfully disappointed if neither you nor Deborah are able to attend the fair."

Mama's cheeks got very pink. She looked like a girl, with her feathery curls and her soft muslin dress. "I don't know if that would be proper, Bernard."

"The Nortons are still here," Lord Bradford pointed out gently. "And we are related now as well. It will be perfectly proper, I assure you. And after the fair is over, I will escort you home in my own chaise."

Mama shot me a worried look.

My face felt frozen. "It is up to you, Mama," I said. "You know that you are welcome to accompany me and Reeve back to Ambersley. In fact, we had assumed that you would do so."

Mama's eyes went back to Lord Bradford's face. "I do feel that Bernard is right when he says that the village ladies will be very upset if neither of us attends the fair. We have been working on it with them for several weeks now."

She was going to stay.

I couldn't believe it.

"You must do what you think is best, Mama," I said, my voice very grim.

Lord Bradford gave me a long, measuring look.

Mama said nervously, "You don't mind, darling?"

"Of course I don't mind."

I wanted to pick up one of the tomatoes that were growing nearby and squash it into Lord Bradford's face.

"Very well then." She turned to the powerfully

built man who was standing beside her. "I will accept your invitation, Bernard, and remain for the fair."

He inclined his head. "I am very glad, Elizabeth. It will be my pleasure to have you as my continued guest."

I turned on my heel and left.

This whole business of Mama and Lord Bradford made me feel sick as a horse.

Dinner was rather a quiet affair. I had caught both Harry and Lord Bradford and my mother before we went into the dining room and told them to say nothing about our going back to Ambersley as I hadn't yet had a chance to talk to Reeve. I planned to wait until I had him in bed before I broached the subject.

I had a feeling that he would consider leaving Wakefield running away and that he wouldn't like it. On the other hand, he would want to protect me.

Another card I meant to play for all it was worth.

Really, I hadn't known I had all of these Machiavellian tendencies. Poor Reeve. He hadn't known what he was getting into when he married me.

It was very late when he finally came upstairs. He and Harry and Edmund had been playing billiards and when I heard the slight slur in his voice as he said good night to Hummond, I realized that they must have been at the wine bottle as well.

He came into the bedroom from the dressing room, a candle in his hand. He stopped in surprise when he saw that I still had the bedside lamp on.

"What are you doing still awake?" he said. His voice was definitely slurred. "It's after one."

"I've been waiting for you," I said, echoing the words I had said to him earlier in the day when we had last confronted each other in this room.

He sighed. "I don't think I'm up to much tonight, Deb. Had a bit too much to drink, you see."

I nodded and watched as he made his way toward the bed.

"I wanted to talk to you," I said.

He groaned. "Can't it wait until tomorrow?"

"I think we should go home tomorrow, Reeve," I said. "I don't want to wait for the summer fair. I want to go back to Ambersley tomorrow."

He untied the silk belt of his dressing gown and let it fall on the floor. The lamp outlined his perfect body with soft yellow light. He swung his legs into the bed beside me and pulled the soft wool blanket up to his waist.

"I thought you were committed to this bloody fair."

"The fair will go off perfectly well without me. And it will go off perfectly well without you, too. We are not the neighborhood gentry around here; we're only visitors. Let Bernard and Harry and the Nortons bear the local standard."

He was frowning, as if he were trying to think clearly.

"But why do you want to go home?" he asked.

"I'm afraid of Robert," I said simply. "When I think of being out in the midst of all those people . . ." I shivered. "I suppose I should feel that there is safety in numbers, but for some reason, I don't. I just feel . . . vulnerable, Reeve. I don't want to go to the fair. It may be silly of me, but I can't help it. I'm afraid."

"Then we won't go," he said immediately. "If that's how you feel, we won't go."

"Thank you," I whispered.

"When do you want to leave? Tomorrow?"

"Could we?"

"I suppose so. Bernard won't be happy about our missing the fair, but that can't be helped." He yawned.

Now we were getting onto tricky ground.

I said tentatively, "I did talk to Mama about leaving."

"Mmmm?" He was sounding very sleepy.

"She felt she ought to stay for the fair so that the local people weren't completely deserted. So she mentioned our plan to Lord Bradford, and it was all right with him."

He yawned again. "What was all right with him?"

The wine was definitely fogging Reeve's brain. He was not usually this dense. I explained carefully, "It was all right that we leave and that Mama remain for the fair. He said that he would escort her back to Ambersley himself after the fair is over."

Reeve rubbed the top of his head. His eyes looked very heavy. "Deb, is it all right if I turn out the lamp?" he said.

"Yes."

He reached over to extinguish the lamp, and darkness descended on the room. I heard him turn over onto his side, the way he liked to sleep.

I thought with a mixture of pain and pity that he had probably gotten himself drunk so that he would have an excuse not to have to sleep with me. He probably was afraid he might get me with child, and he wouldn't want to do that while the situation with Robert was still so dangerously unresolved.

I really did understand his mind very well.

The problem was: How did I go about changing it?

CHAPTER
twenty

A STORM BLEW IN OVERNIGHT FROM THE CHANnel and when we awoke the following morning it was to low-hanging gray skies and strong, gusting winds.

I would have loved to stay in bed with Reeve, but he was up and gone by the time I awoke.

He was going to give me problems, I knew it.

Susan was waiting to help me get dressed, and she said that Lord Cambridge had told her to delay packing, that we would not be leaving until after we saw what was going to happen with the storm. When I got downstairs I inquired after Reeve, and a footman told me that he had gone out with Harry to visit one of Lord Bradford's tenants, who had lodged a complaint about a neighbor's grazing his sheep on his fields.

I decided I would go to the morning room to get some breakfast, but before I sat down at the table, I stepped outside to the terrace to view the sky.

It was truly magnificent, with angry gray clouds racing along its vast expanse at a tremendous pace. The wind was whipping through the garden, but I was standing close to the house, sheltered by the French doors behind me and the tall yew bush on my right side, and the wind only rippled my skirt. The scent of the sea was strong in my nostrils, and I could smell the coming rain.

I never meant to eavesdrop. I realized too late that I was hidden from the occupants of the morning room by the drapes that were drawn across the French doors, but that I could hear what was being said because I had left the door slightly ajar when I had come out onto the terrace.

This was how I came to overhear a conversation that had never been intended for my ears.

At first the sound of voices within meant nothing to me. I just thought it was people having breakfast and that there was no reason for me to make my presence immediately known. I was enjoying the fresh air and the feeling of the coming storm. I have always liked wild weather.

It was when I heard Lord Bradford say, "You are so extraordinarily sensitive to people's feelings, Elizabeth, that I know you must have recognized how dearly I have come to love you," that I realized what was actually going on inside the room behind me.

I froze in my spot next to the yew bush. This was what I had feared all along. Lord Bradford was trying to steal my mother.

Mama said in a shaking voice, "Don't, Bernard. Please don't say it."

She is going to refuse him, I thought in relief.

It wasn't until that moment that I realized how afraid I had been that Mama's feelings had been engaged as well as Lord Bradford's.

"But I must say it," he was going on. "I love you, and I want to share the rest of my life with you. Will you marry me, Elizabeth?"

Mama's voice was even more shaky than it had

been before as she answered him, "I can't, Bernard. I can't."

I smiled.

"Why not?" he asked. His voice was very gentle. "Not only can I offer you love, but I can also offer you a home of your own, a place where you will be valued as you ought to be."

She has a home, I thought indignantly. *She doesn't need you to give her one.*

"Please," Mama begged. "Don't."

I value her, I thought, becoming more and more enraged as I thought about what Lord Bradford had just said. *No one can possibly value my mother more than I do!*

"I had hoped that you might be coming to care for me as well," he said a little sadly.

"Oh, Bernard, I do care for you," Mama said. "But I can't marry you. I can't marry anyone. Not ever."

There was no mistaking the anguished tone in her voice. I frowned.

"Is it Deborah?" Lord Bradford asked. "I know she's jealous of my feelings for you, but she'll get over it."

Jealous? The nerve of the man.

"No," Mama said. "It isn't Deborah. Deborah would never stand in the way of my happiness."

I felt a twinge of guilt.

"I can't say anything more," Mama was going on. "You must just believe me when I tell you that I cannot marry you."

By now the wind was whipping my skirts, even here in the shelter of the yew bush.

Lord Bradford repeated, "Not me or anyone else?"

"That is right."

A branch came skudding across the stones of the patio, its green leaves ripping away in the fiercely gusting wind.

"Well, you are going to have to tell me, Elizabeth," Lord Bradford said. He sounded utterly determined.

"I can't." Mama sounded desperate.

"Listen to me, my heart." I couldn't believe that Lord Bradford was capable of sounding so tender. "Whatever it is, we can resolve it together. But you must tell me."

Mama sobbed.

My fists clenched until my nails dug into my palms.

"I just cannot be a wife, Bernard. I cannot . . . bear . . . it. To be touched. I cannot . . ."

She was crying hard by now.

I wanted to rush to her and take her in my arms.

The wind was rattling the yew bush so loudly now that I had to strain to hear what was being said in the morning room.

Lord Bradford's voice was incredibly gentle. "What happened, Elizabeth, to make you feel this way?"

Muffled sobs. It sounded as if her face were pressed against something. I thought it was probably Lord Bradford's shoulder.

"Was it your husband?"

My heart pounded. *My father? Did my father do something dreadful to her?*

"No, it was not Edward." Mama's voice was only a whisper. I sidled closer to the open door so I could hear it. "It happened when I was still a governess. He . . . he came to my room one night. He forced his way inside. He said that if I ever told anyone, I would be turned away without a reference. He . . . oh, God, he hurt me so much, Bernard. I was so afraid."

I stood like a statue. I couldn't believe what I was hearing.

Lord Bradford said in a truly terrible voice, "Was it John Woodly, Elizabeth?"

My hands moved to my mouth, as if to stop the scream that was on the verge of coming out.

After a long silence, Mama whispered, "Yes, it was."

The wind was still increasing. A few strands of hair had pulled loose from my ribbon and were flying around my face.

"What a shame that he has disappeared," Lord Bradford said in a voice that sent shivers up my spine. "I would very much like to put a bullet in him."

For the first time ever, I found myself actually liking Lord Bradford.

Mama went on, "Shortly after it happened, Edward asked me to marry him." She was not crying as hard now. "I never told him what his brother had done to me."

"Why didn't you?" Lord Bradford asked grimly. "A monster like that didn't deserve to be protected."

"John would have denied it, of course, and I didn't know whom Edward would believe. I was just so grateful that I would have a husband, that I would never again find myself the prey of a man like John. But then, on my wedding night . . . oh God, it all came back."

Mama sobbed again.

"I wouldn't put you through that, Bernard. It could

not have been pleasant for Edward, being married to a woman who could scarcely tolerate his embrace. I tried. Truly, I tried. But every time he touched me . . ." She began to sob harder.

"Don't cry like this, my heart," Lord Bradford said. "Please don't cry."

"I . . . I am trying . . . to compose myself," Mama said.

After a minute, Lord Bradford asked quietly, "What did you tell Lynly to explain your repulsion?"

"I told him that I had been raped once by a former employer. He was as kind as one could expect under the circumstances, but I would never put another man into that situation, Bernard, particularly a man I loved. And that is why I won't marry you."

Silence fell within the morning room. I stood outside on the terrace, my knuckles pressed to my mouth, thinking of my poor mother and the terrible thing that had happened to her.

I thought of Robert and what he had tried to do to me. Would I have been able to respond so joyously to Reeve if I had had that kind of appalling violation stamped in my memory?

I didn't think so.

I thought of John Woodly and the way Mama had nearly fainted when we met him in Brighton. At last, I understood.

"We can work this out together, Elizabeth," I heard Lord Bradford saying persuasively. "It has been many years since that unspeakable thing happened to you. And I am a very patient man."

Mama surprised me by giving a watery chuckle. "No, Bernard," she said. "You're not."

"With you, my patience will be endless." He sounded as if he meant every word.

"I can't," Mama said. "I know it is just me. I see how my daughter looks at Reeve, and I know that physical love can be beautiful for a woman, but I've been crippled, Bernard. And I don't think I will ever get over it."

I had had no idea that my feelings for Reeve were quite that obvious.

There was another short silence from the morning room. Then I heard Lord Bradford say gravely, "Elizabeth, who is Deborah's father?"

The blood ceased to run through my body.

I don't want to hear this, I thought. I shut my eyes and all my muscles tightened in rejection. *I don't want to hear this.*

But I couldn't leave. I stood there, trapped by my own eavesdropping, incapable of moving lest I betray that I had been listening all along.

"Oh God," Mama said, "I don't know. I was married so shortly after John did that to me that I don't know, Bernard. *I honestly don't know.*"

I stood there, frozen, until my mother and Lord Bradford had left the morning room, then I ran upstairs to change into my riding clothes. All that I could think of was that I had to get away from the house. I wasn't the person I had thought I was all my life, and I couldn't face anyone until I had had a chance to try to deal on my own with what Mama had revealed.

They didn't want to give me a horse in the stable.

"There's a big storm coming, Lady Cambridge," the head groom argued with me. " 'Tis not the time to be takin' out a horse!"

For the first time in my life, I used my new position. "I don't want to argue with you, Tomkins," I said imperiously. "Bring me my horse immediately—do you hear?"

He folded his lips disapprovingly. "Yes, my lady," he mumbled, and had Mirabelle, the bay mare Reeve had brought to Wakefield for my use, saddled and brought into the stable yard.

The wind was blowing wildly by the time I mounted up and rode away from Wakefield Manor. Mirabelle snorted and jumped and sidled, fearful of the noise of the wind and of the branches that were cracking and coming down in the woods. I decided to get the both of us away from the trees and steered her along the path that would take us to the sea.

When I asked for a gallop the mare responded instantly, running flat out, as if she were trying to outrace the storm. In reality, of course, we were running into the storm, which was sweeping in off the Channel. The wind tore my hair loose from its ribbon so that it streamed out behind me as we rode, and it whipped Mirabelle's black mane and tail straight out in a similar fashion. It had not yet started to rain, but I could smell the salt in the air, and I knew that the rain would be coming shortly.

I hadn't thought at all rationally about where I was going. I only knew that I wanted to get away, and I ended up by going to the place where I had spent some of the most enjoyable moments of my stay at Wakefield Manor.

I went to Charles Island.

I realize now, of course, that this was a colossally stupid thing for me to do. I can only plead my distraught state of mind as an excuse. I was so full of my own misery that I scarcely even noticed the fact that the tide was coming in extremely quickly, with waves that were very much higher than usual. Already the sand causeway was far narrower than it ordinarily was, and the tide was not due to be at its highest for another three hours.

Mirabelle and I galloped over the strip of causeway and onto the island. The finer sand on the north side was blowing into the mare's face and I turned her west, toward the path that would take us to the rocky south shore.

The wind was throwing up salt spray from the water and was howling through the pines that formed the central part of the island. As we galloped along the narrowing beach, a particularly large wave crashed close to the shore, spitting up a cold foamy mist that sprayed Mirabelle and me. Then the wave came churning up onto the beach path, covering the mare's legs up past her fetlocks. She screamed in fright and reared high in the air. I grabbed on to her neck, but when she came down, she went the other way, arching her back and bucking high. I was totally off-balance, and, after two such bucks, I came off.

I landed on the mixture of sand, gravel, and shells that formed the beach path on this part of the island, and Mirabelle galloped off, back the way we had come.

There was no doubt in my mind that she was on her way home to her stall in the cozy Wakefield stables.

I picked myself up.

I was wet and cold and horseless, but in my mind all I could hear was Lord Bradford's voice saying over and over and over: *Who is Deborah's father, Elizabeth? Who is Deborah's father?*

Even worse came the constant repetition of Mama's reply: *I don't know. I don't know. I don't know.*

What if John Woodly were my father? How could I face the rest of my life, knowing that I was the daughter of a monster like that? How could I be Reeve's wife? The mother of his children?

Oh God, how could I even *live?*

I trudged on, unseeing, unthinking, along the shore of the island, noticing but not noticing that the water was coming in faster and faster and that the pathway between the water and the cliffs was getting so narrow that it was scarcely a foot wide.

I hardly even noticed that I was getting wetter and wetter. The salt water on my face was mainly from my tears.

At last, at a little distance in front of me, I saw the arched entranceway of Rupert's Cave. Waves were already washing in through its opening.

For the first time, my misery lifted long enough for me to take a good look at my surroundings.

The cliffs of the south side of the island towered above me to my left. The storm-tossed water of the Channel raged to my right. And as I looked down at the narrow strip of scree upon which I stood, a wave rolled across it. The water withdrew, but within a very few minutes, the pathway would be covered as well, and I would find myself standing in the ocean.

I pushed my wildly tangled hair out of my face and drew a deep, steadying breath. The first truly rational thought I had had since hearing Mama's confession crossed my brain. *Better get out of here before I drown.*

I turned westward, to retrace my steps.

And that was when I first saw the man on foot who was coming after me.

It took me exactly two seconds to recognize the broad, powerful form of Robert.

I froze.

How could I have been so stupid?

I looked around frantically, searching for someplace I could hide. I was under no illusions about Robert's intentions in following me here.

He was out to kill me.

I looked up at the cliff above me. Could I climb it?

Not here, I couldn't. A little bit farther to the west, the cliff was less steep, but here it was a sheer wall of rock. Unfortunately, Robert was to the west of me. To the east, the cliff dropped precipitously into the sea, which crashed around it in foamy fury, making all thoughts of a climb utterly impossible.

A very large wave came rolling out of the sea up onto the tiny path upon which I stood. It struck me in the thigh with enough force to knock me against the cliff wall, then receded in a swirl of foam. Ten seconds later another, stronger wave hit me again.

I couldn't remain there. I could feel the drag of the undertow and knew that I would be pulled out to sea if I waited much longer.

Robert was still coming steadily forward. The beach near him was not yet underwater, as it was here.

With a horribly sick feeling in the pit of my stomach, I waded through the ever-deepening water toward the entrance to Rupert's Cave.

Reeve had told me that the cave had been a favorite haunt of smugglers because, even though the entrance was underwater during high tide, deep within it remained dry. It looked to me as if my only hope of surviving both the storm and Robert would be to take refuge within the depths of Rupert's Cave.

There were two serious problems with this course of action.

The first was that I wasn't at all sure if the insides of the cave would remain dry in the face of a major storm such as this one.

The second problem was that I was utterly terrified of being trapped in small, dark, enclosed spaces. I had always felt that way, ever since I was a small child.

The thought of spending hours, in the dark, in the remote recesses of a cave, made my breathing double its normal rate, clammy sweat break out all over my body, and my stomach heave. The further thought of being trapped by water coming ever nearer to me and perhaps, eventually, covering me, was enough to make me seriously consider the alternative of tackling Robert.

But it would be too easy for Robert to get away with my murder. All he would have to do would be to hit me over the head and throw me into the sea. The grooms at the stable would vouch for the fact that I had insisted upon taking Mirabelle out in the storm. There would also be the return of the riderless mare to attest to the fact that I had had some sort of mishap.

It would all look so tragic. And Reeve would inevitably think that—somehow—he was to blame for what had happened to me.

I simply couldn't let Robert get away with killing me. I had to fight to stay alive.

I waded with ever-increasing difficulty through the deepening, storm-roiled water to the entrance to Rupert's Cave. By now foam was crashing into the cliffs to the east of the cave, and large waves were rolling into the entrance of the cavern itself. I hoped I had not left it until too late, that I would still be able to get inside without being drowned.

I pressed as close to the cliff wall as I could until I had reached the cave. I entered, once again keeping close to the wall, my fingers scrabbling to get a grip on any outcrops of rock I could find.

I looked inward. The cave was pitch-dark.

I shut my eyes and said a prayer.

You can do this, Deborah, I said to myself. *You have to do this, or Robert will kill you.*

A particularly strong wave knocked me to my knees, and the cold salt water drenched my skirt even higher and trickled inside my riding boots. I kept going, deeper into the cave, deeper into the dark, following the cold, wet, rocky wall with my outspread hands.

The noise of the water at the mouth of the cave increased to a roar as I went deeper.

I strained my ears to hear the sounds of Robert following me, but all I could hear was the roar of water.

Would Robert come after me? Surely the entrance

was impassable by now. I thought that he would be far more likely to retreat to where he could climb to the safety of the clifftop. He would come for me when the tide had receded, and the cave was open once more.

Meanwhile, the water within the cavern was growing deeper and deeper. I fought down rising panic as I wound farther and farther into the cliffside. Finally, the ground beneath my feet began to rise a little and the water, which had been at the level of my thighs, began to lower: to my knees; to my ankles; until finally I reached a place where the ground was freezing cold and damp, but there was no water.

The only problem with this "safe" area was that the ceiling of the cave was quite low, so low that I hit my head on it as I worked my way in. I would have to sit down, with my head bent on my knees, and wait until the tide went out and the water receded from the cave.

I could see nothing.

I thought about Robert, waiting outside for me, and realized that I would have to find some kind of a weapon to use against him. But for the moment I just didn't care. The thing I was worrying about most was if I could possibly make it through the next six hours in this tiny, dark, enclosed place without going utterly and completely insane.

CHAPTER
twenty-one

THE DANK, SODDEN, AIRLESS CAVE WAS SUFFOCAT-
ing me. Even though there actually was enough air to
breathe, my terror of enclosed spaces was greater at this
point than my sense of reality.

Stay calm, Deborah.

This is what I told myself as I huddled there in the
dreadful dark.

*Stay calm. Don't panic. Just concentrate on
breathing.*

In and out, in and out, in and out. I pulled the air
into my lungs and released it, trying to maintain an even
rhythm, trying to think about nothing but the life-giving
air going in and out.

I could feel panic rising, like bile in the back of my
throat. I couldn't even sit up straight in the spot where I
was wedged. I couldn't see anything. No matter how
hard I strained my eyes, they met only blackness.

I felt as if I were being buried alive, waiting in the
dark for the dirt to cover my face and smother me completely.

If I let the panic get the upper hand, I would surely
go mad.

*Occupy your mind with something else. God knows,
you have enough to think about.*

I was soaking wet and freezing cold, and the dripping stone walls of the cave were cutting into my back. My teeth were chattering already. What kind of condition would I be in in six hours?

Think about the enemy, I told myself. *Think about Robert and what you have to do next.*

I clasped my arms around my knees, buried my face in my wet, salty skirt, and forced myself to imagine what would likely be happening outside this horrible cave once I was missed at Wakefield.

They would institute a search for me, I thought. They would see the sand on Mirabelle's legs, the salt on her bay coat, and they would know that I had been on the beach. Reeve would come out to the island to look for me.

If he could get across the causeway in the storm. It was probably underwater by now.

I thought about the huge waves I had seen out on the Channel and knew that there would be no chance of him taking a boat out of Fair Haven either.

I could hear the sea roaring through the cave. The tide was continuing to rise, and it might yet reach my hiding place. I was still far from safe.

The thought of drowning almost panicked me into trying to force my way out of the cave. It seemed to me that nothing could be worse than to be trapped and suffocated, like a rat in a hole.

I would rather face a fatal blow from Robert any day than die like that.

It was only the realization that I would most assuredly drown if I tried to get out through the now-flooded cave that kept me in my place.

Oh God, oh God, oh God, I thought. *Give me strength, dear Lord. Help me to get through the next few hours.*

Second by interminable second, the hours crawled by. The water in the cave continued to edge forward until it finally reached the very tips of my feet. I couldn't see it, of course, but I could hear it lapping, and occasionally I would crawl a little forward to feel for it with my fingers.

I was cold through to my bones, and I struggled desperately not to think about what would happen if the water should eventually fill the entire cave.

When the flow finally reached my feet, it stopped and didn't come any closer.

When I realized that the tide must have reached its height and I would not die horribly, trapped alone in this monstrous cave, I burst into hysterical sobbing. It was quite a while before the extreme discomfort of my physical condition overcame my emotion and brought my mind back to my still-dire present situation.

I was so cold that I didn't think I would ever be warm again. My skirt was soaked, and my feet were wet and freezing inside my boots. My light wool jacket was wet as well, but it wasn't soaked through and consequently was the only piece of clothing I wore that afforded me any protection at all against the bone-deep chill of the cave.

The panic about closed-in places was still there, hovering in my stomach and chest, like a beast ready to pounce.

I fought it. Again and again, I wrenched my mind

back to my problems. I thought about Mama. I thought about the infamous thing that had happened to her, and the terrible way it had affected her life.

She had said that she was a cripple.

My mother. My beautiful, wonderful, loving mother. That man had done that to her.

That man—who might be my father.

But he might not be, either. I held on to that thought with a desperate kind of hope. Mama had said that she did not know which of the brothers had fathered me. It could have been Edward and not John.

It could have been.

But maybe it wasn't.

How could I face the world knowing I had the blood of a man like John Woodly running in my veins?

If Mama truly suspected that I was his child, how could she have loved me the way that she did?

For that, at least, I never doubted. My mother loved me, had always loved me, would always love me.

If Mama could love me, thinking that perhaps I was the child of John Woodly, then perhaps I could . . .

My mind shied away from the thought. I could not accept it. I wasn't ready to accept it. Not now. Perhaps not ever.

I remembered Mama's face when she had come to my rescue the time Robert had tried to rape me. What horrendous memories that sight must have brought back to her.

Water dripped down the side of the cave onto my head and trickled down my neck beneath my jacket. I shivered and shivered.

I remembered how excited I had been about my

first view of the sea. I thought now that if I never saw the sea again for as long as I lived, I would be perfectly content.

I rocked forward onto my knees and reached out in the dark to feel for the inch-deep pool of water that had been lying near my feet. I had been checking that pool of water for what seemed like ages, and this time all my fingers encountered was the wet floor of the cave. I crept carefully forward on my hands and knees until my fingers once again encountered a puddle of cold salt water.

At last, at last, at last, the tide was starting to go out.

The time had come to think seriously about what I was going to do about Robert.

I had recognized long before this that he had me trapped. All he had to do was wait at the entrance of the cave and he would have me at his mercy when I followed the receding tide out.

With great reluctance, I came to the bitter conclusion that, desperately as I needed to get out of this cave, it would be impossible for me to surrender to that need without giving Robert all the advantage. As I had learned before, he was much stronger than I, and if it should come to a physical struggle between the two of us, I was the one bound to be the loser.

My only hope of surviving would be to use this hateful cave to my advantage, to lure Robert inside, where it was dark, and he could not see me.

Then, perhaps, I could be the one to prey upon him.

I would need a weapon, I thought. When the tide receded a little farther, I would see if I could find something to use against him.

*   *   *

I waited for what seemed like forever, and then I began to follow the cave floor down the incline that had saved my life. Water sounded everywhere inside the cavern: dripping from the ceiling, running down the walls, continuing to roar in the entrance. I slipped several times as I made my way along in the pitch-dark, and one time I felt as if I had cut my knee on something sharp when I landed. I reached down with my fingers, searching for the sharp edge, wondering if perhaps it might be something I could use as a weapon.

Finally I touched it. It was stuck into the packed sand and gravel of the cavern floor, and I dug around it trying to free it. Finally it came loose and I realized that I was holding a large shell in my hands. Its edge was sharp enough, but unfortunately it was too fragile to be used as a weapon.

I tossed it aside and continued on, using the wall as my guide through the inky darkness.

The fact that I could stand upright in this part of the cave helped my feelings of confinement immeasurably.

A few moments later, I heard water splash around the ankles of my boots. I had reached the edge of the receding tide and would have to wait until it went out some more.

I bent down and felt around the cave's bed, looking for a good-sized rock.

It took me a while to locate what I wanted. The stone my fingers finally closed around was large enough for me to lift and maneuver yet heavy enough to render a man unconscious if it was wielded properly.

I thought bravely that if Mama could knock Robert

out with a crystal vase, this rock would most certainly do the job.

My biggest problem, of course, was: *How was I to get at him?*

The ideal situation would be for me to stand along the cave's wall, cloaked in darkness, and wait for Robert to follow the central channel past me. Then I could step forward when he was just past me, crack him on the head with the rock, and run for safety.

This, in fact, had been my plan, but the more I thought about it the more I saw that it had a number of problems. The chief one was that while Robert wouldn't be able to see me hiding against the wall, neither would I be able to see Robert. It would be just my luck to end up hitting him on the shoulder, or missing him completely, and then I would be in very deep trouble indeed.

There had to be some way to make him vulnerable.

Could I try to slip past him in the dark? The cave was so noisy with the sound of water, that perhaps I might be able to do that.

Of course, when the entrance finally cleared, the roaring would die away. The only sounds that would be left then would be the more muted noise of dripping. Moreover, the ground underfoot was uneven and it was impossible to get over it without stumbling and slipping.

He would hear me.

On the other hand, I would hear him, too.

If I could not rely on my sense of sight to pinpoint Robert's position, my sense of sound would have to do. I didn't see that I had any other choice.

Clutching the rock in my icy hand, I made my way to the freezing wall, which still had water running down it, and pressed up against it, making myself as small as possible and trying not to shiver too uncontrollably.

I waited.

The roaring of the water in the entrance became quieter and quieter, softening into the sound of waves breaking normally. The opening to the cave had to be clearing.

How much longer until Robert came in?

He couldn't afford to wait any longer than necessary, I told myself. He had to get this done and be out of the way himself before Reeve got to the island to rescue me.

I strained my ears to listen.

Then, at last, I heard it. The sound of feet scrabbling on the sand and pebbles and rock that made up the cave floor.

I listened intently and finally I realized that there was another sound too, a sound I had not expected to hear. I frowned, trying to decipher what it was that I was hearing.

I had a feeling that it was very very important.

I pressed my back against the wall of the cave, and listened hard. What could it be?

Slowly, steadily, the steps came on.

What? I thought. *What?*

Then I realized. It wasn't what I was hearing that was alarming me, it was what I wasn't hearing.

There wasn't any splashing.

My plan had been that Robert would come up the central channel of the cave and that I would pounce on him from the side. But if Robert were coming up the center of the cave I would hear the sound of his feet splashing in the small stream of water that was still running out of the cave down the middle of its floor.

Stupid, I thought. *Stupid. Stupid. Stupid. You used the wall to guide yourself in the dark. Why shouldn't Robert?*

Now I had to get away from the wall and into the central channel myself without his hearing me.

I took one tiny little step away from the wall. The crunching sound made by my feet sounded as loud as a gunshot to my petrified ears.

I stopped, but there was no unusual sound from Robert. His own steps came steadily on.

The noise made by his own footfalls would drown out mine, I told myself firmly. And slowly, carefully, resolutely, I moved away from the wall and into the running water that formed the central channel of the cave.

Because of the rut worn by the running stream of water, the central floor of the cavern was lower than the floor along the walls, which took away some of my advantage. But I was tall, thank God. I would have no trouble reaching Robert's head.

The trouble would be finding it.

His steps came on. My heart was hammering in my chest so loudly that I felt sure that he would be able to hear it. My fingers tightened on my rock.

Then I could hear his breathing. I concentrated intently, trying to place him in the dark. He had almost reached me. Just a few more steps . . .

I lifted the rock, rushed toward the wall and, bringing it down as hard as I could, I struck.

I knew the moment it landed that I had missed his head.

Robert grunted with surprise and pain, but he spun around and grabbed out at me. His hand tangled in my loose, salt-stiffened hair. He pulled hard, dragging my head back.

"*Deborah,*" he said, his voice sounding horribly triumphant. "*At last.*"

I still had the rock in my hand and I struck out at him again, aiming once more for his head. I got him in the face instead. I thought I could hear his nose squish. He cursed vilely, and I wrenched away from him, dropping to my hands and knees, trying to escape into the darkness. But he was after me like a shot. I felt his arms come around me from behind as he clasped me around my waist so tightly that the air was crushed right out of my body.

The both of us were sprawled in the small stream of water that ran down the middle of the cave. It was freezing.

"You and I have some unfinished business, bitch," Robert said in my ear. "And then I'll say goodbye to you forever."

I screamed and kicked and tried to free myself. There was no one there to hear my cries, but I couldn't stop myself.

He laughed. He liked it that I was so afraid.

I was lying on my stomach with Robert's weight crushing me into the ground. I had to turn my head so that my face wasn't pressed into the water.

I couldn't see a thing, but my hands were spread out over my head and I groped with my fingers in the stream bed, searching for another rock.

Robert will rape me, I thought in panic. *He'll rape me and then he'll kill me.*

Reeve, I screamed in my mind. *Help me, Reeve.*

But Reeve was trapped on the mainland, and the only person who could help me now was myself. My mother wasn't going to come running to my rescue this time.

My God, my God, my God. Was I going to die here in this horrible cave?

I won't, I thought. *I won't.*

I got my knees up under me a little and bucked as hard as I could, trying to throw him off me. His hands moved up from my waist to my breasts and pinched. The pain made me lose my breath again. He had pressed himself against my thigh and I was horrified to feel that he had an erection.

I screamed again and thrashed under him, trying to break free.

"You'll hang for this, Robert," I yelled. "Even your father knows you for the monster that you are."

"The only thing I regret is the dark," he panted. "I wanted to see your face as I slammed into you."

At that moment, my hand connected with another rock.

I grasped it in my fingers and struggled to turn over, so that I would be facing him.

He laughed again, a chilling, inhuman sound. "You're only making it worse for yourself by struggling this way, Deborah. Relax and enjoy it."

I reached up with the hand that was not holding the rock to feel for his face. I didn't want to miss my aim this time.

He grabbed my hand and stretched it over my head, the way he had the last time he had tried to rape me. Before he could locate my other hand in the dark, I struck.

I brought the rock down as hard as I could onto the place where I hoped his temple was. This time I connected with bone, not flesh, and I thought I felt something giving way beneath the weight of my blow. He didn't make a sound, but fell across my body, where he lay, as still as the stone I still clutched in my hand.

I crawled out from underneath him, crying hysterically. I dragged myself to the wall and leaned against it because my legs refused to hold me up. I don't know how long I huddled there, shaking and weeping. Finally I pulled myself together enough to realize that I had better not wait around for too long in case Robert regained consciousness.

My knees were trembling so badly that I could scarcely walk, and my joints were so stiff with cold that they would hardly bend, but I managed to feel my way along the wall of the cave, heading back toward the entrance. At last, far in the distance, I saw the first faint glow of light.

It seemed as if I had been buried in this horrible place for centuries, and I hurried forward, longing with every fiber of my being to step out into the clean light of day.

The entrance to the cave was completely clear of water when I reached it, and the sun actually broke out as I exited onto the rough beach. I looked up to the blessed sky and saw that it was still full of clouds, but that patches of blue were blowing in from the south. The storm was apparently over.

I leaned against the cliff wall and drank in the scene before me. Never again would I take for granted the gift of light.

At last I took stock of my own situation.

There was blood on my jacket, but when I opened it to check myself, I could see no injuries.

Then I remembered how I had hit Robert in the nose. The blood was probably his.

Good, I thought. *I hope it's broken.*

I pulled up my skirt and took a look at my knees. They were a sorry sight, but all the cuts would heal. The same with my hands, which were slashed in a number of places from my searching in the cave bed for rocks.

I drew a long, shaky breath. It could have been so much worse.

The thing to do now, I thought, was to get back around the island to the causeway. As soon as it was open, I would make my way to Fair Haven and have someone drive me home. That is, if Reeve didn't get to me first.

I didn't even make it all the way to the south side of the island before I saw two horses cantering toward me along the beach path.

"Deb!" Reeve's frantic shout was as clear as if he were standing next to me. His was the first horse, and he came tearing up the beach toward me, his horse in full gallop. I leaned against the cliff wall and waited for him.

In less than a minute, he had reached me, was out of the saddle, and had me clasped tightly in his arms. I buried my face in his shoulder and began to cry.

"You're freezing," he said, and, still holding me, he

managed to shrug out of his riding jacket and put it around my shoulders.

I cried harder.

"Are you all right?" I could hear the effort he was making to keep his voice calm. "Don't cry, Deb. Can you tell me what happened?"

I couldn't. I couldn't talk. All I could do was cry.

"All right, love. All right," he said, still in the same determinedly calm voice. "We'll get you home and dry, and you can tell us when you are feeling better."

I realized then that Robert was still lying in the cave.

"Robert," I gulped. "Robert tried to kill me, Reeve. I hit him over the head. He's in Rupert's Cave. I hit him and I ran away. He's still there."

"Robert," said a weary, disgusted voice that I recognized as belonging to Harry.

Reeve's arms tightened painfully. "Did he hurt you, Deb?"

"N . . . n . . . no," I sobbed.

I couldn't say any more. I couldn't speak yet of my ordeal in that cave. All I could do was press myself into Reeve's warmth and cry.

Harry said, "Put her up on my horse and get her home, Reeve. You can send my father and some extra horses back here for me. In the meanwhile, I'll go and look for Robert."

Reeve said to me gently, "Can you ride by yourself, Deb, or do you want to ride with me?"

I tried very hard to pull myself together. "I can ride by myself," I said.

Harry dismounted, and Reeve lifted me up onto his

horse. I was so stiff with cold that at first I didn't think I would be able to stay on, but Reeve took my reins in his hand and told me to hold on to the front of the saddle.

There were still several feet of water on the causeway as the horses waded across it, but the wild waves that had whipped it six hours earlier were considerably calmer. I held on to the saddle, and shivered and cried the whole way back to Wakefield.

We rode right up to the front door of the manor, and Reeve lifted me out of the saddle. Mama came running out onto the front steps.

"Deborah!" she cried. "Thank God!"

It was terrible, I knew, but I couldn't face her.

"Please, Reeve," I murmured. "I just want to go upstairs to bed."

He gave me a very worried look, but said, "All right, Deb. Whatever you want."

He put his arm around me to help me, and I leaned gratefully against him as we mounted the stairs together.

"She's all right, Mrs. Woodly," I heard Reeve assuring Mama. "She was caught in Rupert's Cave by the tide, and she needs to warm up. I'm going to take her upstairs to bed and cover her with blankets. Perhaps you could have some hot soup sent up?" His voice was quiet as he addressed Mama. "And tell Bernard to get out to Charles Island as fast as he can. I brought Deb home on Harry's horse, so he needs to bring a horse for Harry. And one for Robert, too."

"Robert? Robert was out on Charles Island with Deborah?" Mama said. "Dear God. Is it true that you're all right, darling?"

"Y . . . yes," I said, and started to cry again.

"Do you want me to help you with her, Reeve?" Mama said.

He must have felt me shake my head, because he said, "No, Mrs. Woodly. She'll be fine with me." We entered the house, and he began to walk me toward the stairs.

As we passed Mama I refused to look at her. I just couldn't bear to.

At the first stair, I stumbled, and Reeve startled me by swinging me up into his arms. I put my own arms around his neck and let my forehead rest gratefully on his shoulder. He carried me all the way up to our bedroom.

"*Susan,*" he roared as we came into the room.

My maid must have been lurking at the dressing-room door, for she opened it immediately. "Yes, my lord?"

"Get me the warmest robe her ladyship owns. Then get hot bricks for the bed. And check in the kitchen to make sure they are going to send up some hot soup."

"Yes, my lord."

Reeve began to strip my sodden clothes off me himself and when Susan came into the room with my robe, he took it from her and made an impatient gesture for her to be gone. Once he had my clothes off, he held up the robe for me to put on, his eyes scanning me quickly before he covered me up again and tied my sash so that the warm robe was snug around my shivering body.

"Your knees and your hands are all cut," he said.

"They'll be all right," I quavered.

"Deb." His dark eyes met and held mine. "What happened?"

We were standing at the bottom of the bed, facing each other. I met his eyes, thought of what I had to tell him, and shivered even harder.

Someone knocked on the door. It was Mama with the soup.

"Reeve," I whispered to him urgently. "Please don't let anybody in. I only want you."

He looked at me in silence, then he leaned forward and, in a grave and oddly formal gesture, as if he was sealing a pact, kissed me on the forehead.

"All right, Deb," he said. "Just the two of us."

I managed to give him a shaky smile of gratitude.

He took the soup from Mama and gently sent her away. When Susan came with the hot bricks, he put them in the bed, and, after I had finished the soup, he made me get under the covers. Then, when I still could not stop shivering, he took off his boots, got in next to me himself, and held me.

And then, at last, when the shivering had finally stopped, and I was lying quietly in his arms, he asked me the question I most dreaded having to answer.

"Deb, why in the name of God did you go out in that storm?"

"It's a long story," I said in a very small voice.

"I'm not going anywhere," he replied a little grimly.

And so, of course, I had to tell him.

CHAPTER
twenty-two

I PULLED BACK FROM REEVE'S ARMS BEFORE I TOLD
him about what I had learned John Woodly had done to
Mama. I didn't deserve to be there until he knew the
whole truth about me.

He was horrified, of course. "Do you mean that
monster actually *raped* your mother?"

"Yes." I rubbed my eyes. "That is why she acted so
strangely that time we met him in Brighton."

Reeve said in a hard, angry voice, "It's also why he
thought he could get away with cheating her out of what
your father would have wanted her to have. He knew
that she would never voluntarily have anything to do
with him. He could rob her with impunity."

Your father.

Wait until Reeve heard the rest of the story.

"Yes," I agreed in a very small voice.

"Christ," said Reeve. "What a quandary for poor
Bernard. If he does truly love your mother, and it cer-
tainly sounds as if he does, then he is a victim of John
Woodly as well."

"I suppose so," I said.

We were sitting side by side in the bed, pillows
propped behind us. Reeve was still wearing his shirt and
breeches, and I was wearing only the blue-velvet robe

that had been part of my bridal clothes. I was not cold any longer, I was only very very weary.

Reeve said in bewilderment, "But Deb, I still don't understand why you felt it necessary to take a horse out in that storm. Tomkins said he told you it was dangerous but that you wouldn't listen." I could feel him looking at me. "You also knew that you were in danger from Robert if you went out alone. It isn't like you to behave recklessly like that."

"No, that's your style, isn't it?" I shot back.

He didn't reply.

I sneaked a glance at his rigid face and bit my lip. "I'm sorry, Reeve. That was mean of me."

He said with uncharacteristic patience, "Did something else happen that you're not telling me about?"

I had to tell him the whole truth. He deserved to know. And more than that, I needed him to know. This was a burden I could not carry alone, and he was the only person alive with whom I could share it.

So I told him what Bernard had asked Mama and what she had replied.

"She told him she didn't know which brother was my father, Reeve," I said wretchedly. I was staring intently at the landscape of the Downs that hung over the fireplace so that I did not have to look at Reeve's face. "She married my fa—Lord Lynly, that is—so soon after John did that horrible thing to her that she never knew for sure which man was my real father."

"Oh my God," Reeve breathed.

"It . . . upset . . . me to hear that," I went on wretchedly. "That is why I went out in the storm. I felt I had to get away from the house, away from Mama. I knew I couldn't face her and behave normally. I was just running away, I suppose. I never even thought of Robert."

A little silence fell in the room, just a few seconds of dead quiet, but it was long enough for me to begin to feel sick to my stomach at what Reeve might be thinking.

Then, "Come here to me," he commanded. I dragged my eyes away from the landscape and turned to look at him. He was holding out his arms. I flung myself into them and pressed myself against his strong, solid body. He held me close, his lips buried in my horrible, salt-stiff hair. "Listen to me," he said. "What happened in your mother's past has nothing to do with you. Nothing. Do you hear me? You are who you are. That is all that is important to me, and it is all that should be important to you as well."

How did he know exactly what words I needed to hear? I didn't know if I believed them, but I was immensely grateful to him for saying them.

"That horrible, horrible man," I wept into his shoulder. "Oh God, Reeve, how can I bear it if I carry his blood?"

"You carry his blood any way you look at it," he said in an ordinary, pragmatic voice. "If he is not your father, then he is your uncle."

I closed my eyes and listened to the steady beat of his heart. It was an immensely comforting sound. "Is that supposed to make me feel better?"

"Nothing can make you feel good about this, Deb. On the other hand, think of Richard. He is a fine person, and you share the same blood with him."

"Richard!" I cried, drawing back and staring up into

Reeve's face. "Oh God, he may not be my brother after all."

I had never thought that I would be dismayed by such a thought.

"If he's not your brother, then he is your cousin. He's your family. Family is like that, Deb. You have to take the good as well as the bad. Look at poor Bernard. He's stuck with Robert."

I nodded slowly, thinking of Robert. He was certainly as bad as, if not worse, than John Woodly.

"There's nothing wrong with Harry or Sally," I said tentatively.

"Nor with Bernard, either. And my Aunt Maria was a very nice woman," Reeve said. "Robert's evil is confined to his own wretched, violent, greedy person. As is John Woodly's."

What Reeve was saying made sense.

"What do you think makes men do things like that?" I asked him in bewilderment.

"God knows, Deb," he said wearily. He smoothed his thumbs along my cheekbones. "I certainly don't."

I gazed up into his wonderful dark eyes and said slowly, "Do you know what I am thinking, Reeve?"

He shook his head. A strand of hair fell across his brow.

"I'm thinking that the both of us have had dreadful things happen in our past."

He did not try to avert his gaze from mine.

I continued, the words coming from someplace deep inside me. "I'm thinking that we can either put them behind us and get on with our lives, or we can let them destroy us. Either way, the choice is ours."

He nodded. His face was very grave. "I think you're right," he said in a low, somber voice.

I leaned forward into his arms once more.

"What happened out there on the island today?" he asked me, as he held me close.

I told him everything. I told him about being trapped by the tide, and about my struggle with Robert.

"Christ!" he said when I had finished. "Robert has lost total control of himself."

I nodded. "Will we ever be safe from him, do you think?" I asked fearfully. "Is there anything we can do to stop him?"

He didn't reply.

"He tried to kill me, Reeve." I rubbed my cheek against his shoulder. "I would go before a magistrate and testify to that if I had to."

"That could be a little problematic," Reeve said. "Bernard is the local magistrate."

I said stubbornly, "Then I'll talk to someone else."

"Let me talk to Bernard," Reeve said. "Obviously something will have to be done."

After a few more minutes of lying clasped in each other's arms, Reeve's lips slid from my hair down to my temple. "Do you know how frightened I was when I learned that you were missing?" he asked huskily.

"I'm sorry," I said.

His lips slid along my cheek. "No matter what may have happened in the past, Deb, we have each other now. And that's what counts."

I tipped my head back to look up at him. "Do you mean that?"

"Yes," he said, and his lips moved to capture mine.

My whole body went up in flames at that blatantly sexual kiss. I had been so close to death and now here I was, safe in Reeve's arms. Suddenly I wanted him with a single, mindless, burning desire that I had never felt before.

I ripped his shirt open and covered his throat and chest with kisses. Then my hands moved lower to tug at the waistband of his breeches.

"Hold on," he grunted. "I'll do it."

He had them off in a moment, and I felt him pressed against me. He was hard as an iron rod.

My fingernails dug into his shoulders, my need was so intense.

"Reeve," I panted. "Reeve."

He pushed me back on the bed, opened my robe, and swung himself over me.

I lifted my legs to receive him.

He drove into me violently, and the sensation was searingly powerful and intense. I closed my legs around his waist and tipped my hips upward, so that he came so deep inside me that he must have been touching my womb.

He pounded into me, driving me up the bed until my head was crammed against the headboard. I held on to him desperately, feeling the life in him, the oneness with him, the defiance of death we were performing together in this wild act of creation and love.

When it was all over, we lay clasped together, our bodies pressed so close that it was hard to tell where one left off and the other began. When I finally felt him move, I opened heavy eyes to see his face bending over mine.

"You need to sleep, Deb," he said gently. "You're exhausted."

It was true. I was suddenly incredibly tired. I managed a smile. "I love you," I said.

"And I love you," he replied. He bent to place a tender kiss on my mouth. "Shall I send for Susan?"

"Later," I managed to say. And then I fell into the welcome darkness of regenerating sleep.

I dreamed that I was trapped in the cave, in the pitchy darkness, with the tide coming relentlessly in. I woke in a sweat of terror and wondered if this was a nightmare that was going to haunt me for the rest of my life.

I got out of bed painfully. I felt stiff and sore, and my knees and hands hurt from the cuts that had been inflicted by the rocks in the cave. I went over to the mantel to look at the clock and saw that it was eight o'clock. Outside my window, the summer twilight was moving in.

Moving like an old woman, I went into my dressing room and looked at myself in the pier glass. The sight was enough to make me shudder. My hair streamed around me like a witch's mane, and there were scratches on my forehead and on my cheek.

My whole body itched with dried salt.

I rang the bell for Susan. I wanted a bath, and I wanted desperately to wash my hair.

It was nine-thirty by the time I had bathed and dressed. I had Susan plait my still-wet hair in a single thick braid, which I fastened on the top of my head so that it did not get my back wet.

Then I went downstairs to face the family. I was determined to confront Lord Bradford and insist that he do something about Robert. He was simply too dangerous to be allowed to go free.

By the time I got downstairs, the men had finished with their port and the house party was gathered in the back drawing room. Mary Ann was playing the piano, and Harry was turning the pages for her. Sally and Edmund were sitting at a table in the corner, working on a jigsaw puzzle and talking together in low voices. The rest of the house party, including Reeve, were scattered around the room, ostensibly listening to Mary Ann. In truth, they all looked as if they were lost in their own thoughts.

Reeve was the first one to see me.

"Deb!" he said. He got to his feet and, coming to the door, took my arm. It was such a protective gesture that I looked at him in a little bewilderment.

Mary Ann stopped playing and swung around on her chair to look at me.

Mama said gently, "How are you feeling, darling?"

I looked at her and was almost surprised to discover that she didn't look any different than she had before I had learned the dreadful truth about her past.

"I'm fine, Mama," I said.

Then I noticed that Lord Bradford was missing.

"Reeve told us about how you got caught in Rupert's Cave by the tide, Deborah," Sally said. "What a dreadful experience. You must have been terrified, all by yourself in the dark that way."

She sounded very subdued, not at all her usual lively self. In the normal way of things, I should have thought Sally would have considered being trapped in Rupert's Cave a great adventure.

As I looked around the room I saw that Sally's solemn look was repeated on every face. Anxiously, I looked up at Reeve.

"We have had some bad news," he said to me gently. "Robert is dead."

I felt my knees buckle. "Dead?"

"Yes. Come along into the morning room with me, Deb, and I'll tell you about it."

He put his arm around my shoulders and led me away from the eyes of all of the people in the drawing room. When we reached the morning room, he made me sit down in an embroidered cabriolet chair, and he sat in the matching chair facing me.

I searched his face with strained eyes. "Did I kill him when I hit him over the head?"

He reached out and took my hand. "No. He drowned, Deb."

"Drowned?" I repeated, not understanding. "But the tide had left the cave, Reeve."

He said gently, "When Harry got to Robert he found him lying facedown in the stream of water that was emptying out of the cave. He was unconscious from the blow you had given him, you see, and so he couldn't move."

I remembered how I had turned my own face when I had fallen in the stream. It had not been deep, but if one had lain in it facedown . . .

I stared at Reeve, appalled. "Oh my God, Reeve. I didn't even think of that! I was just so frightened . . . all I wanted to do was to get away as fast as I could. I never even thought that Robert's face was in the water!"

"Of course you didn't," he replied. "After the ordeal you had been through, no one expects that you would have thought of it."

"I killed him," I said blankly. "Oh God, and it wasn't even in self-defense. When I hit him with the rock, that was self-defense. But I could have turned his head before I ran away. I could have done that."

"You couldn't even see him, Deb," Reeve said. "How could you know that his face was in the water?"

I pulled my hand away from his.

"I could have felt for him."

He shook his head decisively. "No, you couldn't. Suppose he had come around and gone for you again? You had no choice but to do as you did—which was get out of there as quickly as you possibly could."

I said doubtfully, "I suppose you're right."

"Of course I'm right. You'll see that when you think it through."

I shuddered, and said, "Robert may have been a horrible man, but it's not pleasant to know that you've killed someone, Reeve."

"Believe me, Deb, I know that," he returned.

We looked at each other.

I got up and went over to stand next to his chair. I put my arms around him and held his head against my breast.

"Yes," I said. "I see."

"It doesn't matter where the fault ultimately lies," he said bleakly. "There is always that feeling of guilt."

I held him tighter and repeated our talisman. "We have each other."

He turned toward me, put his arms around my waist

and burrowed his face between my breasts. "Thank God," he said simply. "Thank God."

Lord Bradford came home at eleven. He had been in Fair Haven, where they had brought Robert's body after they had removed it from the cave.

"He'll come home tomorrow," he said as he drank a glass of port in front of the drawing-room fire that had been lit against a surprisingly chilly summer night. "I want to bury him from Wakefield."

We all made indistinguishable murmurs of sympathy.

"What a tragedy that Robert could not make it to the back of the cave, like Deborah," Mrs. Norton said.

Lord Bradford looked utterly exhausted. "Apparently he left it until too late," he said. "The tide caught him in the middle of the cave, before he could get all the way through to safety."

I was grateful that Lord Bradford had come up with a story other than the truth to account for Robert's demise. I didn't even care if he had done it to save Robert's good name. All I cared about was that my part in Robert's untimely end was not going to be made public knowledge.

"The water was very rough," I murmured. "The sound of the waves roaring through the cavern was utterly terrifying."

Everyone was silent as they contemplated the picture of Robert caught in this maelstrom.

I stared into my teacup and decided that, no matter how unpleasant it was to realize that one has killed another human being, I was not sorry that Robert was dead. Alive, he would always be a threat to Reeve and to our future together.

He had been an evil man. I was sorry I had been the instrument of his demise, but I was not sorry that he was gone.

This honest acknowledgment of the situation made me feel a little better.

I looked up from my teacup, and my eyes fell on my mother. She was gazing at Lord Bradford with such a mixture of pain and longing on her face that it took my breath away.

She loves him, I thought. *She really does love him.*

This thought did not bring the stab of jealousy that it had always brought in the past. For it was jealousy that I had felt about Mama and Lord Bradford. Both Bernard and Reeve had seen it, if I had not.

How selfish of me to want to keep Mama only for myself, I thought. *I have Reeve now. She should have someone of her own, too.*

But John Woodly and what he had done to her stood like a malevolent monolith between Mama and love.

There had to be a way out, I thought. It simply was not right that the rest of her life should be ruined because of one act that had not been her fault.

I drank my tea, and thought, and did not hear a word of the discussion that went on around me pertaining to Robert's funeral.

At last, Mrs. Norton rose to her feet. "Time for bed, Mary Ann," she said to her daughter.

"Mama," I said, "may I see you and Bernard for a few moments alone?"

My mother's blue eyes darkened. "Why . . . I suppose so, darling." She looked at Lord Bradford. "If it is all right with you, Bernard?"

He looked so tired. "Of course, Deborah," he said with implacable courtesy. "Shall we go into the library?"

He had a footman light the library lamps, and then he gestured Mama and me to the settee that was placed in front of the fireplace.

"I hope you don't mind if I stand," he said with a wry smile. "I'm afraid that if I sit down, I might fall asleep."

Before I could bring up the subject that had been the impetus for this meeting, I had to say something else first.

"I am very sorry about Robert, Bernard," I said quietly. "I did not mean it to happen. If I had known that his face was in the water, I would have turned it."

"I believe you, Deborah," he replied. He rubbed his hands across his eyes, as if he might be rubbing away tears. Next to me, I saw Mama's hands clench in her lap.

Bernard went on steadily, "But I am glad that you did not realize it. It grieves me more than you will ever know that I must say this, but we are all better off with Robert dead."

He was right, and Mama and I knew it.

I folded my own hands in my lap and regarded them with steady concentration. I didn't quite have the courage to look at either of them as I confessed to my eavesdropping.

"I imagine that Reeve has told you what happened between Robert and me in the cave," I said.

"Yes," Bernard replied tersely.

"Did he also tell you why I was out on Charles Island in the first place?"

"No." His voice took on a little more life. "And I, for one, would like to know the answer to that question, Deborah. Your disappearance terrified your mother. It was very wrong of you to have done that to her."

I drew a deep breath, closed my fingers tightly around each other, and said, "I overheard a conversation I was not supposed to hear, and it upset me a great deal. That is why I ran away. I needed time to think before I could face Mama again."

The silence in the room was thick with tension. I could hear the clock on the wall ticking the seconds away. Finally Mama said in a constricted voice, "What conversation, Deborah?"

Still I stared at my hands. "I was standing on the terrace outside the morning room when you and Bernard were talking over breakfast, Mama. At first I didn't realize that the conversation was private, and by the time I did, I couldn't move without letting you know that I was there and had overheard."

"*Oh my God.*" Mama's voice was agonized.

"What a horrible, horrible man," I said. My voice had begun to shake. "I agree with Bernard. I would like to shoot him."

Lord Bradford stood like a statue before the fireplace and didn't say anything.

"How . . . how much did you hear?" Mama quavered.

"I heard it all," I returned. "That is why I was so upset, you see. That is why I ran away."

Mama was wringing her hands. "Oh God, Deborah. I would have given my soul to keep that information from you. I never never wanted you to know . . ."

I turned to her abruptly and flung my arms around her. "I'm all right, Mama. I talked to Reeve about the whole thing, and he helped me. I'm all right. It's you I'm worried about. It's you whose whole life has been blighted by that awful man."

I could feel her fragile frame quivering under my touch. I held her close, her feathery blond curls against my cheek, and finally I turned to look at Lord Bradford.

"You were right when you said that I was jealous of you," I said. "But I'm not anymore. I think you would be a wonderful husband to my mother."

"I can't . . ." Mama choked. "I'm afraid . . ."

I kept looking at Lord Bradford, and he looked steadily back.

"Reeve and I will leave for Ambersley right after the funeral," I said. "A few days after that, I would appreciate it if you would escort Mama home to join us." I added very deliberately, "And if it should take you several days to reach Ambersley from here, Reeve and I will certainly never notice."

Bernard's gray eyes widened slightly. At last, I had succeeded in surprising him.

I said to him softly, "If I were a betting woman, I would wager a great deal that you can succeed in making Mama forget all about John Woodly."

Mama pulled herself out of my arms. "What are you saying, Deborah?"

I looked into the eyes that were so like mine. "I'm saying, Mama, that you won't marry Bernard because you're afraid you can't be a normal wife to him. But what if you discovered that you *could* be a normal wife. Would you marry him then?"

She looked shocked.

"Deborah! Are you suggesting . . . ?"

"Yes," I said. "I am."

"I have always thought you were a splendid young woman," Bernard said to me approvingly. The fatigue had miraculously left his face.

Mama began to sputter.

"Go along to Reeve, Deborah," Lord Bradford said to me with a smile, "and leave your mother to me."

I smiled back at him and left the room to go upstairs to the bedroom I shared with my husband.

EPILOGUE

ALL THE FAMILY CAME TO AMBERSLEY FOR THE christening of my daughter. Mama and Bernard had come early, so that Mama could be with me for the baby's birth. Sally arrived after Helen was born, as my conservative mother did not think it was proper for a young girl to be in the house at such a delicate time. Richard and Charlotte arrived the day before with their infant son. Richard was to be Helen's godfather, and Sally was to be her godmother. Lastly, Harry came up from London, where he was still attending the Royal College of Physicians.

Of course, Reeve had dozens of other relatives, but a christening was a private affair, and we had invited only those people to whom we were closest.

It goes without saying that I had been enormously grateful for the presence of my mother during my baby's birth. She had been a great source of strength and comfort to me. I had also been grateful for the presence of Bernard. If he had not been there to restrain Reeve during the six hours it had taken me to deliver Helen, I truly believe that my distraught husband would have charged into our bedroom and demanded to see me.

"Thank you, Bernard," I told him gratefully when he visited me and Helen several hours after the birth. The last thing I had needed during that very trying time was a wild-eyed husband, convinced I was on the verge of extinction. In childbed, Mama's calm and steady support had been far more welcome.

At first I had been a little fearful that Reeve would be disappointed that his firstborn child was a girl.

In fact, he had been absolutely delighted. One look into Helen's large, blue-gray eyes, and he had fallen utterly and completely in love.

"Her eyes are going to be blue, like yours," he had said.

In fact, I rather thought that her eyes were going to turn dark, like his, but I didn't say anything. I didn't want to get in the way of his obvious enchantment.

"Perhaps our next one will be a boy," I said.

"Perhaps," he said carelessly. "Look at her hands, Deb. They're so tiny yet so perfect. And her skin!"

"I think Reeve is secretly delighted that he doesn't have to share you with another male," Bernard said to me with a laugh.

I myself thought that it might be more complicated than that. Reeve had named the baby after his mother, and I thought that in some obscure way the existence of Helen Maria Elizabeth Ann was a way for him finally to reconnect positively with the parent he had so tragically lost.

It was a crisp, clear October morning the day I stood in the great front doorway of Ambersley and watched the christening party getting into the carriages that would take them to the church. Sally was carefully carrying the baby, her face aglow with tenderness. Helen was wearing the dress and cap that generations of Lambeths had been christened in. She looked adorable, and I had fed her just before they left, so I hoped that she would not cry.

I was relegated to waiting at home until they returned.

"Rest, Deb," Reeve commanded me before they left. "I don't want you to exhaust yourself with all this entertaining."

He had been hovering over me like a mother tiger with one cub all during the last few months of my pregnancy, and he had not been much better since the baby was born. It was sweet of him, but it was starting to get on my nerves.

"I am perfectly fine, Reeve," I said impatiently. "The doctor said that I am a strong and healthy young woman, and there is no reason for me to pamper myself."

He frowned.

"Go along." I gave him a push. "They're waiting for you."

As soon as they had left, I went down the back stairs to the kitchen to make certain that everything was in train for the luncheon that would be served when the christening party returned from the church.

My arrival in the kitchen caused scarcely a stir. This had not been the case when I first stopped in after Reeve and I had come to Ambersley to live. Then I had met with icy disapproval from my servants. It was quite obvious that in their view of the world, the lady of the manor did not just stop into the kitchen for a snack and a chat.

I had persevered, however. Ambersley might be as large as a palace, but it was still my house, and I was determined to feel at home in all of it.

My resolution had paid off, and now my staff and I were perfectly comfortable with each other.

It hadn't hurt that I had had a brand-new stove installed for the cook, and last winter had bought warm wool blankets for the beds of all the servants.

Unlike the aristocratic Lambeths who had inhabited the house before me, I knew what it felt like to be cold.

"Would you care to sample the soup, my lady?" the cook asked me.

I shook my head. "I'd love to, Mrs. Wilson, but I'd better not."

I had shed most of the extra weight I'd gained with the baby, but I still had a little more to go. Once I could get out on horseback again, I knew the weight would melt away, but at the moment I did not think it was a good idea to indulge myself too freely with treats.

The elderly woman who was our cook gave me a reproachful look. "Ye can certainly afford a wee sip, my lady. Ye're naught but skin and bones."

I looked at Mrs. Wilson's comfortably upholstered body and thought that she was hardly the judge I would choose for such a matter as my proper weight.

I smiled at her. "I know it is delicious, and I promise to eat my fill at luncheon."

"Ye need not worry, my lady," she said placidly. "I'll serve 'em a grand meal, that I will."

"I wasn't worried at all," I reassured her. And I wasn't. Mrs. Wilson was a wonderful cook.

After I left the kitchen I went along to the red drawing room, which opened off the black-and-white-marble hall in the front of the house. This was the room that we were using today for the christening party. Reeve's father had had Ambersley's drawing room and dining room redone by Robert Adam, and the result in the drawing room was nothing short of sumptuous. The walls were hung with red Spitalfields silk, the brilliant carpet and much of the red-silk-upholstered furniture had been designed by Adam himself, and the ceiling was gaily patterned with octagons which enclosed colored circles. An immense gilt-framed mirror hung over the white-marble fireplace, and the rest of the walls were hung with equally immense portraits of Reeve's ancestors.

This was not one of the rooms that Reeve and I used on a daily basis, but it was certainly a grand place to have a party. Actually, I was looking forward to doing a bit more socializing than I had been able to of late. Reeve had gone up to London a number of times to attend Parliament, but I had not been in London since our engagement had been announced. This was because at first we had had an obligatory period of mourning for Robert, and then, of course, I had been carrying Helen.

Sally was to make her postponed come out this spring, under Mama's aegis, and Reeve and I were going to spend the Season in London as well. I was looking forward to it, and even Reeve said that perhaps it would not be so bad as long as I was there.

When the christening party finally returned from the church, I brought the baby upstairs to her cradle, which would be in my dressing room while I was still nursing her, fed her again, and then returned to the drawing room, where the others were drinking champagne.

"Helen was an angel in church," my husband informed me.

Sally was indignant. "Reeve! She screamed until she was red in the face when Mr. Liskey poured the water on her forehead."

"She stopped screaming as soon as I took her from you," Reeve pointed out smugly.

I looked at him and thought that we had better have another child soon or this one was going to be spoiled beyond saving.

Mama said, "It is good luck when a baby cries like that."

Did I mention that my mother was proving to be as doting a grandmother as Reeve was a father?

My eyes inadvertently met Bernard's, and we shared a smile.

Richard said to me, "Wouldn't it be jolly if my Dickon and your Helen should marry one day?"

"I would like that very much," I said.

Charlotte laughed. "Richard! The children aren't out of their cradles yet. Besides, parental matchmaking is no longer acceptable. This isn't the Middle Ages, you know. It's the Nineteenth Century."

Richard was unperturbed. "I didn't say I would insist that they marry, Charlotte. I just said that it would be jolly."

I might mention here that Richard's affairs were making a continuous and steady recovery from the depredations of Uncle John, who had continued to be a missing person.

We all hoped very much that he stayed that way.

At this point, Harry said, "I have an announcement to make."

Conversation died, and we all turned to look at him

expectantly. "Mary Ann Norton and I are going to be married," he said with a grin.

"Harry!" I shrieked. "How wonderful!"

His grin broadened. "Yes, it is, rather. We settled it between us a few weeks ago." His eyes went to Reeve, who was sitting on the red-silk chair placed next to his. "I didn't write because I wanted to tell you the news myself."

Reeve clapped him on the shoulder. "Congratulations, old fellow. She's a grand girl."

Harry sobered. "She is. I was afraid that her parents might object to her marrying a mere physician, but they have been very reasonable."

I thought cynically that the fact that the "mere physician" would also be the next Lord Bradford probably had something to do with the Nortons' "reasonableness."

"Will you remain in London to practice?" Richard asked.

"No," Harry said. "I shall be returning to Sussex. There are more than enough physicians in London and not nearly enough in the country."

Reeve got to his feet and raised his champagne glass. "A toast to Harry and Mary Ann," he said. "May they be as happy as Deb and I"—he bowed to me—"And Richard and Charlotte"—he bowed to Charlotte—"and Bernard and Elizabeth"—he bowed gracefully to Mama.

"Hear, hear," we all said, and raised our glasses to drink the toast.

As if on cue, my butler appeared in the doorway. "Luncheon is served, my lady," he announced.

We all filed into the drawing room, still congratulating Harry.

All of our guests were remaining overnight, and Reeve took the men shooting in the afternoon, while the women and I walked through the Ambersley gardens. Even though the summer was over, the huge gardens were still enormously impressive, with their statuary, and their many ponds and fountains, and their huge variety of plantings.

It wasn't until later in the evening, as I was sitting at the dinner table talking to Bernard, that fatigue suddenly struck me like a blow. I thought I managed to conceal it, but when the ladies left the table to retire to one of the small drawing rooms for tea, Mama said to me in a firm voice, "Deborah, it is time that you sought your bed. I will pour the tea for you."

I did not argue.

I went upstairs, let Susan help me undress, and then fed Helen, who was fussing.

My baby, I thought, my lips pressed tenderly against the silky golden fuzz of her hair. *How much I love you.*

I was asleep moments after I curled up in the big velvet-hung four-poster that I shared with Reeve.

Four hours later, I awoke automatically. It amazed me how quickly my body had synchronized itself to the baby's feeding schedule.

Reeve was not in the bed beside me, and I assumed that he was still downstairs, playing billiards or some such thing with the men.

There was a night candle burning in the dressing room when I went next door. The candle was hardly necessary, however, as the light from a full harvest moon was pouring in through the window, illuminating the room with a pale white glow.

I thought I had closed the drapes earlier, and I looked toward the window in surprise.

Reeve was standing there with the baby in his arms. The moonlight glinted off the darkness of his hair and made his eyes look almost black against his moon-bleached skin. He was gazing at Helen with an expression on his face that brought tears to my eyes and a prickly feeling to the back of my throat.

It was such a private moment that I hesitated and would have retreated back into the bedroom if he had not looked up and seen me.

"Deb." His smile was radiant.

I walked over to join the two of them by the window.

"It's almost time for her to eat," I said. "That's why I came in."

"I know. She was crying a little, but when I put my finger in her mouth she sucked on it and stopped."

I rested my cheek on his shoulder and the two of us looked at our baby.

"I never thought I would feel this way about her," he said a little wonderingly. "She's . . . she's like a miracle to me."

I looked at Helen Maria Elizabeth Ann Lambeth, and thought that perhaps she was a miracle. Even more for Reeve than she was for me. For me, she was my deeply loved child. For Reeve, in some strange way, she was redemption.

The miracle fluttered her eyelashes and began to cry.

"The finger trick lasts for just so long," I informed my husband. "I'm afraid you're going to have to hand her over to me."

He grinned at me. I looked at that boyish, happy expression, and my heart rejoiced.

No one was ever going to call him the Corsair again.

DON'T MISS JOAN WOLF"S NEXT
DELECTABLE NOVEL *GOLDEN GIRL*
COMING SOON FROM WARNER BOOKS

Sarah opened the drawing room door and stepped into the room. She could feel the anger seething inside her.

"Your Grace," she said, and stared at the Duke of Cheviot with undisguised hostility.

Somber, gray-green eyes looked back.

One forgot, she found herself thinking, that he really was this beautiful.

"Damn," the Duke said. "It's even worse than I feared it would be."

His words surprised her, but she knew exactly what he meant. "Yes," she said. "It is."

He gestured with one slender, ringless hand. "It really isn't quite as ugly as it appears to be, Sarah. I'd like you to know that."

"I don't want to know anything," Sarah said. "I just want you to go away."

"I don't blame you," he answered. "I deceived you, and you are angry. You have every right to be angry, but I ask you to allow me just ten minutes of your time, so that I may tell you how all this came about."

"I know how it came about," Sarah said. "You need money."

A look of ineffable weariness came across his face. "I need a huge amount of money," he agreed in that soft, deceptively gentle voice of his. "My patrimony from my father was a pile of debt that amounts to over two million pounds."

Do not dare to feel sorry for him, Sarah commanded herself.

She said in a hard voice, "So you decided that the only way to remedy your financial situation was to marry a girl who had money."

"Yes," he said. "But I must stress to you, Miss Patterson, that I regarded such a marriage as one that would confer benefits upon both parties. I would receive the money I so badly needed, yes; but my wife would receive one of the highest titles in all the country. It is worth something, you know, to be the Duchess of Cheviot."

"I'm sure it is—for some girls ," Sarah said, making it very clear by her tone of voice that she was not one of those deluded creatures.

"I liked you," she said. "I thought you were a nice man. And all the time you were lying to me."

He leaned slightly forward in his chair. "Sarah, I want you to listen to me carefully. I think you should marry me and I want to tell you why."

Sarah expression changed from scorn to incredulity.

"Just listen to me," he said. I beg you."

After a minute she crossed her arms over her breast. "I'll listen, but that is all."

He lifted his hand, as if he were reaching out to her. "You are a good painter, Sarah, but in order for you to become a great painter you need to look at many paintings by artists who have the same interests as you. You need to go to Amsterdam, to Paris, to Italy—the places where those pictures are to be found. If you marry me, I will take you to those place, Sarah. Who else do you know who will do that for you?"

Sarah's fists were closed so tightly that her nails were biting into her palms. "You are diabolical," she whispered.

❦

GOLDEN GIRL coming fall 1999